British Muslims Between Assimilation and Segregation

HISTORICAL, LEGAL AND SOCIAL REALITIES

*Mohammad Siddique Seddon,
Dilwar Hussain and Nadeem Malik*

THE ISLAMIC FOUNDATION

Published by

THE ISLAMIC FOUNDATION
Markfield Conference Centre
Ratby Lane, Markfield
Leicestershire LE67 9SY, United Kingdom
Tel: 01530 244944/5, Fax: 01530 244946
E-mail: info0@islamic-foundation.org.uk
publications@islamic-foundation.com
Website: www.islamic-foundation.org.uk

Quran House, P.O. Box 30611, Nairobi, Kenya

P.M.B. 3193, Kano, Nigeria

British Library Cataloguing-in-Publication Data

Seddon, Mohammad Siddique
    British Muslims between assimilation and segreation:
historical, legal and social realities
1. Muslims – Great Britain – Social conditions – 21st Great Britain
2. Muslims – Great Britain – Attitudes 3. Muslims – Great Britain
– Public opinion 4. Group identity – Great Britain 5. Public
opinion – Great Britain
I. Title II. Hussain, Dilwar III. Malik, Nadeem
305.6'97'0941

ISBN 0 86037 354 1

Cover/Book design & typeset: Nasir Cadir
Photography: Sakir Cadir. Reproduced with kind permission by
Murad Associates, www.muradassociates.co.uk

Printed in Great Britain by Antony Rowe Ltd, Chippenham, Wiltshire

Contents

Foreword

British Muslims, and the wider environment in which they live – Britain and Europe, are undergoing some rapid changes. Only with a historic perspective and through the vicissitudes of time, will we be able to truly evaluate the significance of these days – but they seem tumultuous enough. Perhaps as a result of the complex search for its own identity, European society seems to come to terms with the reality of the new Muslim presence with some difficulty. Some argue it has always been thus – that Europe and Islam have mutually defined themselves in opposition to each other. The Muslim communities of Britain and Europe in the post 9/11 world face some serious challenges in which loyalty, identity, citizenship and belonging are constantly questioned. Yet these debates did not begin with 9/11, and neither will they end if, and when, that chapter of human history is complete. Neither can such debates be held in isolation when Muslim identity is as much a result of state policy as it is a result of an Islamic worldview, or of ethnic and cultural influences. In June 2002 the Islamic Foundation, together with the Citizen Organising Foundation, held an important seminar on the subject of *British Muslims: Loyalty and Belonging*, the proceedings of this seminar were subsequently published in 2003. The current volume continues that discussion further and looks at some of the pertinent issues refluxed in that seminar.

Three British Muslim academics present a vibrant discussion on some of the most hotly debated issues within Muslim circles today. Issues such as identity and political participation, citizenship and legal protection are taken up along with contextual discussions of the changing nature of British identity and a review of some of the most salient writings on the British Muslim presence to date. It is noticeable that few Muslim writers have, so far, contributed to the academic discourse on contemporary British Muslims and this book, while not claiming to be the final word in such matters, is a valuable addition. As such, these discussions are relevant not only for a Muslim audience, but for anyone who connects with the Muslim community and wishes to understand some of its inner dynamics.

It is interesting to note that much of the content of this book is forward looking and positive. At a time when there is a sense of severe frustration with community leadership and the political structures of society, this is an important message. Ultimately, the power of faith is in providing hope to people. It is my expectation that this publication will create, or at least add to, a debate on the priorities of the British Muslim community and show that black and white answers, while being simple enough to espouse, are not the solution to the highly complex challenges that face British Muslims.

The Islamic Foundation
July 2004

M Manazir Ahsan,
Director General

Introduction

Muslims are not new to Britain and their individual presence can be traced to the fifteenth century, if not before. Muslim communities have existed in some form or other in the industrial heartlands since the late eighteenth century. In the beginning the Muslim presence was transient and temporary, largely facilitated by British imperial expansion. The Empire brought Muslims to the motherland via a number of means: as merchant sailors or 'lascars', servants, nannies, footmen and personal teachers of the returning 'nabobs' of the British East India Company, or as wealthy oriental merchants, scholars, travellers, princes and princesses or colonial civil servants.

As the empire expanded so too did the numbers of colonial subjects to Britain and by the end of the nineteenth century there were many diverse Muslim communities throughout the country, from dockland Lascars and affluent city traders to indigenous converts. Perhaps because of Britain's dominant civilisation and global hegemony, which had reached its zenith, the various communities of Muslims present here were not perceived as either significant or envisaged as a 'threat' to British culture. Therefore, little or no attention was paid to these nascent communities, apart from the philanthropic and evangelical concerns of a few individual Church missionaries.

However, the presence of larger Muslim communities as a phenomenon of post-war, industrial migration has produced intense academic scrutiny of the 'migration experience' covering a multitude of scholastic disciplines and sociological theories. Further, as the beginning of the twentieth century was perhaps marked by indifference to the newly forming Muslim communities, in stark contrast, the beginning of the twenty-first century has conversely witnessed a proliferation of studies with a particular emphasis on placing British Muslims culturally, religiously, politically and socially within the wider society.

The first generation migration story is now quite familiar but in contrast, their offspring, the second and third generation British-born progeny have an almost untold narrative. Also, the growth of the Muslim communities in the country's urban areas has presented various challenges to Britain's multicultural and religiously plural social mosaic.

At times mainstream British society seems almost reticent of its emerging, diverse, social realities. Often viewed in terms of their 'otherness', British Muslims have, in their settlement and community formation processes, encountered social exclusion and racism.

While ethnicity and race are still relevant factors in cross-community cohesion, minority communities are now (increasingly) likely to identify themselves by their faith as well as by their ethnic or racial origins. This developing sense of religiosity, coupled with a greater engagement in civil society, is an increasingly normative experience for Britain's Muslims.

There are estimated to be around two million Muslims living in Britain today and a general lack of knowledge and understanding about their religion and culture as well as their socio-political situation is often a source of tension and misunderstanding. Oft-quoted 'flashpoints' have increased the misunderstandings and misrepresentations between British Muslims and wider society. The Runnymeade Trust Report, *Islamophobia – a challenge for us all* (1997), highlighted some of the reasons for this phenomenon. The impact of the Human Rights Act of 1998, is also significant and it necessitates more inclusion and facilitation of minority faiths and an increased interaction and dialogue.

Whilst faith-based initiatives have been recognized more widely, through the EU Employment Directive incorporated in 2003 and the inclusion of religious affiliation in the 2001 census, Britain has witnessed a recent marked increase in anti-Muslim sentiment or 'Islamophobia', which has resulted in a rise in verbal abuse, and personal attacks on Muslims, their property and their mosques. The reasons for the alarming increase in these racist and anti-Muslim aggressions can be linked to historical events such as the *Satanic Verses* Affair, the Gulf War, the summer race riots in the north of England and the horrific terrorist attacks on the US in September 2001.

The resultant invasions of Afghanistan and Iraq by allied forces and the increased securitisation of Europe and America, have increased suspicions of Muslim minorities by the general non-Muslim populace. Further, it has raised fears and concerns amongst the Muslim communities despite government assurances and words of comfort from leading ministers and politicians. But, unprotected due to the absence of any laws on religious discrimination, the media have continued to provide fuel for racist fears of being overrun by Muslim asylum seekers and refugees. They also irresponsibly present many British Muslims as a sort of 'fifth column'.

The changing European political climate also affects the way Muslim communities are viewed and the rise of Nationalism in Eastern Europe gave rise to a brutal exercise of 'ethnic cleansing'. Fascism has found favour in mainland Europe giving hopes to Britain's far-right and the British National Party who gained a number of seats in recent local council elections.

The secular imposition, prohibiting religious dress and symbols in French schools and official places will only further polarise anti-Muslim feeling in Europe and beyond. The increase in xenophobia perpetuates the view that Muslims *are* 'other' and therefore do not belong here. All of these events belie the fact that a MORI poll in November 2001 found that 87% of British Muslims declared that they are, 'loyal to Britain'.

When British Muslims disagree with their government on issues of political, moral or religious values as with the Satanic Verses Affair, the Gulf War or the recent events in the middle-east, their contentions should not be viewed in terms of their specific loyalties or belonging to Britain. Rather, their alternative views should be interpreted as an expression of their democratic right to oppose government policies and as an indicator of active integration, that Muslims are aware and concerned with government policies. Increasingly, British Muslims are choosing to define themselves in respect of their national and political loyalties and belonging with an emphasis on the mutualities and commonalties with the wider non-Muslim society experienced recently through participation in the Anti-war Coalition, Human Rights activism and the anti-globalisation movement.

The pressing need to explore the 'how and why' and the 'here and now' of British Muslims has never been greater. This book seeks to offer an analytical account of the current situation of Britain's second largest faith community, charting their historical settlement, legal facilitations and the social realities and challenges they face as a community now well-established as a part of the British religious and cultural landscape.

The publication also seeks to explore some of these issues in detail, raising questions for both the Muslim community to consider as well as the wider British society. In the opening chapter, *Muslim Communities in Britain: A Historiography*, Mohammad Siddique Seddon offers a chronological overview of some of the major studies on the various Muslim communities in Britain, from transient settlers and English converts to post-colonial economic migrants and their British-born offspring. This chapter explores the various studies on patterns of migration, settlement and community formation through the diverse ethnicities, races and theological divisions towards the apparent emergence of hybrid religio-cultural identities which are manifest both locally and globally.

The second chapter, *Equality? The Treatment of Muslims Under the English Legal System*, by Nadeem Malik examines the rights of British Muslims in relation to the English legal system. Even with recent changes to legislation in Britain and Europe, there is still inadequate protection in terms of the religious discrimination that Muslims increasingly face. Historically, Muslims have had to pursue cases of discrimination under the Race Relations Act of 1976. Although this has provided some redress for the initial cases of discrimination that were mostly motivated by difference of culture and colour, the changes in the nature of discrimination over the last two decades, where religion has become an issue, have meant that there has been an increasing awareness of the need for new legislation that would deal with this problem directly.

The chapter presents the limitations of the Race Relations Act and then looks at developments in English law such as the European Convention of Human Rights and its domestic application via the Human Rights Act 1998. It also addresses very recent developments such as the Anti-Terrorism, Crime and Security Act 2001 and concludes that the anomalies that exist with regard to religious discrimination against Muslims are inexplicable from a legal or ethical perspective, thereby paving the way for claims that there is insufficient political will for necessary reforms to take place.

In chapter Three, *British Muslim Identity*, Dilwar Hussain looks at the debates within the Muslim community, especially among young Muslims, and seeks answers to why the notion of a British Muslim identity is important. This is placed within the broader context of how Muslims adapt to their life in the West. The author relates this to the early Muslim community at the time of the Prophet Muhammad, peace be upon him (pbuh), and the chapter examines the notions of identity, belonging, community formation and the encounter with different cultures and beliefs that took place in the formative period of Islam.

British multiculturalism is also addressed and contextualised within the history of immigration into Britain and the debates around race in the 1960s and 1970s. The chapter asks 'what comprises a Muslim identity?' and defines this from Islamic sources. Finally, it also confronts some of the objections that are raised by young Muslims and challenges these in light of Islamic teachings and concludes by looking at the changing notions of Britishness and the implications the debate around identity has on the contributions that British Muslims can and should make to the future of Britain.

The mass migration to Britain by Commonwealth and post-colonial communities have helped to change and reshape our definitions and interpretations of what it means to be British. The presence of significant racial and religious groups have created a modern, ethnically-diverse and religiously-pluralistic British society. But whilst multiculturalism may be a new way of describing 'Britishness', exclusive definitions of 'Anglo-Saxoness' are still perpetuated.

Some questions regarding the 'Britishness' of new communities are still asked particularly in the political sphere, often simply as a means of gaining votes. However, politically being British has no relation to ethnicity or colour and these restricted ideas are associated with historical definitions of 'Englishness' and 'Anglicanism' and not Britishness. In such exclusive interpretations of what it is to be British, all non-white non-Protestants simply remain outsiders or others. Religious and racial equality within the new cultural, political and social realities of modern multicultural Britain is an on-going debate particularly when national identity is constructed around exclusive definitions which not only restrict the inclusion of outsiders, but perpetuate them as the 'other'.

Locating the Perpetuation of Otherness: Negating British Islam, by Mohammad Siddique Seddon, traces the formation of exclusive definitions of Britishness, through the politics of racism and the development of 'national identity' as a consequence of the modern nation-state via the Reformation and discusses the implications of ethnicity and race within the concept of a multicultural Britain. In this chapter, the author also explores how Muslims in Britain are often historically perceived by others and their own self identification in terms of their Britishness. Seddon asserts that it is a persistent misconception that Muslims cannot synthesise their religious and national identities into the new definitions of Britishness and that the reality of this hybridisation of British 'Muslimness', although increasingly experienced, is often difficult to express due to marginalisation and social exclusion.

As a religious community that identifies itself both locally, as British Muslims and globally as members of the universal family of Islam, issues of loyalty and belonging are often raised as questions concerning the citizenship of British Muslims. Where do Muslims place themselves in the context of nationality and citizenship? In, *Friends, Romans, Countrymen?* Nadeem Malik raises a number of pertinent points relating to what he terms the 'citizenship link'. What makes us citizens and what is the connection between legal recognition as a social minority and the concept of citizenship?

In offering answers to these central questions on citizenship, the chapter rolls back the debate to tackle important core issues for British Muslims. 'Is Islam compatible with the West?' 'Can Muslims be British citizens' and 'do Muslims want to engage with society?' Addressing these fundamental questions, Malik suggests, can only be done by examining the obstacles and challenges to citizenship, particularly in the context of a religiously pluralistic and ethnically diverse multicultural society.

Achieving community cohesion in the absence of comprehensive and protective legislation against religious intolerance, racism and Islamophobia may remain a utopian dream. Furthermore, without the fair opportunity to engage as equal and full British citizens despite differences, can minority faith communities and other social sub-groups become participatory members in civil society? Turning these fundamental questions about citizenship on their head, Malik locates a general 'break-down' and 'dissatisfaction' within mainstream British society which is manifest in a disengagement with civil and political spheres, an increase in rates of crime and the presence of widespread discrimination on the grounds of race and gender.

This chapter sets out the theoretical definitions and frameworks for citizenship and discusses the inhibiting factors and practical reasons why inclusivity based on civil engagement and participatory political representation, through the paradigms of multicultural citizenship, are somewhat unattainable for British Muslims under existing law.

The maxim 'when in Rome...' is often directed at migrants in a new place as an informal instruction to give up their religious, cultural and moral beliefs for those of their hosts. To some degree, for the purposes of cohesion and co-existence, 'doing as the Romans do' is quite necessary, even practical. But, asks the author, 'where do the limits lie...and...where are the walls of Rome'. Further, 'how and where do Muslims place themselves as participants in mainstream British society'?

Chapter Six, *Councillors and Caliphs: Muslim Political Participation in Britain*, addresses the subject of how Muslims have engaged with the British political process. Here, Dilwar Hussain looks at the dangers of disengagement from the political process and the consequences this can have on community cohesion. The inquiry begins by looking at how the British Muslim community has gradually entered the political arena, albeit led by external influences, often international issues.

The chapter goes into some detail in examining the debate among Muslims about participation in non-Islamic politics and it explores a broad spectrum of ideas ranging from the views of Ḥizb al-Taḥrīr to those who advocate democracy. Further, it looks at the different approaches of engagement/ disengagement with British politics and identifies six different models, making special mention of the number of Muslims that have become councillors in mainstream political parties. It ends by considering the implications of participation and non-participation and refers to Maslow's theory of human motivation to examine why Muslims have initially focused on very parochial concerns. There is also a brief discussion of the notion of power and how the political process is not the only way of empowering and influencing the lives of people.

We hope that this publication will be a constructive addition to the discourse on British Muslims and in the process of trying to reach greater understanding and formulating proactive policies and recommendations that affect Muslims and their inclusion and exclusion into the wider British society.

Finally, we believe that this collection of essays will serve to give an insider-outsider perspective on some of the contemporary debates that are prevalent among British Muslims. One may find herein great parallels with the issues discussed within other communities that are in a similar phase of acculturation into the British religio-cultural landscape. As such, it should be a useful reference source for people wishing to engage with the Muslim community as well as those Muslims who are living through some of the challenges mentioned, not just as detached observers, but as engaged actors in the great theatre of life.

The Islamic Foundation   The Authors
July 2004

Transliteration Table

Consonants. Arabic

initial: unexpressed medial and final:

ء	'	د	d	ض	ḍ	ك	k
ب	b	ذ	dh	ط	ṭ	ل	l
ت	t	ر	r	ظ	ẓ	م	m
ث	th	ز	z	ع	'	ن	n
ج	j	س	s	غ	gh	هـ	h
ح	ḥ	ش	sh	ف	f	و	w
خ	kh	ص	ṣ	ق	q	ي	y

Vowels, diphthongs, etc.

Short: ـَ a   ـِ i   ـُ u

long: ـَا ā   ـِي ī   ـُو ū

diphthongs: ـَوْ aw

  ـَىْ ay

The Authors

Mohammad Siddique Seddon is a Research Fellow at the Islamic Foundation in the *Muslims in Europe* unit and is currently completing his doctoral thesis in the Religious Studies Department at the University of Lancaster. He is a member of the Executive Committee of the *Association of Muslim Social Scientists (UK)* and has been employed in specialist posts relating to Muslim youth work, education, teacher training and interfaith initiatives. He has published a number of works relating to Islam in Britain. He is married and lives in Leicester with his wife and children.

Dilwar Hussain is a Research Fellow at the Islamic Foundation, Leicester. His primary interests are Citizenship, Muslim communities in Europe and Muslim Identity. Dilwar is involved in a number of Europe-wide and UK based research networks and projects and sits on the Church of England's Commission on Urban Life and Faith. He has a number of published articles, chapters and reviews based his research. In addition to academic research on Islam he is involved with various community organisations including the Forum of European Muslim Youth and Student Organisations and the Citizen Organising Foundation. He regularly speaks on his research areas and also runs diversity training courses on Muslim culture. Dilwar is married with two daughters and lives in Leicester.

Nadeem Malik is a Partner of BK Solicitors. He serves as a Trustee of a number of charities focusing on social engagement and active citizenship. He has worked as a Barrow-Cadbury Research Fellow at the Islamic Foundation as well as Legal Affairs Consultant to the Citizen Organising Foundation. His professional background has included specialising in Discrimination and Employment Litigation and he has represented people across the country whilst working for, *inter alia*, the Commission for Racial Equality. He was Course Director of the Islamic Foundation's Cultural Awareness Training Courses and responsible for the Muslim Participation in Civil Society and Religious Discrimination Research Projects. He is a founding member of the Association of Muslim Lawyers and served, until recently, as its Deputy Chair. He also serves on the National Council of the Islamic Society of Britain. He is married with one son and lives in Birmingham.

Chapter 1

Muslim Communities in Britain: A Historiography

Mohammad Siddique Seddon

Introduction

It would be impossible to give a definitive history of Islam in Britain, the subject area is vast and developing research is continiously uncovering and discovering new historical points of contact. This chapter, therefore, will instead focus on the more recent phenomenon of the formation of the sizeable presence of Muslim communities in Britain. In particular, it will analyse how these various communities of Muslims have been observed and studied from 'outsider' perspectives by focusing on some of the major works undertaken. The objective is to help to formulate a general consensus of how British Muslims have been and are now perceived.

To date there exists a growing bibliography of studies on Muslim communities via a number of academic disciplines from ethnic and cultural, sociological and anthropological to theological and religious studies. All of these works have added to the developing research and chronology. They are useful contributions to the cataloguing of the historical and social development of Muslim communities and provide a valuable insight into how they have formulated and established communities in Britain. But they also have their limitations, sometimes the information is deliberately void of detail and instead seeks to offer a panoramic perspective of Muslims in Britain. An interesting example can be found in Paul Weller's religious directory.[1] Conversely, some studies are limited by the specifics of the subject area and the particular sub-groups observed.

Ron Geaves has produced a monograph concentrating on the national 'sectarian' influences present within the Muslim communities in Britain.[2] His work pays particular attention to how these theological and ideological groups impact on communities both locally and internationally. The book contains useful information that adds to the general understanding of British Muslims. However, the study is specific to South Asian Muslim settlers and nothing is offered on the Muslims of Arab, Turkish or African descent and their 'movements'. Overall, many studies are limited in their real understanding of the religious dynamics and paradigms that shape and mould the Muslim community. Instead, studies often tend to exclusively observe the imported cultures and customs of various ethnic sub-groups that constitute Muslim communities, focusing on the preservation of the variant cultures and traditions; how they are impacted and transformed by new social conditions and environments. Few research studies exist that explore how the religion and the religious identity of the various migrant communities transports and transforms itself into a new setting.

The expansion of Islam has since its nascent period, seen Muslims migrating and travelling to new domains. Indeed migration, its impact and process, is at the heart of understanding the establishment of the *ummah*.[3] The Prophet's migration or *hijrah* from Makkah to Madinah was the turning point in the creation of the first community of Muslims and the Islamic citadel. It is through the *hijrah* of the Prophet Muḥammad (pbuh), his migrating Companions and the indigenous Muslims of Madinah who facilitated them, that the Muslim *ummah* have been collectively and continuously able to identify themselves religiously, socially, morally and politically.[4] It is therefore, the paradigm for the migration experience, community formation and the notion of the global Muslim community – the *ummah*. As a relatively new occurrence in the West, the migration, settlement and formation of Muslim communities, beyond their particular ethnicities, has largely been overlooked. With almost 60% of Britain's Muslim population now born in the UK it is evident that the term British Muslim is a social reality and not a politically engineered 'tag'.[5] In an endeavour to highlight this deficiency in understanding the dynamics of religious practice and identity, this chapter will offer a brief overview of major studies on Muslim communities from the late nineteenth century to date. The chapter, a historiography of Muslim communities in Britain, will not only provide a chronological contextualisation of these communities and their migration, settlement and formation, it will also demonstrate that despite the diversities in ethnicities and race and beyond theological divisions, Muslim communities in Britain are bound together by virtue of their religious identity into a single entity – the *ummah*.

THE FIRST MUSLIM COMMUNITIES

The earliest studies of Muslim communities in Britain written in the middle to late nineteenth century are unfortunately largely incomplete accounts of their emergence, settlement and ethnography. Two records, one a short and vague reference and the other a brief study limited to a small chapter are represented in the writings of Arnold[6] and Pool[7] respectively.

Apart from the obvious limitations of Arnold's work, it contains one of a few rare references to the British *Shaykh al-Islām*, Abdullah Henry William Quilliam. Arnold records his conversion to Islam whilst travelling in Morocco in 1884 noting that Quilliam was struck by the sobriety and good morals of the Muslims. He documents how Quilliam returned to his home city of Liverpool and began establishing a 'Muslim Mission'. This brief reference is a tantalising glimpse into the early Liverpool Muslim Community. Unlike other works written about Quilliam's activities in the same period Arnold is distinctly non-judgemental. Whether Arnold met Quilliam or visited the Liverpool Community, as Pool did, is hard to establish but it appears to be unlikely given the very limited information in his book – it is contained in just one paragraph. Perhaps Arnold believed the Liverpool Muslims to be of no significance whereas Pool seemed alarmed by their existence and was pessimistic in respect of their efforts, influence and future. Arnold's observations of this new emerging Muslim community in Britain imply a hybrid form of Islam with a distinctly British identity. This is influenced by the missionary converts to Islam who, Arnold notes, are "profoundly ignorant of the vast literature of Muhammadan theologians". As a result he further observed:

> They have introduced into their religious worship certain practices borrowed from the ritual of Protestant sects, such as the singing of hymns, praying in the English language etc.[8]

Arnold does not see these innovations as an abrogation of Islam, rather he considers them to be defining features of a religion that can, "adapt itself to the peculiar characteristics and the stage of development of the people whose allegiance it seeks to win".[9] Pool is far less accepting of the presence of Muslims in Britain and his attitude perhaps reflects the pervading view of Islam in the late nineteenth century. Pool's work, what he describes as a 'comparative study' between

Islam and Christianity, is presented as a polemical transposition of his personal fear and dislike of Islam. He prophesies Islam's imminent demise and expresses his hope for the future of Christianity as "the true religion of the Western world". Christianity was, at the time of Pool's writing, still the normative religion and a prominent feature of Western European life despite the onslaught of post-enlightenment secularism.

However, written in the climate of nineteenth-century religious polemics and fuelled by global political and economic tensions, the book typically reflects the anti-Muslim sentiment that was predominant and is often reflected in the works of other Orientalists like Muir and Margoliuth.[10] Throughout the study Pool is vitriolic and he reinforces perpetuated myths and stereotypes about Islam in order that the reader would conclude the superiority of Christianity. However, beyond Pool's diatribe, what is uniquely important is his chapter entitled, 'Islam in England'. This chapter offers another yet more detailed contemporary insight into the Liverpool Muslim community and its charismatic founder and leader, Quilliam. The chapter title is misleading in that it represents a study of the Liverpool Muslims with nothing more than a passing reference to other British Muslim communities in existence in London, Woking and Manchester.

Pool visited the Liverpool Muslim community in the autumn of 1891 and spent four days as a personal guest of Quilliam. Like Arnold, the author does not concern himself with the details of the community's specific demography and ethnography. Instead, he is primarily concerned with the community dynamics of proselytising the Islamic faith. This preoccupation with religious mission, unfortunately omits important information regarding the members of the Liverpool community. In studying the religious observances of the Liverpool Muslim community Pool, like Arnold after him, has recorded the peculiar features of congregational worship, which adhered to and catered specifically for its Christian participants. After reviewing the community's missionary efforts and activities, Pool gives a passing reference to one hundred and twenty 'Moslems' in London, but he says, "they are orientals". He then comments further that in Manchester, "there are forty of the Faithful, but only four of them are English converts".[11]

Pool's information regarding the Manchester Muslim community is inaccurate. Manchester had by the end of the nineteenth century a well-established Muslim community comprised of Moroccan, Syrian, Lebanese and Egyptian Arabs. Many from this vibrant Arab community were wealthy cotton traders. This early Muslim community had been established since the 1830s and has been referred to in an article by Halliday.[12] Pool's condemnation of Islam is perhaps due to his Christian zeal yet it is strange that his 'prophecy' regarding the Liverpool Muslim community, dying a 'sudden death' should come true. However, the demise of the community was as a result of global rather than local factors. Although the community did face some local hostility and anti-Muslim prejudices, under the guidance and leadership of Quilliam it continued to thrive. However, when the Turks allied themselves with the Germans in the First World War, Quilliam, who was officially honoured as the *Shaykh al-Islām* of Great Britain by the Ottoman Sultan, was suspected along with other British Muslims of being an enemy agent. There are two contemporary studies that make a detailed reference to the Liverpool Muslim community of the late nineteenth and early twentieth century by Ally[13] and Khan.[14] These later studies offer an in-depth analysis of the community's formation and facilitations in addition to an inquiry into the social problems the community encountered. The achievements and dynamics of the Liverpool Muslims, their mosque, educational institute, weekly and monthly periodicals, printing and publishing house and the orphanage, the 'Medina Children's Home' far supersede most Muslim communities present in Britain today.

THE YEMENIS AND THE SEA PORTS

From what has been written on Muslim communities none, with the exception of Richard Lawless'[15] work, are historical studies and even this particular study is limited to the specific period of the early twentieth century. His book charts the migration and settlement of the Arab community of Tyneside. As one of the oldest continuous Muslim communities in Britain, its origins can be traced to the end of the nineteenth century when they came to England as Lascars, or seamen and firemen, aboard British vessels from the port of Aden in the Yemen. Although many Yemenis claimed British citizenship via British colonial rule as a protectorate of the port of Aden, most were rural farmers, and some were Somalis, who had found their way to the protectorate in search of a better future. As it was virtually impossible to prove otherwise due to a distinct lack of documentation the Arab seamen were usually granted British citizenship. Essentially, this account documents the journey, hardships and struggles that Arab and Somali sailors faced. Their first experience was exploitation at the hands of ruthless Arab Sarongs, or 'middle-men', who acted as brokers between the seamen and the shipping companies at the Aden port. Once in Britain the Lascars suffered a similar fate when Arab boarding-house keepers with whom they lodged between passages also acted as brokers and demanded their 'commission'. As if this wasn't enough, the Yemenis then faced blatant discrimination and racism from white sailors who envisaged them as a threat to their jobs and livelihood.

Racial discrimination took the form of legislation when in March 1925 the Home Secretary implemented a Special Restriction Order under Article 11 of the Aliens Order 1920, which imposed a registration of all 'coloured seamen' in the UK at the local police stations. Ironically, many 'coloured' sailors were actually British citizens. The plight of the Yemeni, Somali and Indian Lascars in Britain[16] had caused much consternation amongst Christian charities and missions some time earlier and their deprivation was recorded in two works by Salter published in the later part of the nineteenth century.[17]

Although the largest migrant Arab communities were centred around Cardiff and Liverpool, Lawless' book focuses on the history of the community of Tyneside. The author refers heavily to an earlier work undertaken originally as a doctoral thesis on the South Shields community by Sydney Collins.[18] Lawless pays great attention to the particular details concerning the employment struggles of the migrant seamen and the internal politics of the community that was often divided by tribal allegiances. However, much of his research echoes another less comprehensive earlier work by Carr.[19] Although Carr's article is largely an observation of the communities current situation and contemporary issues relating to identity, it still contains some historical details. Lawless' account of the difficulties faced by the migrant Arabs and the subsequent racism, race riots, rota-system of employment for 'black' seamen, docklands area settlement, inter-marrying with white women and 'half-caste'[20] children by mixed race marriages, represents a work of social history. Unlike Carr, Lawless sees intermarriages as an assimilation and diffusion of the Arab community rather than an integration or organic evolution of the Arabs into the wider society. In contrast, Carr's article begins by identifying the Yemeni community in South Shields as a model for racial tolerance and integration for the rest of Britain. He maintains that, whilst South Shields may enjoy the luxury of excellent race relations, the history of this development is in stark contrast to the present situation. Carr celebrates the transition of the Yemeni community from migrant Arab settlers into intermarried and culturally integrated 'Anglo-Arabs'. Nevertheless, the fact that he identifies the community as 'black' is perhaps a revealing insight into just how integrated they are in reality despite his claim that, "Black Geordies are 'Geordies' first".[21]

Both Lawless and Carr mirror each other's observations and accounts of the Arab community's settlement and formation up to the post-war period. It is around this time that observers note that the community seems to have developed a heightened sense of its Islamic identity. The religiosity of the Yemenis had always been a feature of their identity and most of the early single-man Arab boarding houses catered for a *ḥalāl* diet and many had a designated area for prayers.[22] After the settlement of the Yemeni sailors in Britain via the many marriages to English wives, the "half-caste" children from mixed race marriages, which had reinforced racist fears of an emerging "mongrel" race, were taught Arabic and recitation of the Qur'ān. While the children may have been neither fully Arab nor English in terms of their racial identity, they were fully Muslim in their religious identity. On this point Zubayda Umar notes:

> This is by no means a minority community which finds itself isolated and alien within a larger English society, but it is rather a long-established one which has integrated with the native population while retaining its own religion and identity.[23]

Lawless does not interpret the development of the Arab community with the same enthusiasm as Carr and Umar, that being the organic development of the ethnic, religious and cultural aspects of their Arab identity into a more 'Anglo-Arab' experience. His final chapter observes the disintegration of the community through assimilation,[24] integration,[25] and acculturation.[26] The increased manifestations of the community's Islamic identity through the establishment of mosques and Muslim schools are interpreted by Lawless as an anomaly. He views these institutions as an expression of out-dated introspectivety by the Yemenis that is in obvious contention with the pervading secularity of the wider society.

The post-war years leading to the present, where the physical presence of the Arab community is less demographically concentrated and ethnically visible, represents for Lawless the demise or 'end of an era' for the Yemenis of South Shields. Umar, like Carr, believes that the dispersion of the community is as a result of the decline of the shipping industry and the community becoming more British and less Arab. Referring to the social exclusion experienced by the community, she says, "The problems of development are financial rather than social or cultural".[27] As a document that traces the origins and early history of the Tyneside Yemenis, Lawless' book provides an invaluable study of one of Britain's first Muslim communities in the early part of the twentieth century.

Halliday has also produced a monograph on the Yemenis in Britain.[28] Unlike the historical and regional study undertaken by Lawless, he examines the migration and settlement process of Yemenis to Britain nationally and includes both historical and contemporary issues from a political perspective. Dalrymple described the Yemeni Arab community as, "the oldest and most successfully integrated Muslim community in Great Britain".[29] His quaint portrait of the South Shields' settlers as successful and fully participating Anglo-Arabs is in stark contrast to Fred Halliday's study of migrant Yemeni communities dispersed throughout Britain. Dalrymple sees a clear synthesis between Islam and the 'Britishness' of the Yemenis, and says, "the South Shields Yemenis are becoming more Anglicised every year. They are becoming English Muslims".[30] Halliday in contrast, refers to the strong cultural and psychological ties with their homeland, describing Britain for the Yemeni migrants as the 'remotest village'.[31] Halliday's description illustrates that despite the migration, urbanisation and industrialisation of the Yemeni community in Britain, their world is still largely viewed, according to the author, through a traditionally tribal and rural Arab society. Perhaps in many ways this experience is not unique to the Yemenis in Britain and similarities may be present in the South Asian migrant communities. Certainly Halliday's observations of migration and settlement patterns largely correlate with the findings of other studies made on migrant communities to Britain. However, in this particular research the author reveals a number of unique features related to the 'two-wave' Yemeni settlement.

Their migration as referred to earlier, can be traced to the late nineteenth century when as Dalrymple and Lawless[32] have also observed, Arab sailors began to arrive at British ports initially staying only temporarily between passages. The establishment of 'Arab only' boarding houses was a solution to the prevalent racism by white boarding-house keepers who refused non-white guests. As with later South Asian migration, it was the poor and largely uneducated rural classes from the Yemen who were forced into migration through dire economic circumstances. Both Lawless and Halliday have mentioned the corrupt process by which at each juncture in the migration procedure 'middle-men' would take their 'cut'. In the context of a tribal and socially hierarchical culture the Yemenis were familiar with the 'middle-man' as a means to a job, travel papers and visa. Halliday, quotes the original rather wry Arabic, "ḥaqq al-qaḥwa",[33] literally meaning 'the right of coffee', a euphemism for bribery or corruption and a necessary means of securing their passage to Britain. This mass movement in search for work in Britain eventually led to a classic form of migration referred to as 'chain migration'. Yemenis who had set-up in Britain would forward sufficient funds to male relatives or fellow villagers who would then repeat the same process. Sometimes whole ships (and later factories) would employ its crew or staff via 'chain migration'.[34]

Yemeni politics are often transported into Britain and conflicts and tensions surface amongst the British Yemenis in microcosm. Halliday's research details the growing politicisation of the Yemeni community and traces the developments and origins of organisations and unions in addition to linking them with the politics and historical changes and events in the Yemen.[35] Al-Ḥakīmī's migration coincided with a major change in the shipping industry and the first transformation of the Yemeni community from a transient docklands community into an urbanised industrial workforce – a transition from sojourners to settlers. After the First World War, in which many British Yemeni sailors died in defence of Britain, the introduction of oil-burning ships as faster and more efficient vessels saw many of the Yemeni sailors without work. The labour-intensive boilerman or 'donkeyman' duties, which had often been allocated to the Yemenis, were no longer needed. This forced many Arabs to seek employment beyond their traditional maritime work. A large number left the seaports for industrial towns and cities. Larger communities began to form in cities like Manchester, Birmingham and Sheffield. The competition for jobs, not just at sea, had sparked-off a number of 'race riots' and the Yemenis like the other South Asian and West Indian migrants were easy visible scapegoats and targets for racism. The influx of other migrant communities to the docklands area in Cardiff where the Yemenis were concentrated became known, somewhat exotically, as 'Tiger Bay'. The visible otherness of the Yemenis has throughout their history in Britain been a 'reason' for racial attacks on them. Halliday has recorded many such racial attacks and has also expressed his personal perception of the Yemenis as the other. On one occasion when he travelled with some Yemenis in Britain he noted:

> One can only imagine what the few Birmingham residents then on the streets to get their morning milk and Sunday morning papers would have thought if they could have understood what these busloads of dark men were singing, attacking British imperialism and the perfidy of the Saudi ruling family.[36]

The fluctuating populations of the various local British Yemeni communities are often linked to the economic situation in Britain and, on rare occasions, to events in the Yemen. Liverpool was traditionally home to a small community of seafaring Yemenis but when the shipping industry declined after World War One most of the community moved to other cities. However, in the late 1960s a small community of Yemeni shopkeepers began to flourish as the city swelled its post-war industrial migrant workforce. When laws on immigration changed in Britain in 1962, there was another serge in Yemeni migrations to Britain. Equally, Halliday notes that when the Yemen relaxed its laws on allowing wives and children of migrant workers to leave in the early 1980s the British-Yemeni communities further expanded.[37] Although Halliday has observed that, "By the late 1980s there were fifth generation Yemenis living in Britain",[38] events in Yemen have helped British Yemenis to maintain very strong ties with their country of origin. They have also contributed in the community's 'incapsulisation' and passive segregation or what is usually called 'boundary maintenance'. Cultural traditions like the consumption of *qat*, a mild narcotic leaf chewed as a social activity, and the continuance of 'arranged' marriages with spouses from the Yemen seem to perpetuate the community's rigid introspectivity and percieved unwillingness to integrate.

It is interesting to note that the objections to what was originally termed as 'arranged' marriage[39] referred to in Halliday's work, have now been replaced by the phrase 'forced' marriages. The terminology has shifted from the association of 'forced' within the tradition and culture of mutually arranged marriage, quite acceptable and encouraged Islamically, to an attack on marriages where mutual consent is absent. It had been generally assumed that 'arranged' marriages were unpopular amongst British Muslims until the community could find a voice and correct this false assumption of 'arranged' being interpreted as 'forced'.[40]

Halliday's sociological study of the Yemenis in Britain leaves one with the impression that despite its long history the community has failed to make any real or visible impact. Whilst in comparison with other larger migrant communities to Britain this may be true, other observers like Dalrymple, Carr and Umar, distinguish the Yemenis from other Muslim communities as a model for 'integration' and 'British Islam'. Halliday, in contrast, sees the Yemenis as 'the invisible Arabs'[41] and concludes that they largely view themselves as 'sojourners'. This view is similar to the experience of some of the migrants from South Asia studied by Muhammad Anwar,[42] who whilst they deem themselves 'sojourners' will ironically never return; they can never be as settlers who have come to terms with their shifting Arab and British identities.

PAKISTANIS IN BRISTOL AND OXFORD

Studies on Muslim communities in Britain become historical social documents by default due to the time-space context in which they were originally written. For example, Patricia Jeffery's book[43] possibly one of the earliest anthropological studies on British Muslims, is very dated in the terminologies used, approaches towards and interpretations of the community observed. Jeffery's work traces the migration and early settlement of Pakistanis to Bristol.[44] As a study of a Pakistani community in Britain her book has some similarities to the work of Philip Lewis.[45] However, her work focuses primarily on the preservation of the ethnicity of the migrant community from an anthropological perspective whereas Lewis' primary concern is the identity and religious development of the community. The author offers an interesting insight into early forms of what are now termed Cultural Studies. As such the book is caught in its own era and reflects, to a large extent, the British concerns with newly forming migrant communities and their expected assimilation into a perceived British mono-culture.

Charting the traditionally established pattern of migration and settlement, the arrival of single males first later followed by wives and family, this work explores several distinct divergences between Pakistani Muslim and Christian migrants. A brief and concise introduction to Islam is offered by the writer as a means of contextualising the customs and culture of the Pakistani Muslims. There is no such introduction on Christianity to serve the same purpose for the Pakistani Christians. The implication is that Pakistani Christians enjoy a unique status in their shared religiosity with the host community. Muslims are seen and described as 'migrants' whereas Christians are expressed in terms of 'refugees'. This is because most Muslims actually intended to return to Pakistan and Christians on the whole wanted a 'new' and 'better', less religiously discriminated life in England. The author writes in expressed terms of 'Anglicization' and 'Westernisation' when referring to the assimilation of migrant families into British society. This terminology reflects the pervading attitudes to new migrant ethnic communities in the late 1960s and early 1970s and thus renders the work somewhat outmoded and dated. However, the author's observations of transported customs and social structures such as the *biraderi* or 'brotherhood/fraternity/kin' are accurately described and documented particularly the development of 'adopted kin' of the newly forming Pakistani Muslim community in Bristol. It is interesting to note that this neo-*biraderi* actually defies the traditional definitions of *biraderi* from within its geographical rural settings in Pakistan. *Biraderi* is in effect 'nearest and dearest' through blood ties, marriage and tribal bonds. In Bristol the hybrid form of kin was apparently created using a criterion based on acquaintance, similarity or shared social class. In profiling the migrants, which was restricted to a small number of informants, the author concentrated on the economic considerations of the community that for her seemed to be a major factor for migration. The writer visited Pakistan and admirably learnt to communicate in Urdu[46] so that she could further strengthen her relationship with her informants.[47] She noted that the majority of her informants were from poor rural areas and were mostly educated to only a very elementary level. In the case of Muslim women there was often no education at all, although one informant had an MA in English and was a qualified teacher. The Pakistani Christian women had all benefited from a missionary school education and as a result most spoke some English unlike their Muslim counterparts who, the author asserts, were disadvantaged because of this.

Pakistani Muslim migrants shared aspirations for what the researcher describes as 'ashrafization', the desire for social nobility through asserted religiosity. The antithesis of 'ashrafization' she claims, would be 'Westernisation', adopting or aspiring to the ideas and culture of the West. An apparent reaction to colonialism, 'Westernisation' is, the author contends, viewed as a negative trait which is perhaps equal to culture desertion or rejection.

The author claims that Pakistani Muslims had also transposed their erroneous ideas about British society and Christianity as an un-Godly society largely devoid of morality and shame. These wrong ideas had been imported to Britain by the Pakistani Muslims exclusively resulting in the formation of a very 'cut-off' or insular community concerned predominantly with the preservation of its culture and religion. The apparent desire for wealth and status 'back home' is portrayed as a kind of cultural 'upward mobility' which for Pakistani Muslims was reflected in the economic transferral of funds to families as dependants and investments in land and property in Pakistan.

Echoed in Muhammad Anwar's later work,[48] Jeffery's book records the acculturation of the second generation Muslims who display a more distinct British identity in contrast to their parents. However, her research, conducted in the early 1970s, does not assume that the majority of Muslims in Bristol would actually settle in Britain unlike the Christians who in the majority had already cut ties with Pakistan. The study asserts that because of a shared religion – although not culture – Pakistani Christians found it far easier to 'assimilate' into British society whereas Pakistani Muslims were far more reticent. Keeping very strong ties with Pakistan had added to the cultural identity of Pakistani Muslims and the establishment of religious and social events such as Qur'ān reading for children and an Asian Film Club had helped to some extent in preserving language and culture. The desire to retain a distinct Pakistani identity through social and cultural institutions is another example of what anthropologists describe as 'boundary maintenance'.

In contrast, the Pakistani Christians although culturally still very Pakistani,[49] generally wanted to break links and ties with their past they tended therefore to immerse or assimilate into their new social environment. By way of example the author refers to the Christian's pastime and preoccupation with visiting pubs and alcohol as an indicator of their willingness to assimilate. Fieldwork in Pakistan had, the author states, confirmed the Christian's claims that they were in effect treated as second class citizens. By the usage of the two terms 'migrant' and 'refugee' there is an implicit suggestion that the 'migrants' are opportunistic self-imposed economic exiles and that the 'refugees' are displaced or diasporic victims of religious oppression.[50] In reality, according to the author, most of the Pakistani Christians did not come to Britain directly from Pakistan; many came via Iran, the Gulf or Canada. One major area of research missing from the thesis is the effects and impact of racism on the communities studied. No observation or inquiry of the pervading societal trends in Britain, particularly the rise of racism and xenophobia, in the late 1960s and early 1970s has been offered. The book is also lacking in any discourse around post-colonialism and how much this featured in anthropological or social studies in the period when the book was written is a significant question. By excluding this background information the author places responsibility for the lack of inclusiveness in British mainstream culture, on the migrants rather than on the obstacles of exclusion by the wider society. In this respect, the terminologies, ethnocentricity, and general assumptions regarding the correlation and approximations between religion and culture and pervading attitudes to new communities and their integration into the wider society seriously date the work.

Alison Shaw has also published an anthropological study of the Pakistani community in Oxford.[51] The research undertakes an observation and analysis of the community's lifestyle, habitat, work and social environments in the context of its culture and faith. The author spent a limited period of seven months in Pakistan with families as a means of gaining further insight into the customs and traditions of Pakistanis. Perhaps typical of anthropological studies, the research details what was observed with precision yet there is little by way of in-depth analysis of the data. Nor does the author give reference to her research methodology or how she came into contact with her informants and how she collected her data. The researcher's interpretations of the intra-dynamics of this community may be unrecognisable to the community studied, but the observations on the living patterns of the community do provide a detailed and useful insight. The study is also specific to the Oxford community in that the author makes no claims that her findings are representative of all Pakistani communities in Britain although she asserts that there would be some correlation.

The 'outsider' perspective does sometimes lead to erroneous conclusions. This is particularly highlighted when the author describes her experiences in all male company in a community that is traditionally male-female segregated. She remarks that white women where often accepted into the all male space as 'honorary men'[52] when in reality it may be that the community was either affording her the status of a near female relative or simply accommodating her Western lifestyle which does not traditionally practise segregation of sexes. Pakistani families generally have a concept of the family that extends marital bonds and blood relatives and would normally even include *biraderi*. In these circles segregation of the sexes is not usually strictly adhered to. It is perhaps because of her interpretations of segregation that Shaw also concludes that married couples in Pakistan rarely spend time together. She claims this is because their husband-wife relationships are not normally one of companionship.[53] Exploring this theme further the writer observes the cultural practice of marrying within the extended family or what she describes as the 'caste' system. The study does not separate cultural practices from religious ones and the uninitiated would not easily distinguish between both. As with other similar works this research is more concerned with the cultural practices of the Pakistanis in Oxford. From an anthropological perspective Shaw's work does explore community cultural dynamics and the impact of the migration process of the customs and traditions of Pakistanis in Britain. However, Islam appears almost coincidental in the interpretations of the community observed.

KASHMIRIS AND BENGALIS IN BRADFORD

Philip Lewis has written a more recent study of a settled Pakistani community in Britain.[54] The title of the book,

Islamic Britain, is perhaps misleading as this research is restricted to the study of the Pakistani-Kashmiri community in Bradford. In focusing on this North Yorkshire city the author has 'honed-in' on a community that is not only predominantly rural Pakistani in its origins, but almost exclusively Mirpuri. The author's descriptive ethnographical research on the religious identity and practices of a remote regional ethnic South Asian community would no more reflect the normative for British Muslims than those of the Hausa Nigerian Muslim migrants in Manchester. Whilst the Bradford community represents a large Muslim urban presence, approximately 16% of the total population of Bradford,[55] their ethnic diversity compared with most other British cities is noticeably limited. Hence the 'Islam' that Lewis encounters is distinctly Asian in culture and traditionally rural. Although the study is able to locate other small ethnic entities of Indian and Bangladeshi origins, it does not engage with their transported cultural practices as it does in some detail with the Kashmiris. Along with the *Barelwis* and *Deobandis*, the book catalogues other Muslim theological and philosophical schisms present within the Bradford community from *Jamāʿat-e-Islāmī* to *Tablīghī Jamāʿat*. This work includes a brief history and development of these various groups in addition to their demography within Bradford's numerous mosques.

Beyond the intra-Muslim politics and theological differences the study examines the challenges of 'multiple identities' among the Muslim youth whose heightened sense of 'Britishness' is seen as being in contention with their traditional Muslim and Asian identities. Lewis seems to suggest that a synthesis of these two identities is not impossible. The researcher's insistence that for this Kashmiri Muslim community, language is indivisible from religion, is a central theme throughout the study. As the author makes a connection between the dependency of Urdu and understanding Islam, the implication is that second and third generation Muslims are distanced from their religion because of their bilingual ineptitude. Even when individual informants are presented as 'self-conscious' Muslims or 'Islamists', the inability to express their religiosity in Urdu is interpreted as a serious religio-cultural disconnection.

Lewis has made positive contributions in cataloguing the development of community facilitation both through mutual co-operation and self-help projects; the numerous mosques, Islamic schools and other social institutions being visible evidence of the communities' evolution. Muslim participation and representation into civic society via both internal organisations like the Council of Mosques and the Muslim Parents Association and outside institutions, such as political parties and the Commission for Racial Equality, are thoroughly studied by Lewis. Local landmark events such as securing *ḥalāl* meat provisions and the Ray Honeyford Affair are fully documented as are the impacts of national (the *Satanic Verses*) and international (the Gulf War) events. The book testifies to the intense media attention paid to the Bradford Muslims during the unfolding of all these incidents. Dubbed Britain's 'Islamabad' by the tabloids, the community is seen as a barometer by which British Muslim sentiment can be measured. It is also through these events that the study highlights some of the theological dilemmas for Bradford's *ʿulamāʾ* who are often at odds in their *fatwās* (Islamic legal rulings) on most of these issues. Commenting on the transition and transformation of this community's Islamic identity, so interwoven with its ethnic customs and traditions, from a rural Muslim majority environment to an urban, multi-cultural and pluralistic society with minority status has, the author claims, left many Muslim scholars 'out of sync'. He rightly observes that their traditional Islamic scholarship based on *taqlīd* (legalistic imitation) within *'dār al-Islām'* (the abode of Islam) has not prepared them for the problems of 'Western' acculturation by Muslims who understand Islam only from within a dominant Islamic society and, therefore, cannot appreciate a functioning minority status Islam, a theological problem addressed by Tariq Ramadan.[56] Lewis observes this phenomenon and offers a solution, like many non-Muslim and *some* Muslim commentators before him, in the form of a 'theological reformation' echoing that undertaken by Western Christendom which would seek to re-examine the way in which the Qur'ān is interpreted and understood as a divine text.

Almost a decade on from these observations and possible developing solutions to the adherence of *taqlīd*, we find within British Islam the evolution of *fiqh* through the re-institution of *ijtihād* (analogical opinion) contributing to a 'time and space' contextualisation of the *sharī'ah*. The researcher does not seem to find a place for *ijtihād* in his analysis and subsequent conclusion of the future for British Islam. This may be because the community he studied is bound to its traditional perceptions of Islam, functioning only via *taqlīd* within *dār al-Islām*. Perhaps this is the danger of representing one distinct community as a British Muslim paradigm.

The Bengali community in Bradford may not seem the obvious choice of location in which to study the newest Muslim community to have settled in Britain from South Asia. East London is home to the largest Bengali community in Britain and almost two-thirds of the population of Bengalis in Britain lives there. The majority of British Bengalis originate from the Sylhet region in north-east Bangladesh, formerly East Pakistan. Bangladesh gained independence from West Pakistan, which was originally split into two geographically separate parts, in 1971 after a fierce and bloody civil war. Stephen Barton's book, a study of the Bradford Bengali community,[57] pays particular attention to the religiosity of this community and closely examines the role of the mosque and the community's religious leader, the Imām. At the time of the research (1986) the author estimated the population of Bengalis in Bradford to be at one thousand. Islam came to the Bengal region of South Asia via Arabian and central Asian traders, scholars, soldiers and Sufis. Each of these travellers introduced various expressions of Islam, according to their particular interpretations and manifestations. The result has been a quite distinct and 'localised' form of religion that has fused Bengali customs and culture with Islam, producing a predominantly charismatic Sufi expression of Islam quite unique to the region.

The Bengali migration to Britain conforms with other South Asian migration patterns although their physical presence in Britain is far smaller than the Pakistani and Indian communities. The ability of the Bengalis to formulate functioning communities, which could form leadership and political representation, has been dominated and hindered by the rural village culture and traditions that pervade in Bangladesh. Traditionally communal and tribal, the community in Bradford was led as in Bangladesh by elders and leaders. The author noted that, "organisations were not related to the needs of the community but to the influence of certain people".[58] The researcher found that the best form of introduction by which to study the Bengali community was by using the public space of the mosque. As a meeting point and community centre it is a good means of establishing personal relationships with potential informants and to observe their religious practices. The small and intimate size of the Bradford community seems to have provided a better, more manageable, environment with easier access to informants for data gathering and study.

The community established its first mosque in 1960 to facilitate the growing number of women and children joining their husbands and fathers in Britain. In addition to the mosque the Twaqulia (sic) Islamic Society was formed, to 'secure its (the community's) unity and autonomy'.[59] When the society purchased two adjacent buildings to establish a meeting hall for celebrating weddings and religious festivals which also included accommodation for the Imām and a schoolroom, or *madrasah*, for teaching the Qur'ān and Bengali language, the result was a heightened sense of the community's Islamic and ethnic identity. The author's research clearly records that the establishment of a religious centre and the appointment of an Imām resulted in an increase in the community's religious observances. Despite social environments and conditions in Britain and Bangladesh being distinctly different, the author noted that, "the migrant community has preserved the system of *purdah*[60] in a variety of forms, both rigorous and flexible".[61] A whole chapter of the work has been devoted to the role of the Qur'ānic *madrasah* in traditional Muslim societies and within the newly forming Muslim communities in Britain. Barton has outlined in detail the institution and history of the Qur'ān school as an elementary form of religious education and a continuous tradition throughout the Muslim *ummah*. He traces the development of the *madrasah* in India during the time of colonial rule and records how the British effected the course of Islamic education by creating their own *madrasahs*. The general response was a boycott and a rejection of Westernstyle education, which was largely seen as indicative of colonial rule. New forms of Islamic teaching did however emerge which sought to integrate old and new methods of teaching. The after-school Qur'ān class is a feature of both traditional Sylheti culture and the new communities of Muslims in Britain. This particular traditional style of rote learning has come under much scrutiny by non-Muslim educationalists who largely view it as an outdated teaching method. The author acknowledges the possibility of social and psychological conflicts that may arise as a result of being caught between what he describes as, "ancient Islamic" and "modern Western" schooling. He sees the educational objective of Muslims thus: "they aim to develop Islamic concepts and institutions that will yet make use of the resources and insights of Western scholarship".[62] To emphasise this objective the author refers to the development of Islamic educational material in various European languages. Barton sees much value in this system as a means of forging a link between children and their religion. He dismisses criticisms of the traditional system as views that are, "mainly ignorant of the value of this practice to the Muslims and of the function of the school in the community".[63]

As a very traditional Muslim community rooted in their Islamic faith as an integral facet of their identity, the Bengali community still has great respect for the Imām. Barton traces this reverence to the early days of Islam when the Imām and Caliph both upheld and exemplified Islamic law and Muslim integrity, enjoining congregational acts like the observance of prayer and the payment of zakāt, the compulsory almsgiving. In the local setting of the Bradford community the Imām appears to have very little authority outside of the mosque. Whilst his congregational duties had actually increased because of the pressures and problems faced by many Muslims coming to terms with their new status and new cultural environment, the Imam's salary was in real terms, "less than he had received in his previous post in Sylhet".[64] The Imām was acutely aware of the impact of secularisation on his community and sought to redress the balance by exhorting a greater learning and adherence to the Qur'ān. Twice weekly the Imām gave a congregational sermon, one as the traditional Friday sermon or khuṭbah and a Sunday afternoon dars, or lesson, giving a tafsīr, or commentary on the Qur'ān. The author observed that the Imām tried to make his sermons relevant to the current situation and the community's conditions in Bradford, teaching that Islam should be practised beyond the confines of the mosque. The Imām's message was normally limited to the basic fundamentals of worship in Islam, although he was critical of saint worshipping and theories and theorists of secular thought. He also noted that the Imām was a member of Daʿwatul Islām, an organisation inspired by Jamāʿat-e- Islāmī,[65] and Barton observed:

His theme was taken up by those who spoke at the conferences, exhorting the Bengalis to be faithful Muslims, as individuals and as a community, so that the non-Muslim people of Britain would be attracted to Islam.[66]

Barton's useful research on the Bengali Muslims of Bradford records a community whose ethnic and religious identities are completely interwoven. This observation makes the work distinct from most other studies on Muslim communities in Britain, which focus primarily on the varied ethnicities as the predominant or most important element of their identity. This particular research is meticulously detailed and as a result it highlights how Bengali Muslims differ from other Muslims. It is also evident from the study that, like the Yemeni community in Britain, the Bengalis have a very strong cultural, emotional and psychological connection to their 'homeland'. This appears to result in the preservation of their religious identity in its original 'localised' and traditional form. Changes have occurred and adaptations to new situations and environments are manifest but in comparison to the development of other Muslim communities in Britain the Bengalis represent a very conservative religious entity.

The Pakistanis of Birmingham

There is a growing area of research studies on Muslim communities which focus on their social exclusion and disadvantages. Although most accounts make some reference to racism faced by Muslim communities, many studies seem to view racism as a peripheral problem or a less important feature of social exclusion. Daniéle Joly has, like Philip Lewis, explored how Muslims have combated social exclusion via community facilitation and by participation in mainstream political organisations along with other civic institutions. The study is engaged with the effects and challenges of the industrialisation and urbanisation of an essentially rural migrant Muslim community. Joly, Barton and others refer to an earlier work by Badr ud-Din Dahya[67] that examines the same phenomenon and Joly's book[68] combines both qualitative and quantitative data on the Pakistani community in Birmingham. The monograph is essentially a collation of papers and articles of studies undertaken by the author over a number of years. Some of the articles were originally written in French and published in academic journals in Europe and appear in the book in translation. This sociological study maps out the Pakistani migrant settlement and community formation in Birmingham; from initial ideas aimed at assimilation and acculturation, largely through the education system, to a more realistic inclusive and culturally reflective programme of integration primarily via multiculturalism. Community associations, through the development of mosques and cultural centres, are not, according to the author, formulated to replace kinship groups as Emile Durkheim might argue. Rather, she asserts, these facilitations are an expression of the organic and generic development of the migration/settlement process, 'the more complete the community, the more active the associations'.[69]

Joly's work provides data on the population growth and demography of migrant communities to Britain based on population censuses and surveys. The research brings to light some interesting facts regarding the urban settlement of British Muslims. The statistical data is comparable to those studies undertaken by Anwar[70] and Modood.[71] For example, in some inner city areas Muslims occupy 60% of the run-down and decaying pre-war houses.[72] Whilst unemployment is highest amongst ethnic minorities, in 1991 28.8% of ethnically Pakistani and 31.7% of ethnically Bangladeshi people were unemployed. Yet, self-employment amongst ethnic minorities was 16% compared to a 13% 'British National'.[73]

The study charts the development of the Pakistani community in Birmingham by examining its associations and institutions and their purpose and function in the preservation of cultural and religious community identities. The establishment of mosques for the Muslim community is, the researcher says, "a symbolic representation of the land of Islam".[74] The book observes that mosques have new functions that go beyond the traditional roles as a place of worship and centre of religious education as in South Asia. In Britain they also act as a platform for political issues, locally, nationally and internationally and as community centres. Muslim involvement in local politics has largely been as a means of self-representation firstly through the politics of inter-community relations primarily centred around the local mosques and secondly through involvement in local resident associations. Joly claims that Muslim interaction in these two areas represents, "their material well-being and that of their spiritual well-being in a foreign land".[75]

The book observes the shift in emphasis for those politically orientated Muslims from transnational political issues towards more localised British concerns and she lists a number of organisations and campaigns in which Muslims are involved. A new feature is the emergence of local Muslim councillors from the Pakistani and Yemeni communities in Birmingham. The issues of Muslim children in state schools have been major reasons for growing political representation. Poverty, social deprivation, exclusion, racism and racial tension are given as reasons why Muslims tend to affiliate themselves largely with the Labour Party. As Joly notes, "the Labour Party it would seem then, is supported by Muslims because it favours a social programme from which Muslims themselves could benefit".[76] Although the Conservatives occasionally field Muslim candidates, this is normally done only where a Muslim candidate is running for election with the Labour Party. The author believes that the 'Victorian values' held by the Conservatives are "imbued with imperialistic English superiority" and that they "leave no place for the cultures and religions of previously colonised peoples".[77] Whilst Muslim representation, as a recent phenomenon, has achieved some successes on a local level, the author observed (in 1995) that Muslims felt they had achieved little on a national level, "as exemplified by the absence of a Muslim MP".[78]

The particulars of Muslim needs in the field of education are confined to specific demands on dress codes, observances of religious holidays, *ḥalāl* meat provision, the teaching of sex-education, single-sex schools and collective worship or Muslim assemblies.[79] It is in provision for Muslim children within state schools that Muslims have successfully negotiated recognition of religious teachings. Lewis has also noted these significant gains and accommodations. The first problem was that of compliance with the school uniform for girls. In most cases older girls were required to wear a dress that revealed their naked legs, which is not permitted according to Islamic law. The unwillingness to accommodate religious dress codes led to many Muslim girls being excluded from school. Equally when the *ḥijāb*, or headscarf, was worn by some Muslim girls (again a religious requirement for females outside the home after puberty) was also met with hostility by some headteachers. In addition to exploring how Muslims are facilitated and culturally included or excluded within the state school system, Joly has studied the pervading Muslim parental attitudes and views on the education of their children. The author highlights the shift in emphasis from cultural assimilation through education towards a more realistic approach represented in multiculturalism. Whilst multiculturalist educational strategies are preferred to assimilation, Joly has noted that consultation with Muslim parents has largely been overlooked.

This study provides extensive data acquired through rigorous interviewing of Muslim parents. The increasing numbers of

Muslim 'faith' schools has for some Muslim parents resolved many issues relating to their children's religious identity and the type of education taught in state schools. According to Joly's findings, a commonly held belief by the majority of first generation migrant parents is that a good education is of primary importance for the future of their children and a major factor in their commitment to settling in Britain. Thus, although most parents were only modestly educated the survey showed that parental expectations for their children's education as a means of a better future are high. At the same time many parents would like to see 'mother-tongue' languages taught in state schools and suprisingly many parents believed that the school would provide a better facility and environment for teaching traditional Qur'ānic Arabic. As for the case of single-sex schools, 86% of parents surveyed wanted this provision for their children. Despite a degree of ineptitude in English, Muslim parents tended to display more parental involvement in their children's education than native English parents do.

The author has also offered an interesting exploration of the shifting identity of young British Muslims. Here, once again, the study employed qualitative data from interviews with young Muslims. She examined issues ranging from traditional family values, their relationship with Pakistan and Britain and Islam as a hybrid identity beyond traditional cultural manifestations. Her work acknowledges a growing sense of Muslim 'Britishness' and she notes, "if they are between two cultures, as is often assumed, they combine elements of both and have a new outlook".[80]

MUSLIMS IN LEEDS

An observation of the Muslim community in Leeds was undertaken by Ron Geaves and published in 1995.[81] This particular research has focused on the religious identity of the city's Muslims treating their ethnicities as a secondary component. It includes a brief demography and ethnography of the Leeds community including figures indicating the percentage per population of the various Muslim ethnicities. Into these figures the researcher has also included the 'fluid' and transitory student population which pushes up the total population of Muslims in Leeds to around twenty thousand. Geaves also mentions the impact of the construction of the Mangla Dam in Mirpur that displaced over a hundred thousand people many of whom already had relatives here and therefore migrated to Britain. This study charts the traditional and familiar patterns of migration and settlement and also contains some very interesting information from interviews with pioneering migrants like Chaudri Bostan Khan who came to Leeds in 1946 and a short time later, 'married an English woman who eventually converted to Islam.' Another interesting character is P.G.J. Shah who had first arrived in England in 1924 and later returned to the Punjab before finally settling in Leeds in 1943. Shah also married an English woman and this phenomenon seems to be a common feature of early migrants to Britain, an occurrence that Geaves says, 'bridged the cultures'.[82]

Muhammad Rashid Ali, the son of such a mixed marriage, informed the author how early settlers had preferred to live in Cardiff because, the researcher notes, 'there was a religious teacher to educate the English wives and children of the earliest subcontinent Muslim migrants to the city in the basics of Islam'.[83] Although Ali seemed disadvantaged in his younger days by the absence of a Muslim religious teacher, the situation was transformed when Ahmad Shuttari came to Leeds University to study in the early 1960s. Ali was taught how to read the Qur'ān and became well versed in the teachings of Islam. He later became involved in addressing local institutions, faith groups and organisations about Islam and was the first Muslim to become a magistrate of the city of Leeds.

The study asserts that the attitudes of these early Muslim settlers, in particular their interaction and mixed marriages with the wider community, had a direct and radical effect on the development of the Muslim community in Leeds. Geaves' research also includes population growth comparisons between the Muslim community and other minority faith communities from South Asia, Sikhs and Hindus. He quotes from the research of Roger and Catharine Ballard[84] who note that the 'suburbanisation' process saw the minority Bengali and Mirpuri Muslim communities as being disadvantaged and therefore, some fifteen years behind the development of the Sikh community. The author observes that the formation of the Muslim community in Leeds witnessed a certain amount of irreligiosity amongst many single males in its nascent period but the researcher says his informants were reluctant to confirm this. It also appears that they were a somewhat underdeveloped community compared to other Muslim communities in Britain. The research credits the shift in religious awareness to the presence of a small number of Bengali families in Leeds who sought to establish a mosque.[85] His profile of the Bengali Muslims mirrors the localised Sufi expression observed by Barton's study of Bengali Muslims in Bradford.[86] The Bengalis in Leeds initiated the first acquisition of a mosque, a former Jewish synagogue, then the Pakistani Muslims were invited to join the project when the required funds could not be raised by the Bengalis. Eventually, after much reluctance and negotiation the mosque was jointly purchased and established in 1960.[87] The mosque operated without an officially designated Imām for some time. It was only after the establishment of this first mosque, a joint effort, that others began slowly to appear; some developed from ethnic and theological divisions and others were instituted out of geographical necessity like the University Mosque.

Although the author claims his research is primarily concerned with the religious identity of the community he studied, there appears to be some confusion between what is observed as 'religious' and that which is 'cultural' or 'ethnic'. For example, the book correctly observes, "Islam's injunctions are apparent in many spheres of life" and that Islam employs a holistic approach encompassing, "social relations, marriage, divorce, kinship, economic and political relations" extending beyond the confines of what is traditionally identified as 'religious' here in Britain.[88] However, when referring to the arrival of women and children into the Muslim community in Leeds, the researcher states:

> all these aspects of Islam grew to prominence interwoven with South Asian ethnic customs. Islam was used to promote ethnic awareness as in the case of Halal butchers and other specialised shops and businesses catering to religious prescriptions, and the increased celebrations of religious festivals.[89]

Here, the issues of collective universal religious prescription, such as *ḥalāl* meat, are presented as South Asian ethnic dietary customs and the observence of Muslim religious festivals are portrayed as ethnic cultural manifestations. However, local traditions and customs, such as regional cuisine, dress, native languages, marriage ceremonies and mosque architecture are manifest heterogeneously in accordance with the variant local traditions and cultures.

The research also undertakes a brief description of the theological influences on the community and the author records that the key Muslim leaders in the community were influenced by the "Indian moderate tradition of Islam" by scholars like Muḥammad Iqbāl and Sayyid Aḥmad Khān.[90] The study also contrasts the ideological differences of the other main South Asian schools of thought, the *Deobandis* and *Barelwis*. Geaves notes however that, "although the mosques in Leeds have been equally divided between *Deobandi* and *Barelwi* congregations the attitude to these radically different approaches to Islam has generally been very moderate".[91] He also confirms the findings of many other researchers; an increase in religious interest among young people who, he noted, were mostly British-born and educated and were therefore discovering what Islam means to them directly. Whilst attributing this trend to a general "resurgence of Islam worldwide", the author concludes, "it may also be because Islam has been used by increasing numbers of this generation to resolve identity questions which have arisen from sitting astride two cultures". He adds that British-born Muslims will have an increasing role to play in community leadership.[92] The focus on mixed marriages seems to hold a certain fascination for the researcher who claimed that they had contributed to what he terms, "the moderation of the Leeds Muslim community".[93] The research concludes similarly to many other studies on Muslim communities in Britain, confirming that the migration processes and experiences of first generation Muslims is beginning to have less impact on how Islam shapes itself within the context of Britain.

PAKISTANI MUSLIMS IN MANCHESTER

Beyond the exilic and diasporic experiences of the first generation of post World War Two migrants to Britain is a new emerging community with a developing British character and culture which is increasingly identifying itself in expressed terms of its religiosity rather than ethnicity. This phenomenon has been covered briefly in the earlier works of Joly[94] and Lewis.[95] Jessica Jacobson has undertaken a more detailed research on this transition[96] and it is the subject of Elizabeth Scantlebury's article[97] on Muslims in Manchester. Scantlebury's comments on the increase in studies on Muslim communities in Britain saying that, "Muslims in Britain have generally been categorised within the confines of ethnicity, migrant status and as a facet of race relations".[98] This has been largely as a result of studies undertaken by non-Muslims who perhaps have projected their own interpretations of the importance of religious identity for British Muslims and Scantlebury claims that she seeks to redress the imbalance.

Her study argues that the wider British Muslim community should be viewed as a single unit but her study tends to focus on points of division rather than convergence. She notes that for any Muslim community it is the *ummah* that represents the paradigm for an Islamic society. Although the first community of the Prophet Muḥammad's era provides the ideal universal model, She does not gloss over points of difference amongst Muslims:

> National, ethnic and linguistic differences between Muslims, along with a variety of schools of thought within Islam, suggest that, in reality, diversity is a more accurate description than unity.[99]

The diverse mix of ethnicities and theologies of Manchester's Muslim community represents for the researcher the *ummah* in microcosm. She contends that once one looks beyond the paradigmatic *ummah* there can be an infinite number of segmentations of identities through the fractionalisation of religious ideologies and theologies, ethnic regionalism and racial belonging, tribal allegiances or *biraderi*. All of these observations, according to the researcher, "bypass important questions about what Muslims may have in common that could supersede the boundaries of ethnicity".[100] As a consequence her study endeavours to examine the Muslims in Manchester as a religious 'whole' and the author agrees with Jørgen Nielsen's assertion that British Muslims should be perceived as a single religious community:

> There is quite enough evidence to justify talking of a Muslim community in Britain. The traditional factors of division

continue to exist in some strength, factors of theology, policy, ethnicity and socio-economic background.[101]

The research briefly outlines the historical developments of the various ideological groups and refers to the more detailed studies on this subject undertaken by Robinson[102] and Werbner.[103] Scantlebury argues that the proliferation of mosques in Manchester is evidence of fragmentation along ethnic and theological divisions. The article includes a table which lists the number and location of mosques in Manchester as being nineteen (in 1995) along with the various predominant user groups according to their ethnicity and their theological and ideological affiliations. It could however be equally argued that the establishment of these mosques primarily reflects the settlement patterns of the various ethnic groupings of the Muslim community. Had the table included the date each mosque was established then perhaps a clearer correlation between the migration, settlement and community formation of each ethnic Muslim grouping could be made. Mosques function as very 'localised' religious centres and it would therefore serve no useful purpose to establish a mosque along a specific theological belief in a community that did not already reflect or share that particular school of thought. For example, Scantlebury lists two mosques for the Old Trafford district of Manchester and shows the main user group is Gujarati – *Deobandi*. Both the location of Old Trafford and the theology of the Deoband School of the mosque are traditionally linked to the migration and religious ideology of the Indian Gujaratis. The same can be said of the two Pakistani – *Barelwi* mosques in the Longsight district of Manchester, a traditional settlement area for Kashmiri migrants who, as Lewis' work confirms, are predominantly theologically *Barelwi*.[104]

To support her claim of fragmentation the author details the 'power shift'[105] of the Victoria Park, Central Mosque, established in the 1940s when it was attended by a small congregation of around seventy, mostly from Arabia and some from South Asia. During this period the congregation was theologically eclectic. As the Muslim community grew, due to an increase in immigration, the ethnicity of the congregation became predominantly Pakistani. By the 1970s, when a purpose-built mosque was established, Scantlebury records "the electoral system for the Mosque Committee had the inevitable result that it became, to all intents and purposes, a Pakistani mosque".[106] A further power shift later occurred but this time it was theological. The Imām, originally instated by the newly formed Pakistani committee, was of the *Deobandi* theological school. As the majority of Pakistani Muslims in Britain are theologically *Barelwi* it was perhaps natural that the Central Mosque should reflect the dominant ethnic and theological Muslim presence.

Pnina Werbner's article on migrant settlement shifts in Manchester, adapted from her original doctoral research in the 1970s,[107] charts the early migration of Pakistanis to Manchester and the community settlement into the Victoria Park and Longsight districts of the city.

> The mosque was initially bought and run by the whole Muslim community in Manchester...as the West Pakistani[108] community grew in numbers and spread into Victoria Park and West Longsight, its members came to dominate the Central Mosque. Today although officially the Central Mosque serves the whole community, it is controlled by West Pakistanis, and each of the other communities has its own mosque.[109]

Whilst the geo-political specifics of the spatial conglomeration of Manchester's Muslims would be unfamiliar territory to most readers, the above quoted events serves as an example of how mosques may be divided along ethnic and sectarian groupings. However, beyond the sub-divisions of Manchester's Muslims the researcher highlights a point of fusion with the creation of the Manchester Council of Mosques. As Lewis observes, with the creation of the Council of Mosques in Bradford, its formation in Manchester was also brought about by external pressures, "The Rushdie Affair and the Gulf War have had a profound impact on Muslims in Britain. They have responded by organising themselves together to give a united front."[110] The Council of Mosques eventually suffered a split when an election replaced an Imām in one mosque. The new Imām could not agree with the rest of the Council and so he withdrew taking four other Imāms with him. Despite fragmentation, the Council of Mosques continued to champion Muslim community causes in Manchester. Scantlebury uses the examples of difference as a means of proving that the ideological paradigm of the *ummah* is an impossibility, "at first sight, this would suggest that the ideal of one *umma(h)* remains largely unattainable, only to be experienced briefly during time of threat".[111]

Scantlebury's term 'fractionalisation' is used in the specific context of theological and ideological schisms observed as an increasing feature within the Muslim community of Manchester. Theological differences happened as a secondary feature in the establishment of community mosques in Manchester. The power-shifts documented in the history of the Central Mosque within the Victoria Park district, referred to by the author and Werbner, serve to example this phenomenon. Originally the mosque had been multi-racial and theologically eclectic. Although fractionalism in various forms hinders the ideal of a single harmonious community, many observers see a greater cohesion among the younger generation of emerging British-born Muslims. This study confirms the findings of Lewis, Joly, and Jacobson with regard to the heightened sense of religious identity above ethnic origins amongst second and third generation Muslims. The author notes:

Whereas the progression from fusion to fission may be the continuing experience for first generation Muslim migrants in Britain, the situation alters again for the British-born younger generation. Their perspective looks progressively less to countries of origin and more to interpreting Muslim identity in a British context.[112]

The Muslim Youth Foundation appears in the table of mosques in Manchester compiled by the researcher. Its location is listed as 'city centre', its main user group as, 'N/A' (not applicable) and its school of thought is recorded as 'non sectarian'. The article quotes extensively from the *Islamic Banner*, a monthly periodical of the Muslim Youth Foundation. The quotes used from the periodical are there to examplify the ideological shift of the youth towards the ideal of the *ummah*. One account of an ʿ*Īd* prayer celebration reads:

> It was heartening to see the many different nationalities; Jamaican, Malaysian, Arab, Pakistani, English, Bengali and others at one gathering. This affirms a growing awareness of the need for a Muslim Community devoid of ethnic, territorial, micro-religious or political divides.[113]

The *Islamic Banner* does not hold back on its criticism of elders in the community who fall short of the ideal of a unified *ummah* and instead perpetuate inter-Muslim sectarianism and rivalry. It also invoked the early days of an integrated Muslim community in the Central Mosque, "this original intention of the Central Mosque remained the ideal that inspired the second generation, British-born Muslims".[114] With the larger percentage of the Muslim community in Britain now born in this country, it would seem that a move away from the ethnic and religious divides experienced by the first generation migrants is apparent and a move towards a paradigmatic single religious identity is becoming a perceived reality.

CONCLUSION

The earliest studies of Muslim communities in Britain have observed the development of small groups of indigenous converts to Islam, notably the Liverpool Muslim community in the latter part of the nineteenth century led by Abdullah Quilliam, Britain's first official *Shaykh al-Islām*. These studies have largely been conducted by Orientalists and they tend to reflect the predominant societal attitudes towards Islam in that period. Anti-Muslim sentiment is probably due to religious polemics as Britain was still predominantly a Christian society, rather than it being an early manifestation of what is experienced today through 'Islamophobia'. Ironically, during the height of the British Empire it was Muslims and not Christians that represented the majority of Queen Victoria's Imperial subjects. Pool's account of the Liverpool Muslim community portrays his intrigue and fascination with a religious community which he sees as an anomaly and a forlorn effort of Islam in Britain. Arnold's study is less detailed but he is critical of the distinctly Anglo-centric form of Islam practised by the Liverpool Muslims. He records their forms of worship, which he sees as somewhat erroneous, concluding that this is an expression of Islam's ability to manifest itself in a 'localised' form.

The history of the Yemeni Lascars, their journey and eventual settlement in Britain, is well documented and their presence represents the historical continuity of Muslim communities in Britain. Whilst Lawless is interested in their 'otherness' in terms of their Arab identity, he views their eventual integration and acculturation as the end of an era. The majority of other observers such as Carr, Dalrymple and Umar celebrated their Anglo-Arab identity and example the Yemenis in South Shields as a model for integration. Halliday is less optimistic and sees the situation of the Yemenis more in terms of their introspectivity and invisibility. His observations of the local Yemeni communities throughout Britain reflect a community locked into its exilic and sojourner mindset. However, Joly alludes to the engagement of Yemenis in Birmingham as local councillors and active participants in mainstream British society.

The migration of South Asians to Britain has yielded the largest number of sociological studies and South Asian communities are usually interpreted and represented via their ethnicities and the dynamics of their religious identities are normally overlooked or treated as incidental, even peripheral. Anthropological studies like Jeffery's and Shaw's explore these communities in expressed terms of the 'other'. As a result their works are observations of how specific ethnic minority groups interact within their own member group and with the wider society and new social environments. Lewis and Barton have employed a different method of research through Religious Studies. They have analysed the religious dimensions of two very distinct ethnic minority groups that have settled in Bradford, the Kashmiris and Bengalis respectively. However, the religious expressions observed by these studies present a very distinct 'localised' and traditional form of Islam transported from the geo-cultural origins of these ethnic groups. A similar misinterpretation through confusion between religious, cultural and ethnic expressions also appears in Geaves' study of the Muslims of Leeds. It would be wrong to interpret the religiosity of such sub-groups beyond the contexts of their 'localised' religious expressions as first generation migrants and present them as normative for British Muslims.

The shifting identities of second and third generation Muslims, whose experiences and interactions with mainstream British society is often vastly different from the migration experiences of their parents, is an area of research with a growing bibliography. Joly, Jacobson and Scantlebury have explored to varying degrees the perceived new identities of British-born Muslims. Two distinct observations as a result of research amongst young British Muslims can be made. Firstly, the 'multiple' or 'shifting' identities of second and third generation British Muslims from the specific ethnic and cultural origins of their parents towards a broader feeling of being British, signifies them beyond a mere singular political definition. The new or shifting identity experienced by young British Muslims is often quite complex and difficult to express through generalisations or by essentialising British Muslims through their particular geographical and cultural origins. Qualitative data reveals that notions of what it means to be 'British' are usually expressed as a personal experience or interpretation. Secondly, researchers have noted an intensified sense of religiosity amongst a large number of young British Muslims. This hybrid form of religious identity is removed from the 'localised' and more traditional forms of religious expression manifest by their migrant parents. As the typology on Islam in the vernacular increases, young Muslims feel able to interpret and express their sense of 'Muslimness' within the cultural context of their new identities and environment. This shift from their geographical, ethnic and cultural origins results in their sense of Muslim identity within the global community of Islam – the *ummah* – becoming heightened. Developing their status as a minority faith group within the multicultural and religiously pluralistic framework of British society whilst ideologically connecting with the universal paradigmatic *ummah* has appeared to help young British Muslims negotiate the complexities of their shifting identities. This new confidence is manifest in the number of second and third generation British Muslims who can express and eloquently vocalise their experiences to the wider British society.

Chapter 2

Equality? The treatment of Muslims under the English Legal System

Nadeem Malik

Introduction

Given the current climate of debates on human rights, Islamophobia, multi-ethnic societies and pluralism, the Muslim community has often been the centre of attention. This chapter seeks to examine the rights of British Muslims with particular regard to their position within the English Legal System. In discrimination terms, the only tangible avenue available to Muslims historically has been to pursue an action under the Race Relations Act 1976. This Act has been very limited in application *per se*, and especially limited with regard to religious discrimination, which arguably was never its intent. The chapter presents the limitations of the Act and then considers more recent developments in English law such as the European Convention of Human Rights and its domestic application via the Human Rights Act 1998. The chapter then considers some more recent developments in law such as the Anti-Terrorism, Crime and Security Act 2001 and concludes that all available remedies at present are not satisfactory and that the incredulous anomalies that exist with regard to religious discrimination and discrimination against Muslims in particular, are inexplicable from a legal, moral or ethical perspective and can only be the result of an unsympathetic political regime.

RELIGIOUS DISCRIMINATION

Religious discrimination is well understood by those who experience it, hardly noticed by those who do not experience it, tolerated by those who indulge in it – and largely ignored by those who are in a position to do something about it.[1]

Introduction

Religious discrimination is a topic that has acquired much media attention ever since the Runnymede Trust report, *Islamophobia – A challenge for us all,* was published in 1997. The issue itself however has been significant for a considerably longer period but has neither been recognised by the media nor the law.

The lack of academic or other materials available on this topic serve only to support Mr Thomson's above-quoted assertion. Until recently, very little was written about this phenomenon and it was not included in the debates surrounding equality issues. Even the 'authoritative' texts and bodies such as the Commission for Racial Equality have, until very recently, paid cursory attention to discrimination on religious grounds. It has taken the incorporation of the *European Convention on Human Rights*[2] (hereafter referred to as the *Convention*) into domestic law, in the form of the *Human Rights Act* 1998[3] (hereafter referred to as the *Act*), to raise public awareness and create a situation where discrimination on the grounds of religion is unlawful, albeit in limited circumstances.

Given the above, one could assume that the issue is now resolved and that from October 2000 there has no longer been a problem. This however, would be a fallacious assumption. The Act is limited in application and scope and does not, in itself, provide a satisfactory solution to the problem. Just as the Sex Discrimination Act 1975 and the Race Discrimination Act 1976 did not, in themselves, provide a complete remedy to the problems of sex and race discrimination, the Act does not, in itself, fully resolve the problem of religious discrimination.

In order to assess the particular difficulties and factors that will have a bearing on this discussion, it is imperative that some fundamental questions are answered. These include a brief study of the evolution of race equality legislation, problems faced by such legislation, anomalies that have and continue to exist in law and the categorisation of different forms of discrimination.

Most of the examples will be taken from an employment context, as this is probably the arena in which discrimination most often occurs.

The Race Relations Act 1976 and Religious Discrimination

The Race Relations Act 1976 was enacted during a period of history that witnessed a revolution in equalities legislation. Within a very short period of time, the Sex Discrimination Act 1975, the Equal Pay Act 1970 (which came into force in 1975) and the Race Relations Act 1976 transformed the way in which women and people from minority ethnic groups were perceived by the law. Prior to these Acts, employers could lawfully discriminate against women and could, although unlawfully, discriminate against black people. The 1976 Act made it more difficult for such discrimination to take place because it allowed individuals to pursue their own action against an employer. Although discrimination on racial grounds was actually made unlawful by the Race Relations Act 1965, legal proceedings could only be initiated by the Race Relations Board, which was established by that Act. One may ask why, at that time, was discrimination on religious grounds not also made unlawful?

One can only hazard a guess at the answer, suffice to say that politically, this 'onslaught' of equality legislation was more than enough for the powers that be. The degree to which this whole issue was misunderstood is exemplified by the way in which the Sex Discrimination Bill, which became the model for the Race Relations Act, was drafted. The Bill sought to outlaw discrimination that occurred in a direct fashion only and made no mention of indirect discrimination. It was only during the hearing of the Bill in Parliament that arguments taken from United States law were considered and the Bill was amended to include discrimination on indirect grounds also. The importance of indirect discrimination will be explained in more detail later in this chapter.

For government to legislate against discrimination on grounds of race and sex, in both a direct and indirect context, was a revolutionary step. To have legislated against discrimination on religious grounds may have amounted to 'going too far' in that political climate. Indeed, it took almost another twenty years for discrimination on the grounds of disability to be taken seriously.[4]

In view of the above, it would be wrong to assume therefore that religious minorities have had no recourse against discrimination *at all*. It would also be incorrect to presume that there has been a common view amongst those that make, interpret and implement the law to *actively prevent* people from religious minorities from being discriminated against. Although there is no doubt that this may be the view of some, the majority of the Judiciary have at least attempted to give a wide reading to legislation so as to be as inclusive of minority groups as possible. This interpretation has assisted Muslims on a number of occasions and that cannot be ignored. However, such reasoning is often relegated to the realms of '*obiter dictum*' (non-binding principles) and fails to register in the essential '*ratio decidendi*' (binding judgement).

The ethos and spirit of discrimination legislation was expressed well by Lord Justice Waite in the Court of Appeal.[5] In explaining the governing principles of statutory construction, he said:

> Two principles are in my view involved. The first is that a statute is to be construed according to its legislative purpose, with due regard to the result which is the stated or presumed intention of Parliament to achieve and the means provided for achieving it ('the purposive construction'); and the second is that words in a statute are to be given their normal meaning according to their general use in the English language, unless the context indicates that such words have to be given a special or technical meaning as a term of art ('the linguistic construction').

In explaining the 'purposive construction' he observed:

> The legislation now represented by the Race and Sex Discrimination Acts currently in force broke new ground in seeking to work upon the minds of men and women and thus affect their attitude to the social consequences of differences between the sexes or difference in skin colour. Its general thrust was educative, persuasive, and (where necessary) coercive. The relief accorded to the victims (or potential victims) of discrimination went beyond the ordinary remedies of damages and an injunction – introducing, through declaratory powers in the Court or Tribunal, the recommendatory powers in the relevant Commission, provisions with a proactive function, designed as much to eliminate the occasions for discrimination as to compensate its victims or punish its perpetrators. These were linked to a Code of Practice of which Courts and Tribunals were to take cognisance. Consistent with the broad front on which it operates, the legislation has traditionally been given a wide interpretation.

Lord Waite then went on to quote with approval Lord Justice Templeman who said of the Race Relations Act:

> ...the Act was brought in to remedy a very great evil. It is expressed in very wide terms, and I should be slow to find that the effect of something which is humiliatingly discriminatory in racial matters falls outside the ambit of the Act.[6]

These statements, made by two of the most senior Judges in the country, clearly illustrate a willingness to look beyond the letter of the Act into the purpose that it was created for and to apply the rules of natural justice and equity in deciding any particular case. It is important to bear these principles in mind when considering the impact of any particular piece of legislation. As we will examine, the European Convention and therefore the Human Rights Act introduce other mechanisms of interpretation and particularise methods of limitation, control and integration which will no doubt develop in time.

In order to appreciate the complexities of discrimination legislation and its interpretation, it is useful to explore the various categories of discriminatory conduct and how Muslims have been considered by each. The two main categories are of particular importance, these being direct and indirect discrimination. Before looking at these categories in detail, a general overview of how the Courts have categorised different religious beliefs and individuals within a particular faith is necessary.

Definition of Discrimination

'Direct discrimination' is defined as follows: A person discriminates against another if on racial grounds he treats that person less favourably than he treats or would treat other persons.[7]

This definition is interesting in that it does not presume that the person bringing the claim is from a minority ethnic group, but only that they have been treated less favourably on racial grounds. This means that a white man who was refused a job for having a black wife, can bring a claim of discrimination.[8]

'Indirect discrimination' is defined thus:

A person discriminates against another if he applies to that other a requirement or condition which he applies or would apply equally to persons not of the same racial group as that other but:

1. which is such that the proportion of persons of the same racial group as that other who can comply with it is considerably smaller than the proportion of persons not of that racial group who can comply with it; and
2. which he cannot show to be justifiable irrespective of the colour, race, nationality, or ethnic or national origins of the person to whom it is applied; and
3. which is to the detriment of that other because he cannot comply with it.[9]

The wording is indeed complicated and difficult to understand. Justice Kilner-Brown described this section as "excessively and unnecessarily convoluted".[10] So 'convoluted' is the section that in an earlier case, in seeking to clarify the position, Justice Waite proposed no less than ten questions which should be asked when considering indirect discrimination.[11] The importance of indirect discrimination will become apparent later when it is identified that often the only approach that Muslims can take is to argue indirect discrimination.

Muslim v 'Ethnic' group

One of the particular difficulties that Muslims experience under the Act is the fact that Islam is not a religion confined to a particular 'ethnic' group. It is a trans-national religion and the billion or so Muslims in the world come from almost every nationality. The 'racial grounds' mentioned in s1 of the Act have been defined within the Act as colour, race, nationality or ethnic or national origins.[12] This definition was expanded upon further in the House of Lords case of *Mandla v Dowell Lee*.[13] This was a case involving a boy who was refused a place at school because he insisted on wearing a turban. It was a case of indirect discrimination as there were other Sikh boys at the school who did not wear a turban. The House of Lords in this case said that 'ethnic' should be construed widely in a broad cultural and historic sense. The issue in question was whether or not Sikhs could be considered to be an 'ethnic' group. In a detailed Judgement, the Lords set out certain criteria and characteristics which they said had to be taken into account when deciding whether or not a particular group formed an 'ethnic group'. The issue was whether or not that community was distinct by virtue of certain characteristics. The Lords said that of the various characteristics that could be taken into account, two were essential. Firstly, that the group should have a long shared history, of which the group was conscious and which distinguished it from other groups. Secondly, in addition to the first criterion, the group must have a cultural tradition of its own, including family and social customs and manners – often, but not necessarily, associated with religious observance.

The Lords mentioned five other characteristics that could also be taken into account and held to be relevant. These were:

1. either a common geographical origin or descent from a small number of common ancestors;
2. a common language, which did not necessarily have to be peculiar to the group;
3. a common literature peculiar to the group;
4. a common religion different from that of neighbouring groups;
5. the characteristic of being a minority or being an oppressed or a dominant group within a larger community.

The Lords also stated that a person could fall into a particular racial group either by birth or by adopting and following the customs of the group. The test was that firstly the person feels that they are a member of the group and secondly that the group accepts the person as a member. If these two conditions are satisfied, that is sufficient, and it is not relevant whether or not the person was born into the group.

In deciding the matter, the Lords found that Sikhs were indeed a distinct racial group and were therefore afforded all the protections of the Act. In considering the matter the Lords commented that Jews also met the conditions and were therefore an 'ethnic group'. This has been confirmed in a number of other cases also.[14]

The position with regard to gypsies is similar in that they have been held to constitute a racial group.[15] The reasoning was that whether or not a particular group are identified by their ethnic origins is principally a question of fact. Using the tests in *Mandla*, gypsies are a minority, they have a long shared history and a common geographical origin. They have unique customs, a common language, a history and ancestry passed from one generation to the next. Although the language is very similar to English, almost one fifth of the words are replaced by Romany words. Neither the fact that they do not necessarily share a common biological ancestry nor the fact that many of them no longer live a nomadic life were held to be sufficiently relevant. Given that many of them have assimilated into the general population was not relevant either, as it was held that there was still a clearly identifiable minority which retained its own identity and regarded itself as being gypsies and therefore an 'ethnic group'.

'Irish' has also been considered to be an 'ethnic' origin, whether it be a person from Northern Ireland or Eire.[16] The judgement said that the perceptions of ordinary people should be taken into account. Would somebody regard a person as being Irish even if they were from Northern Ireland? The answer obviously is yes, even though they would be a British citizen.

Various cases have followed a similar rationale and concluded that being 'Welsh' is a separate ethnic group.[17] The position is a little more confusing with Scottish people, although they are most likely a separate ethnic group too.[18]

THE POSITION OF MUSLIMS

Given the above, the position of Muslims is an anomaly. The general position is that Muslims are not a racial group.[19] In *Tariq v Young & Others* the tribunal held that Muslims are defined by their religion and not by their race, nationality or ethnic group. The tribunal distinguished the case from *Mandla* by saying that Sikhs are geographically defined by originating from a particular place in India and that they are bound by their culture as well as their religion.

Even more specifically, in cases where Muslims from a particular geographic background or culture have been considered, they have not been found to constitute a 'racial group' within the meaning of the Act. For example, it has been found that Mirpuris from Kashmir are not a racial group.[20] This decision was reached even though they have a particular language, geographic heritage, ancestral links, common culture and religious values. A similar position exists with regard to Pushtuns from Pakistan.[21] It must be said that individual tribunals decided these particular cases and different tribunals may take a different view. However, this has not been the case to date.

The anomaly is that a black Falasha Jew from Ethiopia, a white Ashkenazi Jew from Russia and a brown Sephardic Jew from Lebanon are all treated as belonging to the same ethnic race for the purposes of English Law – black, white and brown Muslims, Hindus, Buddhists or even Christians from the same areas are not given the same privilege.

Perhaps it was with this in mind that the Commission on British Muslims and Islamophobia said in its consultation paper:

> It has been established through case law that members of two world faiths, Judaism and Sikhism, are fully protected under the Race Relations Act 1976, since they are considered to belong to distinct ethnic groups. It is a serious anomaly that no such protection exists for members of other faiths, even though Muslims (as also Christians) would emphatically not wish to be seen as all belonging to a single ethnic group. A further anomaly is that direct discrimination in employment on religious grounds is unlawful in one part of the UK, Northern Ireland, but not in Great Britain. Officialdom's slowness to recognise these anomalies in anti-discrimination legislation may well be affected by Islamophobia, or by insensitivity to Muslim concerns. If new legislation were to be introduced specifically to outlaw religious discrimination, however, the clear public message would be that Islamophobia is unacceptable and that British Muslims have the same rights as all other citizens.[22]

IS INDIRECT DISCRIMINATION SUFFICIENT?

It will be in order to quote Robin Allen QC on this issue:

> Discrimination law has long recognised that the principle of equal treatment is not just concerned to ensure that the same

situations are not treated differently but also that different situations are not treated in the same way. Where different situations are treated in the same way, then disguised or indirect discrimination can occur.[23]

Robin Allen QC goes on to cite from the American Supreme Court to provide a clear statement about the aims of indirect discrimination legislation:

> Congress has now provided that tests or criteria for employment or promotion may not require equality of opportunity merely in the sense of the fabled offer of milk to the stork and the fox. On the contrary, Congress has now required that the posture and condition of the job seeker be taken into account. It has – to resort again to the fable – provided that the vessel in which the milk is proffered be one all seekers can use. The Act proscribes not only for overt discrimination but also practices that are fair in form, but discriminatory in operation. The touchstone is business necessity. If an employment practice which operates to exclude Negroes cannot be shown to be related to job performance, the practice is prohibited.[24]

Referring to one of Aesop's fables, the fox and stork were both thirsty and wanted to drink milk. If the milk were offered on a shallow dish, the stork would not be able to drink from it because it is physically different. Thus offering the milk on a shallow dish would have a disproportionate adverse impact on any stork, and offering the milk in a deep bottle would have a disproportionate adverse impact on any fox. In order to achieve true equality of opportunity, the milk would have to be offered in either a vessel that both the fox and the stork could drink from, or from two vessels, one suitable for each animal. To ensure further equality, each vessel should contain the same amount of milk. Often, it is the case that not only are the vessels that are provided not suitable for Muslims to drink out of, even when they can access the milk, there is very little of it. For example, an employer may try to limit overt acts of one kind of discrimination, but may 'draw the line' and allow other acts of discrimination.[25] Thus, although the contents of the vessel are accessible, there is very little milk contained within.

The fable, as extended, illustrates very well the limitations of indirect discrimination *vis-à-vis* Muslims. In a case of indirect discrimination involving a black Ethiopian Applicant and a white English employer, once the Applicant had met the conditions to satisfy the claim of indirect discrimination, he would have a clear remedy under the Race Relations Act. The position would be the same if a woman were to satisfy the similar test under the Sex Discrimination Act. If a Muslim were to prove indirect discrimination according to the same tests because the condition applied results in a disproportionate adverse impact on Muslims, although they had met the tests, or managed to access the vessel, there would be no remedy in law, or no milk!

To pursue an action of indirect discrimination under the Race Relations Act it is essential that the person making the complaint meets the criterion of 'racial group'. Therefore, there must be an element of *racial* discrimination before a complaint of indirect discrimination can be pursued. There have been cases involving Muslims who complain of racial discrimination as an integral part of the discrimination that they have suffered on religious grounds.

In the case of *J H Walker v Hussain and others*[26] seventeen employees were dismissed for attending ʿĪd Prayers and claimed indirect racial discrimination. They were successful because they all happened to originate from the Indian sub-continent and were therefore regarded as a minority ethnic group. Clearly, the underlying reason for the discriminatory act was to prevent them from attending ʿĪd Prayer, i.e. on religious grounds, the Tribunal considered that the effect would be to discriminate against most people from the Indian sub-continent and, therefore, would constitute indirect discrimination on racial grounds. If the seventeen Muslims had been white Muslims they would have had no remedy. Similarly, if both the Muslims and the rest of the workforce employed by J H Walker had all belonged to a mixture of different ethnic groups, so that it was not possible to view the seventeen Muslims as belonging to a distinct separate ethnic group, they would have had no remedy.

No matter how extreme the discrimination, often there is no recourse in law for a Muslim. For example, in *Safouane & Bouterfas v Joseph Ltd & Hannah*[27] two Muslim employees were summarily dismissed for praying during their lunch and afternoon breaks. Prior to their dismissal, they had been subjected to a series of discriminatory acts, including having their prayer mats urinated on. The Applicants could not argue direct racial discrimination as the treatment was related to their *religious beliefs* rather than their ethnic origin. The tribunal decided that there was no indirect discrimination either because although the Applicants belonged to the same North African ethnic Arab minority, the Respondents (respectively North African Jewish and North African Coptic) had a good record of employing staff belonging to a number of other ethnic minorities and could not therefore be regarded as being 'racially' prejudiced. The Applicants therefore had no remedy in law.

It is often the case that Muslim women bear most of the discrimination[28] and there are situations when a Muslim woman can seek to challenge the treatment that she has suffered by using the Sex Discrimination Act 1975. For example, in the case of *Sardar v McDonald's*,[29] Sabrina Sardar was summarily dismissed for wearing the *ḥijāb* or headscarf. She challenged the dismissal and was successful at tribunal. However, she won the case not on grounds of religion but on the grounds of sex discrimination. Her legal representatives were quoted as stating:

We fought the case on sexual discrimination grounds and not as religious discrimination, because religion is not recognised in law. If we had taken the case as religious discrimination, we would have lost.[30]

As Ahmad Thomson states in commenting on this case: "In spite of the words used, it is nevertheless clear that Sabrina Sardar was sacked because of her religious practice, not because of her gender".[31] It is therefore clear that although, due to no alternative, indirect discrimination has been a tool used by Muslims to attempt to secure fundamental human rights, it has not been a very effective one.

THE EUROPEAN CONVENTION ON HUMAN RIGHTS[32]

Background

The Convention is an international human rights instrument having a quite unusual feature of giving signatory states the right to allow individual petition, as well as allowing states to bring proceedings against one another. The United Kingdom granted the right of individual petition in 1966.

This has meant that ever since 1966, individuals living in the United Kingdom who feel that one of their Convention rights has been breached has been able to seek redress in international law if they have been unable to achieve a satisfactory remedy in domestic courts. In cases involving the right to freedom of religious thought, there may be a conflict of personal right and public interest. For example, if a Muslim wants to take a slightly longer lunch break on Friday in order to pray his obligatory congregational prayer he may not be allowed that extra time, even though he offers to make it up, because it may infringe on the work conditions of the whole organisation.[33] In conflicting situations such as these, a balance must be struck. The European Court of Human Rights explained this balance thus:[34]

> Inherent in the whole of the Convention is a search for the fair balance between the demands of the general interest of the community and the requirements of the protection of the individual's human rights.

It will be interesting to observe how this balance is maintained across Europe when dealing with varying conflicts posed by different religions. The interpretation which should be given to the Convention is certainly one which should ensure religious freedoms are protected. Section 2 of the Human Rights Act 1998 places on courts a statutory duty to consider Strasbourg jurisprudence when deciding cases that deal with Convention concepts. The Convention is an international treaty and should be interpreted in accordance with the Vienna Convention on the Law of Treaties 1969. The intention being that the Convention is read purposively, giving effect to its central purposes. These being varied and illustrated by case law. For example, the protection of individual human rights,[35] the ideals and values of a democratic society (contained in the preamble to the Convention) and pluralism, tolerance and broad-mindedness.[36] As stated in the case of *Marckx v Belgium*,[37] the Convention is intended to guarantee rights that are not *theoretical and illusory* but rights that are *practical and effective*.

This background is intended to indicate the positive aspects of the Convention and to provide an understanding of how it has been drafted to secure what really are, fundamental freedoms. This, in recognition of the fact that often these freedoms are denied or abused by various people, bodies and systems.

INTERPRETATION

It is important to note, however, that the Convention creates rights against states and not against private individuals, this being an obvious limitation in this context. There are numerous other limitations to the Convention, which follow a basic presumption. The presumption is that a right identified in the Convention is protected and that any subsequent limitation or exception is subject to this presumption. Any general instrument, especially when dealing with matters of human rights, by its very nature must identify basic rights and values, which will always be subject to limitation and exception to make the instrument realistic to implement. This notion is adequately explained thus:

> The Convention seeks to balance the rights of the individual against other public interests. Rights such as the right to respect for privacy and the right to freedom of expression may sometimes compete with each other (see *Kroon v Netherlands* (1994) 19 EHRR 263; *Soering v United Kingdom* (1989) 11 EHRR 439). Equally, individual rights under the Convention – such as the right to respect for private life (under art.8) and the right to freedom of expression (under art.10) – may conflict with other important public interests. These sorts of rights, which engage the rights and freedoms of others too, are necessarily qualified, and the Convention permits them to be limited by the state.
>
> But the object of human rights jurisprudence in democratic systems is to ensure that democracy does not mean that the tyranny of majority causes disproportionate interference with the rights of minorities. The Convention therefore seeks to ensure that the limitations which the majority may place upon an individual's protected rights, in the name of the common or competing interests, are imposed only if they are prescribed by law, intended to achieve a legitimate objective, and are necessary in a democratic society (that is, proportionate to the end to be achieved).[38]

It is unclear as to how this concept of 'proportionate to the end to be achieved' will be interpreted by different courts in different jurisdictions. The same principle will have to be considered when interpreting the Human Rights Act. Some of the Articles have general limitations and conditions attached to them which reveal the ethos and intention underlying their purpose. These limitations provide an interpretative guideline for those negotiating them and are intended to ensure a degree of consistency across member states. An example of such a limitation is Art. 8(1) which states "Everyone has the right to respect for his private and family life, his home and his correspondence". Using the definitions above, this would be the 'presumption' or presumed right. The limitations and exceptions to it are contained in Art. 8(2) which states:

> There shall be no interference by a public authority with the exercise of this right except such as is in accordance with the law and is necessary in a democratic society in the interests of national security, public safety or the economic well-being of the country, for the prevention of disorder or crime, for the protection of health or morals, or for the protection of the rights and freedoms of others.

Clearly, the exceptions listed in Art. 8(2) are open to interpretation by each member state and will be interpreted in the prevailing climate. The obvious fear for Muslims is the fact that there is an increasing level of Islamophobia[39] in European states and this has been well documented in the United Kingdom by the Runnymede Trust.[40]

The Convention is also to be interpreted in ways which conform with certain other doctrines and principles. For example, an underlying principle of Convention jurisprudence is the rule of law. The rule being that, no matter how desirable the end to be achieved is, no interference with a right protected under the Convention is permissible unless the citizen knows the basis for it and that basis is set out in an ascertainable law. Therefore, if no such detailed authorisation by the law is available, any interference will breach the Convention, irrespective of its justifiability. This principle protects the most sacred right of an individual to be conscious of his rights and freedoms. If individuals are to live according to a certain prescribed mode of behaviour, it is imperative that they know both what they can and cannot do. Other Convention doctrines and principles include legitimacy, proportionality, appreciation and derogation.[41]

FREEDOM OF THOUGHT, CONSCIENCE AND RELIGION[42]

Article 9 of the Convention provides that:

1. Everyone has the right to freedom of thought, conscience and religion; this right includes freedom to change his religion or belief and freedom, either alone or in community with others and in public or private, to manifest his religion or belief, in worship, teaching, practice and observance.

2. Freedom to manifest one's religion or beliefs shall be subject only to such limitations as are prescribed by law and are necessary in a democratic society in the interests of public safety, for the protection of public order, health or morals, or for the protection of the rights and freedoms of others.

The unique thing about Article 9 is that it extends to both individuals and to religious organisations. Therefore, a mosque, church or other religious organisation could institute an action on behalf of its members.[43] The other issue worth noting is that the Article includes religious and non-religious beliefs alike.[44]

At first reading, the Article seems to offer such a wide, all-encompassing right that one would be forgiven for thinking that it provides a solution to religious discrimination. This is arguably not the case, as is identified by Wadham and Mountfield:

> However, the Strasbourg case law places considerable weight on art. 9(2) and is relatively narrow when it seeks to balance the right to religious expression and the contractual rights of others, specifically employers. In cases in which discrimination because of the consequences of a religious belief have been alleged, the Strasbourg jurisprudence is extremely restrictive.[45]

This was illustrated in the case of *X v United Kingdom*,[46] which involved a Muslim schoolteacher who was not allowed to attend the mosque on Friday afternoons. The Commission decided that the conduct of the Education Authority did not amount to a breach of Article 9 because he had not disclosed this need at interview or during the first six years of his employment. The Commission decided that a fair balance had to be reached between the Applicant's religious requirements and the Education Authority's requirement to organise the school timetable efficiently. The United Kingdom could therefore rely upon Article 9(2) as their defence. It would be interesting to see how a similar case would be decided today, or what the position would have been if the Applicant converted to Islam and then made the same request.

Although one would hope that the decision would be different now, given more recent decisions, it may not be. For example, in a 1997 case,[47] a Christian employee argued that a requirement to make her work on Sunday breached her Article 9 right. The Commission decided that it did not. The reasoning was that "Ms Stedman was dismissed for failing to agree to work certain hours rather than for her religious beliefs, as such, and was free to resign". This alarming decision when viewed under the light of the aforementioned Aesop's fable, would lead one to conclude that even when the milk is offered, not only is it legitimate to offer it in an inappropriate vessel, but it is also legitimate to say "Well, if you don't drink it out of this particular vessel – you can die of thirst!" These two cases are indicative of the broad scope which the European Court of Human Rights has given to Article 9(2), where contractual obligations are placed before *prima facie* rights, and of the underdeveloped nature of the concept of indirect discrimination in this respect.

In other cases, a different approach has been taken. For example, in the case of *Kokkinakis v Greece*,[48] two Jehovah's Witnesses were convicted of proselytism for door-to-door evangelism. They were prosecuted and fined. The Court accepted that attempting to convert others was an integral part of their belief and that act was therefore protected under Article 9(1). The Court found that the limitation on this right was one prescribed by domestic law and that the intention of that domestic law was to protect the rights and freedoms of others. However, the Court decided that the decision to prosecute was "not justified by a pressing need" due to the fact that no regard had been given to the means used by the couple to evangelise. Had such means been improper then there would have been a breach of Article 9 but as such there was not.

The Convention can, therefore, be most useful in securing fundamental human rights, such as the freedom to religious worship, at European level. The difficulties of interpretation and conflict with other domestic legislation remain and will only be resolved or not, in time.

POST–11 SEPTEMBER 2001 LEGAL DEVELOPMENTS

It is helpful to consider a few of the recent changes that have been introduced in English law which may have a significant impact on both the psychological and practical existence of the Muslim community in Britain. These issues cannot be looked at in any context other than that of the events of 11th September 2001, simply because the events were so significant and acted either as a catalyst to the developments in question or indeed as the sole reason for their introduction at all. Halliday explains the significance of 11th September as follows:

> The events of 11 September 2001 and their consequences are, by any standards, a global event: the explosions themselves killed people of many countries, not least hundreds of Muslims, be they Pakistani and Arab professionals in the World Trade Center towers or the up to 200 Yemeni doormen and workers on the ground. The explosions were watched, with incredulity and fear, across the world. The longer-run consequences are worldwide, affecting military security, the everyday security of people in their own homes, workplaces and travel, the world economy and, not least, relations between peoples, cultures and religions. The events have precipitated a global crisis that will, if we are lucky, take a hundred years to resolve. They are far from being the first acts of violence intended to cause terror, by states of all shades and often of purported peacefulness. But they were in certain senses unique in form and consequences, and acquired a greater impact, occurring as they did, at the start of a new, initially hopeful, age. Political terrorism is a product of modernity itself: but the events of 11 September have punctured a huge hole in the optimism of the new millennium and of that modernity.[49]

The attacks on America created a new tension in the hearts and minds of almost every human being on the planet. The world's sole superpower had been exposed as vulnerable on its own terrain. Globally, every individual alive had a view on what had happened. These views ranged from the completely heartless having no sympathy for either those who lost their lives nor their loved ones, to the other extreme of people feeling that the only way to avenge the dead was to kill countless other innocent men, women and children. The political, social and economic consequences will indeed take decades to settle and become clear. At the time of writing NATO and Russia are signing new treaties to secure borders and join forces to combat the new faceless enemy – 'international terrorism'. Despite the rhetoric of President Bush, most Muslims around the world feel that they can begin to see the outline of that 'faceless enemy' – they fear that face may be their own.

To avoid the predicted 'Clash of Civilisations' that has become the bedrock of so much discussion on the New World Order, and there can be no doubt that such a clash must be avoided at all costs, it is imperative that a common sense of justice and value for human life be instilled in the hearts and minds of all people. This needs to take place at a global political level as well as at a local level. Without a sense of being valued, respected and treated equally, no human being can be expected to want to join hands with those around him and acquire a 'shared' sense of justice. People must be made to feel that they are not all being tarred with the same brush but are treated as individuals, given the same rights and privileges as people of other faiths and have the same legal status as all others. Communities of active, engaged citizens need to be created who are all working together with a common shared purpose and goal. This context is referred to by the Prime Minister as follows:

> Since 11 September, countries have been rapidly revising their relations with others. The stakes are high: we need to get it right. Should we fail to do so, and subside into protectionism, narrow regionalism or even isolationism, we shall pay a heavy price.
>
> But by the same token, the dynamism of globalisation and the speed of events makes this a moment of historic potential for creating international stability and peace, and for bringing economic development to parts of the world left behind. It is an opportunity to harness the power of community for the good of all, to create a world where people everywhere can

see the chance of a better future through hard work and the creative power of the free citizen, not the violence and savagery of the fanatic. And that is an opportunity we should grasp with both hands.[50]

The language of 'free citizen', 'creative power' and 'power of community' is inspiring and hopeful. Utopia does not seem mythical or even out of one's reach if we are to believe that the creation of such a society is possible. Sadly, it is clear that the skewed focus and unjustifiable emphasis of recent legislative change exposes a reality very distant from this utopian dream. It becomes apparent, when considering even fleetingly a few recent legislative developments, that British Muslims are not being given the same rights and freedoms that others enjoy. This fact has already been exposed earlier with regard to the Muslims not having any protection against religious discrimination under English law. If Muslims are to feel that they can be part of this dream, that they too can fully participate in society, struggling against its ills and rejoicing in its goodness, they will need to feel that they are equal in their citizenship. This includes equality in law, economy, media and politics. What we will examine are some of the social and psychological implications of legislation on the Muslim mind, how deep rooted historical Islamophobia plays a role and how current debate around citizenship can exclude Muslims as a result of this context.

The situation for Muslims in Britain is particularly aggravated by racially motivated crime. Given that the vast majority of Muslims in Britain belong to minority ethnic groups, they are often the focus of both racially as well as religiously motivated crime. Racially motivated crime is on the increase in Britain in any event. A recent Home Office study[51] shows that there was an increase of 107% in the reporting of racist crime in 2000. Race crime in England and Wales increased from 23,049 cases in 1998-1999 to 48,000 in 1999-2000. Some areas of England saw dramatic increases such as 459% in West Mercia and 364% in Devon and Cornwall.[52]

A particularly controversial piece of legislation has been the Terrorism Act 2000. However, the Anti-Terrorism, Crime and Security Act 2001 illustrates better how British Muslims were again failed by the English Legal System by being denied the same protection that is granted to some other religious minorities.

THE ANTI-TERRORISM, CRIME AND SECURITY ACT 2001

This Act was rushed through Parliament so quickly that very few people were even aware of its implications. It was considered to be a knee-jerk reaction to the events of 11th September 2001 and received severe criticism from civil rights organisations who considered it to be even more objectionable than the Terrorism Act 2000. It is beyond the purposes of this chapter to seek to enter into a discussion of the various complex areas of this Act and what they mean for civil rights in Britain. The focus will be on Part 5 of the Act which deals with Race and Religion.[53] The key issues here relate to the possibility that the Act could have extended the Public Order Act 1986 to include an offence of incitement to religious hatred and how the Act amends the Crime and Disorder Act 1998 to include religiously aggravated offences. The decision to not include an offence of incitement to religious hatred provoked much debate within the Muslim community which felt let down by Government once again. The reasons for this are explored below.

The intentions behind the Act were to strengthen legislation to protect against any terrorist threat that may occur, especially given recent global events and in particular the close relationship that Britain has with the United States of America. The Act is broad in increasing state powers to deal with these potential threats, providing numerous methods of investigation, detention and punishment for those convicted of an offence. Part 5 of the Act particularly covers issues relating to racially aggravated offences of assault,[54] criminal damage,[55] public order[56] and harassment.[57] These have all been extended to include religion. In its early presentation before Parliament, it was suggested that the Act include a provision to amend Part 3 of the Public Order Act 1986 to include incitement to religious hatred. This clause was withdrawn as it was desired that the Act be implemented as soon as possible and any further debate on this issue would serve only to delay that. The consequences of this for the Muslim community were considered by them to be very serious.

AMENDMENTS TO THE PUBLIC ORDER ACT 1986

On the 13th December 2001, the Home Secretary was forced to withdraw his proposal to amend the Public Order Act 1986. In Parliament he said:

> Coming from Sheffield, I am familiar with the old nursery rhyme about the grand old Duke of York. So I have marched myself up to the top of the hill and I am about to march myself down again. Before anyone can quip about giving way gracefully or otherwise, I shall ask this House to give way to the House of Lords, which has voted twice to remove the incitement to religious hatred clause from the Bill. There we have it. There will be consequences. Every decision we take – be it this House, the House of Lords or people in their individual lives – has consequences.[58]

Obviously it was not an easy decision for Parliament to make. There were clearly reasons for and against the introduction of such a provision on both sides. Arguably however, this is often the case when a Bill makes its way through the Houses and therefore it was nothing new or unduly complicated for Members of the Houses to deal with. This particular clause however was one that could simply not be agreed upon within the time allowed. The arguments that were proposed for and against the clause are considered below.

Reasons for incitement to religious hatred clause:

The major reason for amending Sections 18 to 23 of the Public Order Act 1986 would have been to address the anomaly which exists with regard to the way in which religious groups are recognised within the law. This anomaly has been considered in detail earlier and is specifically that some religious groups are offered protection by the law whilst others are not. This is on the basis that those religious groups that are protected are deemed to be racial groups, i.e. Sikhs and Jews. This leaves the anomalous situation of Muslims and other religious groups not being recognised under the law and therefore not being offered any protection through it. This position was outlined by the Home Secretary during the debate.[59]

The effect of this distinction and the problems it poses within the context of employment law was considered earlier in this chapter. The distinction between race and religion and the legal protection offered to one and not the other has an impact in numerous other spheres of public life also. These include civil matters such as family law, the allocation of resources and public funds (where grants are often made on the basis of ethnic categories as opposed to religious categories) as well as criminal law. For our purposes, the Public Order Act 1986 does not recognise religious groups and this leads to some very sophisticated forms of pernicious discrimination against Muslims to be legally perpetrated.

One such example of this 'legal discrimination' is the case of *R v Director of Public Prosecutions ex parte The Council of the London Borough of Merton.*[60] In this case Merton Council asked the High Court to declare that Muslims should be covered under the provisions of the Public Order Act 1986. This was rejected by the Court which upheld the view that Muslims were a religious group and not a racial group and could therefore not enjoy the protections offered by the 1986 Act. The brief facts of this case were that a community of Muslims living in south London purchased an old dairy and converted it into a mosque. They were subjected to a campaign of abuse and harassment by a group of British National Party (BNP) members. Members of the community were physically attacked, threatened, spat at and abused verbally. The BNP went on to launch a public campaign which included putting up thousands of stickers and posters showing offensive material about Muslims. These were displayed throughout the area including the mosque itself and the local civic centre. The police were contacted and they began proceedings. They arrested the local BNP organiser, Paul Ballard, together with three thousand stickers. He was charged under Section 23 of the 1986 Act for inciting racial hatred. The police however were instructed by the Crown Prosecution Service to drop the charges as they considered that although the material was clearly 'offensive and threatening', Muslims were not protected by the 1986 Act as they did not constitute a 'racial group'. This position was confirmed by Justice Tucker in the High Court.

It is highly likely that if an identical case were to be presented before the Courts today, although everybody concerned would agree that the material is offensive and threatening, once again, nothing would be done about it. Obviously if the 1986 Act had been amended, Mr Ballard would have been convicted and sentenced appropriately. If the campaign had been against a Sikh Temple or a Jewish

Synagogue, there is no doubt that Mr Ballard would have been convicted.[61] One only needs to visit the BNP website to see exactly how well they have used this loophole in the system to legitimately discriminate against Muslims.

What messages does this kind of reasoning send out to the British Muslim community? Are they expected to believe that these are simple oversights which the British Parliament and Judiciary have been making for the past thirty odd years? Or is the position not that the will is not there but that the debate is so complex and to legislate for such protection would be so difficult that it is impossible to do? If it is the latter, British Muslims ask themselves why it is that other groups can then be legislated for – are the issues not the same or are they more complex when it comes to Muslims? If it is that the position with regard to Muslims is indeed more complex, then how is it that so many other legal systems around the world manage to protect Muslims against religious discrimination? Whichever argument one accepts, it seems at best illogical and at worst a malicious confirmation that those in a position to protect Muslims, simply do not want to do so.

An argument against the adoption of the clause was that it would stifle freedom of speech and thereby infringe on the basic human rights of others. Indeed, this is a valid fear that the Muslim community shared. Just as every other just-minded person committed to living in a democratic plural society, no Muslim would want to stifle the legitimate right to free speech enjoyed in Britain today. As a matter of fact, this cherished right is not enjoyed by many Muslims living in so-called Muslim countries and is therefore even more cherished by British Muslims. Further, no Muslim would want their right to speak freely curbed in any way either. It is submitted however that this would never have been the case if this clause were to have been implemented. In order to protect an individual's right to free speech and strive to reach a balance between that right and the right of another not to be offended, various safeguards would have been included within the Act itself. These would have been firstly that it must be shown that the person accused of inciting religious hatred used threatening, abusive or insulting behaviour. Intent would also have to be shown – that either there was a clear intention to cause incitement or that there was a likelihood that religious hatred would result from the use of such language. The word hatred itself is a safeguard as it signifies very powerful feelings, the level of which would have to be proven. This would obviously rule out jokes or simple observations.[62] It is hard to imagine any person innocently discussing the behaviour, beliefs and customs of another being convicted of inciting 'hatred'. The clause would also have been drafted to refer to a group of people rather than an individual and would further have required that the incitement be in the public domain. Finally, no prosecution could be pursued without either being instituted by the Attorney-General or with his consent.[63] These provisions would render it almost impossible for a person without malicious intent and a powerful manifestation of that intent to harm a group of people to be prosecuted unfairly.

REASONS AGAINST INCITEMENT
TO RELIGIOUS HATRED CLAUSE:

Ironically, the Muslim community shared one of the main reasons for why the incitement to religious hatred provision should not be included in the Anti-Terrorism, Crime and Security Act 2001. That reason was simply that it was inappropriate to include such a provision in an Act that was primarily designed to tackle terrorism. Given the climate of Islamophobia and the generally unhealthy attention being paid to Muslims in particular, it was felt that to include the provision at this stage would not only be inappropriate but would serve to strengthen the stereotype that there is a link between Muslims and terrorism. This led to an unusual situation where Members of both Houses who had campaigned for a number of years to introduce protection against incitement to religious hatred found themselves opposing the same provision when it came before them. The main argument being that rather than protect Muslims and minority faith groups, it would serve to increase tensions instead. It was also argued that it would be perceived that the provision was being introduced to simply protect one faith group, Muslims, whereas this was not the case.[64]

Another argument to exclude the provision was that there is a distinction between religion and race. Whereas race is a genetic attribute, something that one is born with and cannot change, religion is a matter of choice.[65] In matters of choice one must be subject to criticism and those being critical should not be disallowed that right. Indeed, it is through such criticism of religions that often many people end up choosing to follow them.[66] There was also concern about the degree to which the protection would extend and how innocent commentators may fall foul of the provision. The counter argument to this point has already been presented above.

The traditional argument of how to define a religion arose again in this discussion. This argument was considered earlier with regard to implementing legislation to protect against religious discrimination. The amended 2001 Act would not have provided a definition for what constitutes a 'religion'. The situation legally is not clear and there is an argument that some sects and cults could use the provision to justify not only the private practise of their beliefs but also public manifestation of and invitation to them.[67] Any criticism of such beliefs would then become unlawful.[68]

Another criticism was that by extending the legislation to include religion, other forms of incitement to hatred were being excluded. These included incitement to hate on the grounds of gender, sexual orientation and political views.[69] Indeed, the severity of the problem of inciting hatred is highlighted in various recent academic publications.[70]

Finally, it must be pointed out that the incitement to religious hatred provision was not the only one taken out of the Bill. Other provisions considered inappropriate such as powers of the police, retention of communications data and disclosure of information were also withdrawn.

To summarise this part of the 2001 Act, although there were clearly understandable reasons and complications with regard to the implementation of the incitement to religious discrimination provision, it would have been a historic opportunity to introduce legislation that would not only protect and put British Muslims on a level playing field with other minority faith groups, but it would also have sent out powerful clear signals that Muslims are indeed welcome, honoured and respected in British society. This, at a critical time in history when Muslims are feeling more victimised and persecuted than ever before. Had this provision been introduced, the xenophobic conduct of the BNP and others could be prevented and perhaps the civil unrest experienced in northern English cities in the summer of 2001 could have been avoided (this is discussed in more detail in the next chapter). It seems that whenever there is a balance to be struck between the religious freedom and rights of British Muslims and some other matter (such as how to define religion), Muslims often suffer.

AMENDMENTS TO THE CRIME
AND DISORDER ACT 1998

Parts (1) to (6) of Section 39 of the Anti-Terrorism, Crime and Security Act 2001 amend Sections 29 to 32 in Part 2 of the Crime and Disorder Act 1998. These sections deal with 'racially aggravated' offences which, as amended, become 'racially or religiously aggravated' offences. Section 28 of the 1998 Act, which provided the meaning of 'racially aggravated' will now read:

1. An offence is racially or religiously aggravated for the purposes of Sections 29 to 32 below if:

    a. at the time of committing the offence, or immediately before or after doing so, the offender demonstrates to the victim of the offence hostility based on the victim's membership (or presumed membership) of a racial or religious group; or

    b. the offence is motivated (wholly or partly) by hostility towards members of a racial or religious group based on their membership of that group.

2. In subsection (1)(a) above – 'membership,' in relation to a racial or religious group, includes association with members of that group; 'presumed' means presumed by the offender.

3. It is immaterial for the purposes of paragraph (a) or (b) of subsection (1) above whether or not the offender's hostility is also based, to any extent, on any factor not mentioned in that paragraph.

4. In this section 'racial group' means a group of persons defined by reference to race, colour, nationality (including citizenship) or ethnic or national origins.

5. In this section 'religious group' means a group of persons defined by reference to religious belief or lack of religious belief.

These amendments now render it unlawful to commit an offence under the 1998 Act against a person because of either their race or their religious belief. Further, it also introduces this concept into the aggravated offences. Sections 29 to 32 of the 1998 Act deal with aggravated offences which can now be on the basis of race or religion. Aggravated offences carry a higher penalty than the offence that they are based upon and it was therefore most important that the amendments introduced with regard to religion apply to them also.

Sections 39(5) and 39(6) of the 2001 Act amend sections 29 to 32 of the 1998 Act to include religiously aggravated offences as well as racially aggravated ones. These sections deal with assaults,[71] criminal damage,[72] public order offences[73] and harassment.[74] All of these offences can now be charged with being religiously aggravated.

The purpose of these amendments was to ensure that people of any faith, who have not committed any offence and are innocent citizens, are able to practise their faith protected from any fear of violence.[75] The reality still remains that Muslims are increasingly under attack and that both individuals and places of worship continue to be the target of unjustifiable violence. However, these amendments are certainly welcomed by the Muslim community that can be vaguely reassured that at least a little is being done to protect them from religiously aggravated prejudice and attack.

Conclusions

It is clear that the position with regard to Muslims suffering religious discrimination is at best unclear and at worst regarded with indifference or hostility by both those who interpret law and those that make it.

It is absolutely essential that this situation is resolved urgently, as the degree of suffering and inequality pervading a 'civilised, democratic Europe' on the basis of religion has been increasing daily. The position is articulated well by Lord Lester of Herne Hill[76] who stated:

The fundamental question raised, with great power, cogency and eloquence by the noble Lord, Lord Ahmed, and the noble Baroness, Lady Uddin, is the problem of Islamophobia. It is the problem of how to give British Muslims the right to effective remedies for arbitary discrimination and unequal treatment of the kind that people like myself have if we are discriminated against as Jews on racial grounds.

I personally find it strange that I should have a remedy if I am discriminated against on racial grounds but, for example, the noble Lord, Lord Haskel, should not have a remedy if he is discriminated against on religious grounds. When, as an officer in the Army, I experienced discrimination, I could never tell whether the anti-Semitism was on racial or religious grounds. Other noble Lords have referred to the complications, as did the Right Reverend Prelate the Bishop of Oxford in his important speech.

There surely has to be an effective legal remedy for the wrong of religious discrimination as well as the wrong of racial discrimination. I suggest that those who raise technical objections to the framing of legislation should concentrate on the need for a legal remedy for British Muslims that is as effective as that which exists for other minorities in this country. That is the pressing social need that must be addressed.

When I hear technical objections being raised I wonder whether we ever look at the laws of other countries. Almost every other Commonwealth and continental European country, as well as Ireland, have in their written constitutions guarantees of equal protection of the law without discrimination on any ground, including religion. It is only because we do not have such constitutional guarantees that we have the incoherent patchwork of laws that act in their place. Surely, it is absurd that my rights as a British citizen should depend on whether I happen to live in Great Britain or Northern Ireland. How can it make sense that religious discrimination is forbidden in Northern Ireland and not in Great Britain? I know of no other country like that.[77]

Perhaps the issue of fundamental rights and freedoms will only begin to be resolved when the wisdom of Lord Lester dawns upon all those involved in the Judicial process.

Clearly then, there are significant anomalies and contradictions that exist within the English Legal System with regard to the treatment of Muslims. How long will these anomalies be allowed to exist and is it possible to resolve them? These and other pertinent questions need to be answered not only very quickly, but also in a fashion that ensures equality of treatment and equitable grounding for future developments. The desired statues of having a vessel that is suitable for all to drink from, and which will provide all with equal amounts of milk, will not be achieved without considerable thought, sensitivity, research and change.

The Race Relations Act 1976 has proven itself to be limited in scope and flawed in construct. Over twenty-four years its effect and impact has been highly suspect and limited even in terms of race discrimination, let alone religious discrimination. The differentiations of direct and indirect discrimination and the very definition of 'race' that have evolved serve only to complicate matters and exclude large numbers of minority communities. The intended purpose of the Act, to provide an equitable platform and prevent discrimination against members of minority communities, has certainly not been achieved in the case of Muslims. This, even for Muslims who come from minority ethnic backgrounds. Surely there is now an established need to review and amend the Race Relations Act to remedy these glaringly obvious defects?

The very language that has been shaped by the various discourses on 'equality' debates has created a culture that is not 'religion friendly'. This is why bodies like the Commission for Racial Equality and Race Equality Councils will not provide assistance to those suffering from discrimination on 'religious' grounds. A knee jerk reaction automatically rejects the likelihood of any remedy existing in English Law being pursued and renders the victim paralysed. The work of the Runnymede Trust has done much to address this issue and to bring attention to the use of language and stereotyping[78] and has highlighted the need for further study in this area.

Given this, there may be small windows of opportunity which exist for Muslims from minority ethnic backgrounds, but there are absolutely no remedies in law at all for converts to Islam who are discriminated against because of their faith. An almost unbelievable state of affairs results in a person being able to lawfully discriminate against another on religious grounds, even though the other person may look like, act like, have the same ethnicity as, even have the same name and family as the perpetrator of the discrimination!

As to the European Convention and Human Rights Act, both are clearly also limited in scope. The provisions are subject to limitations and controls and the cases decided to date show that once again, Muslims will not be treated equally. How the Convention rights will be treated within these limitations and constraints by domestic courts remains to be seen. One can only assume that, as required by the Act, the lead will come from the European Courts. If this is the case, as mentioned, the treatment of Muslims will most probably not be very favourable.

What then is the solution to this problem? This may seem a difficult question in the light of the existing complexities and pervasive attitudes. However, as with most issues in law, a relatively simple answer can be given by referring to basic principles which can then be translated into a legal instrument by adding the requisite terminology, limitations, qualifications and interpretative construct. The questions that need to be answered are: Is it proper that in a democratic, pluralist, civilised, Western society people are allowed to be discriminated against on religious grounds? Is it proper that when such discrimination takes place, victims are left with no clear remedy in law? Is it proper that the powerful tools of language and media are allowed to dictate which groups are allowed to have their universally accepted fundamental freedoms protected?

It is only when these questions are answered that the situation will become clear and the obvious needs of those suffering discrimination on religious grounds will be met. Perhaps then, the essential prerequisite is a political change, an acknowledgement of the particular problems encountered by the Muslim community in the light of the pervading climate of Islamophobia. The United States Senate has recently made such an acknowledgement where the following Resolution was passed on 1st July 1999:

That:

1. the Senate condemns anti-Muslim intolerance and discrimination as wholly inconsistent with the American values of religious tolerance and pluralism;

2. while the Senate respects and upholds the right of individuals to free speech, the Senate acknowledges that individuals and organizations that foster such intolerance create an atmosphere of hatred and fear that divides the Nation;

3. the Senate resolves to uphold a level of political discourse that does not involve making a scapegoat of an entire religion or drawing political conclusions on the basis of religious doctrine; and

4. the Senate recognizes the contributions of America's Muslims, who are followers of one of the three major monotheistic religions of the world and one of the fastest growing faiths in the United States.[79]

Such commitment and awareness holds out a ray of hope and a touch of optimism in an otherwise deeply troublesome scenario.

In short, although Muslims have, in the past, been largely unprotected from religious discrimination, some hope now exists in the form of *Council Directive* 2000/ 78/EC *of 27th November* 2000 (on the implementation of the principle of equal treatment in employment and occupation – but not in any other spheres of life – without discrimination "on grounds of religion or belief, disability, age or sexual orientation"). It has been adopted under *Article* 13 *of the EC Treaty* as introduced by the *Treaty of Amsterdam.* This Directive was implemented by the United Kingdom on the 2nd December 2003 in respect of religion or belief, so as to be compatible with the rights set out in the *ECHR*. Despite its obvious limitations, it is a step in the right direction. Furthermore, in July 2004 the Home Secretary again proposed a law against incitement to religious hatred. This was welcomed by the Muslim community as well as the Commission for Racial Equality which argued that any potential law should have wider application and also cover the delivery of goods and services. While these positive developments are acknowledged, British Muslims are concerned about the way in which they have generally been, and still are, treated under the English Legal System. Ranging from lack of legal recognition to specifically being targeted under the Terrorism Act and by being excluded even when the opportunities to offer them limited protection arise, such as under the Anti-Terrorism, Crime and Security Act, British Muslims feel disadvantaged. This situation needs to be addressed urgently; if it is not, British Muslims will never feel that they are truly equal citizens.

Chapter 3

British Muslim Identity

Dilwar Hussain

INTRODUCTION

Of all the internal debates that face Muslims in Britain perhaps one of the most vigourous is about identity. The identity of those who migrated to the UK from various parts of the world, the first generation of the settled communities, is perhaps easiest to define. Those who lived their formative years in Pakistan, Bangladesh or Egypt would rarely deny that they are Pakistanis, Bangladeshis or Egyptians who live in Britain. The issue becomes somewhat more complex for those who have been born in the UK, second and third generation Muslims who will be the primary focus of discussion (and address) here. I am not going to delve into the issue of identity among converts to Islam directly or specifically, though this is an interesting and worthwhile area of study that has some significant parallels with the case of second and third generation Muslims.

Why is the issue of identity so important? Because without being able to psychologically take up the identity of being British, people whose ancestors have settled on these isles, will not feel that they are 'at home'. Hence, they will be condemned to remain as 'migrants', never really putting down roots. Or will be perceived as a 'minority' even though some of Britain's boroughs are now over 50% non-white. This chapter will look at the issue of British Muslim identity and examine why this is an important debate for Muslims. On a methodological note, it should be mentioned that while such a discussion would initially seem very sociological, a solely sociological approach when dealing with a phenomena such as British Muslim identities may create a discourse that is too reductionist in nature. Such a subject has explicit social, political, and theological dimensions, (not to mention perhaps also psychological and economic ones implicitly) and it is therefore difficult to have a proper discussion of contemporary Muslim identity without also engaging with at least the political and theological dimensions of the subject matter. The chapter therefore takes these three perspectives into account and presents an insider view of British Muslim identity, primarily addressing a second generation, British Muslim audience.

What is a British Muslim? Can such a creature exist? A simplistic definition might be: anyone who carries a British passport and is a Muslim. But obviously the situation is far more complex. A look at the root of the word 'identity' will show that it implies some degree of 'sameness' hence the word 'identical', yet it also connotes difference,[1] suggesting that an identity is an individual, differentiating phenomenon. One may therefore say that identity is relational with 'another' and not an entirely isolated matter. Thus, identity, which can have many facets – social, personal, psychological, political, etc. – is the (self) definition of a person or group, in relation to others. The reason for pointing this out is that, logically speaking, from the outset a discussion of identity cannot be an entirely isolationist one, as by definition there has to be interaction. What is up for discussion, however, is the degree and nature of this interaction.

Entwined with this discussion are the many debates surrounding Britishness itself. What does it really mean to be British? Of course this question could be broadened to cover almost any national identity, yet with Britain there is a peculiar factor, the difference between being English and British. In order to look into what this difference may exactly be, one has to really look at the history of Britain, the precise meaning of the terms English and British and how they have come about. Another important factor to consider is how these terms are defined. Is it simply a matter of what is commonly accepted, or is it by self-definition? Are these differences based on race, culture or language, or are the differences deeper? It is perhaps due to the very complexity of this debate that it has remained a contentious one for so long.

For many there seems to be a crisis of identity among young Muslims in Britain; however one needs to be cautious of generalising and drawing such conclusions hastily. For while in the minds of some young people there is a genuine sense of crisis – they are not sure as to what their identity should be – one finds many others that are comfortable with their individual identity, but because different people have adopted different means of self-definition, collectively there is not as much congruence as one would have presumed, leading to a sense of chaos or 'crisis' in collective terms.

The events of 11th of September 2001 and the ensuing 'war on terrorism' have placed a spotlight on Muslim communities across the world that is difficult to avoid. This has been further exacerbated by the wars in Afghanistan and Iraq. In the UK, Muslims have come under considerable pressure from the media, with accusations of disloyalty to their country being levelled in some cases. New laws have been rushed through Parliament that affect not just terrorism, but immigration, asylum and a host of other matters. The Home Secretary's call for a language test has been seen by some as a departure from Labour's traditional defence of minorities. However, one can see some reasons for concern. The riots that broke out in Oldham and Bradford in 2001, the condition of inner city areas, the 'segregated lives' that people are leading, are all constantly challenging the boundaries of the many debates around being Muslim and British.

Recent research among Muslim youth shows that many young people are blending the local identities of their environment and friends and the culture of their parents to come up with new, hyphenated identities such as 'British-Pakistani-Muslim'.[2] While most Muslims would comfortably include Britishness in their self-description, and those living in Scotland and Wales quite easily self-define as Scottish or Welsh, it seems that few of those living in England would say that they are English. Yet moving to the regional level many would quite easily identify themselves as a 'Scouser' or a 'Brummie'. This difference between regional, English and British identity is one that will be considered briefly here but deserves further exploration.

Although a poll undertaken by MORI reported that 87%[3] of Muslims surveyed feel 'loyal to Britain', notions about being British are by no means unanimous within Muslim circles. The real debate is raging on within the minds of young people who are faced with different influences from their parents, 'the community', school, peers and the broader influences of British society. Yet despite the fact that the debate hovers above the heads of Muslim youth, it would be naïve to think of this as a new debate within Muslim circles. The settlement of the early Muslim communities in Europe refluxed the question of how much of European culture could be adopted and how much should be rejected. In 1865 two opposing *fatwās* were formulated about Muslims wearing hats that originated in the West.[4] And going back to the early days of Islam, one would, no doubt, find similar debates among the Muslim communities that migrated from the Arabian

Peninsula to other parts of the world as they encountered Persian, Byzantine, African, Slavic, Chinese or Indian Culture.

To make matters more serious and controversial, the debates around identity touch upon crucial questions – the whole nature of the relationship between the Muslim world and the West, and the nature of the relationship between Islam and modernity.[5] How much of Muslim legacy and tradition is sacrosanct and therefore 'non-negotiable' or firmly established (*thābit*) and how much is a matter of interpretive application, and contextualy bound to a particular era and geography, and therefore subject to change (*mutaghayyir*) over changes of time and place? This debate has aroused the passions of the Muslim world and led to a wide spectrum of responses ranging from complete rejection of anything Western to challenging the validity, in the contemporary world, of the Qur'ān and/or the *Sunnah*.

IDENTITY

The Definition of Self

In modernised societies there is a heightened sense of the individual and self-identity. The daily choices we make about clothing, food, the newspapers we read, the television programmes we watch, all speak volumes about who we are and send out images, consciously or sub-consciously, about the type of person we think we are. Choices of belief, personal philosophy, career, relationships, similarly give out such signals. Yet this is not just one-way traffic, for we constantly influence others and are influenced by external factors, be it the people around us or the pervading culture. Because of the individualisation of society and the break from traditional modes of social roles, this notion of self-identity becomes more powerful. The individual has achieved a greater scope of choice to shape his/her self, to be an individual. As Giddens puts it:

> What to do? How to act? Who to be? These are focal questions for everyone living in circumstances of late modernity – and ones which, on some level or another, all of us answer, either discursively or through day-to-day social behaviour.[6]

The individual however is not completely free to act alone. For Giddens there are connections between the most 'micro' aspects of society – individuals' internal sense of self and identity – and the bigger picture of the state, multinational corporations, and globalisation, the 'macro' level.[7] Sociology cannot make sense of each of these levels by looking at them in isolation. If, for example, one is to consider the changes in morality in Britain post World War Two – looking at relationships outside marriage, increases in crimes of an immoral nature or the increase in sexual imagery in the public domain, such changes cannot be accounted for adequately by looking at either the micro or macro levels. They were not led by social institutions or the state, yet neither did individuals spontaneously change their minds about moral behaviour. Most of such changes were influenced by a decline of religious authority and were perhaps coupled with the rise of materialism in British society. These changes were in turn affected by other social factors and influences. Changes in laws regarding family and gender roles would have come from the macro level, yet their demands would have stemmed from the micro level. The change within the micro level would have been caused by social movements at the macro level, which of course would have come from people's experiences and dissatisfaction at the micro level. Change is therefore a result of a very complex interaction of micro and macro forces.

The Media

There are few influences in the modern world as great as that of the mass media. Whether it is in the form of popular entertainment, documentaries, chat shows, or news magazines and papers, the media is likely to shape our images of self, others and the relationships between the self and the other. It may not be an exaggeration to say that no such 'force' existed in the past in visual, electronic, audio and print format; constantly on, constantly interacting with us. Ranging from a reflection of what happens in society to allowing us to escape from what happens in society, the media constantly nudges and challenges us. While news and documentaries may inform us or 'report' to us, such information is also reappropriated by society and a cause and effect loop is set up. Hence information in the media does not merely reflect the world, but constantly shapes it as well.

Transient and Multiple Identities

Michel Foucault looks at identity as something that is not within a person, but rather as something that results from people interacting. People do not possess a real identity; an identity is a temporary construction that is constantly shifting. For Foucault the notion of self is related to power. Power, which may be defined as the ability to influence the environment, or the ability to act, is something that individuals engage in. Power is not possessed, it is exercised. And where there is power, there is bound to be resistance. Hence identities are not given, but are the products of ongoing processes, meaning that identities are constantly produced and transformed through social interaction.[8] It is the reality of the world that individuals, despite being single entities rarely occupy or appropriate single identities. An individual may be a father, husband, son, cousin, uncle, office worker, sportsman, etc. all at the same time. Shifting effortlessly from one role to another or indeed juggling different roles at the same time while negotiating his way through life. Similarly when considering a religious and national group such as Muslims living in Britain, multiple layers of identity come into play.

Multiculturalism

The invitation of a migrant labour force from the Commonwealth Countries after World War Two, with the existence of push-pull effects,[9] led to a rapid influx of migrants during the 1960s and 1970s. While those arriving into Britain may have already been 'British Subjects' it was for the first time in recent history that such large numbers of people, so visibly different were taking residence in the British Isles. It became clear that with such migration the idea of Britishness would inevitably change. The experience of fascism across Europe had meant that most people were not willing to support notions of racial exclusion as a popular ideology. The tension that this created was significant. Enoch Powell in his (in)famous speech of 1968 said:

> We must be mad, literally mad, as a nation to be permitting the annual inflow of some 50,000 dependants, who are for the most part the material of the future growth of the immigrant-descended population. It is like watching a nation busily engaged in heaping up its own funeral pyre.

Powell continued to elucidate the dangers that the settlement of migrants would pose,

> For these dangerous and divisive elements the legislation proposed in the Race Relations Bill is the very pabulum they need to flourish. Here is the means of showing that the immigrator communities can organise to consolidate their members, to agitate and campaign against their fellow citizens, and to overawe and dominate the rest with the legal weapons which the ignorant and the ill-informed have provided. As I look ahead, I am filled with foreboding; like the Roman, I seem to see "the River Tiber foaming with much blood".[10]

Powell's 'rivers of blood' speech may sound unacceptable to us now, but it seemed to have articulated the sentiments of the nation. Opinion polls showed that 75% of people supported Powell.[11] Just prior to this, in 1964, a Conservative local candidate in Smethwick won using the slogan "If you want a nigger for your neighbour, vote Labour". Policy makers embarked on a twin track policy of 'limitation' and 'integration', as Roy Hattersley summed it up, "without limitation integration is impossible, without integration limitation is inexcusable,"[12] showing how laws to curb immigration were linked to legislation aiming to outlaw racial discrimination and creating a place for 'blacks' in British society. It was Roy Jenkins who took this a step further, articulating the early British notion of Multiculturalism:

> ...a flattening process of uniformity, but cultural diversity, coupled with equal opportunity in an atmosphere of mutual tolerance.[13]

What do we mean by Muslim Identity?

In order to understand British Muslim identity, let us take a step back to look at *Muslim* identity. It is proposed here that the most important elements that impinge on the formation of a Muslim identity are:

- The concept of self (who/what am I?)
- The concept of territory (where am I?)
- The concept of community (the people I live with).

1. *Self*

Muslim notions of the self are forged by the complex interchange of numerous factors, perhaps the most influential among these being the concept of God and man's relationship with God. For a Muslim, God is One (a concept known as

Tawḥīd) and is the Loving and Merciful Creator, Sustainer and the final Judge of all affairs. He is the Lawgiver and the Sovereign (among other attributes), but above all He is Compassionate, Forgiving and Just. And while man is created in a natural state of purity and goodness as vicegerent of God (*khalīfah*), he is capable of weakness and forgetfulness. Man is therefore deputed (*istikhlāf*), but encouraged to constantly bear his Lord in mind (*dhikr*) in order to be conscious of God (*taqwā*) and fulfil his duty as *khalīfah* with justice and diligence. This strong relationship between man and God is designed to keep God at the hub of human life such that the Divine Spirit touches all of man's actions whether this worldly or other worldly – in fact such a division is artificial, for God is the Guide in all affairs. In order to remind mankind, throughout the ages, God has chosen messengers and given them inspiration and revelation to remind people. This role now rests with the believers who are encouraged to 'call unto good things', to 'promote what is right and discourage what is wrong'. This spiritual relationship and divine context (*rabbāniyyah*) sets the scene for man's many and varied roles in life.

The Muslim is therefore a subject of God, in fact His deputy, who lives not for himself only but to bring goodness to humanity. The concepts of *tawḥīd, istikhlāf, dhikr, taqwā* and *rabbāniyyah, inter alia,* form the core of a Muslim's being and essence.

2. Territory

Traditional Muslim societies were not based on the nation-state and it is largely a European influence that led to the creation of the many Muslim nations that exist today. Nationalism was embraced by some, but initially vehemently rejected by others. The days before the nation-state saw the Muslims living in territories where it was not uncommon to see people of various ethnic and linguistic backgrounds sharing the same geographical space. To this day, the debate goes on as to how legitimate nation-states are within the Islamic framework.

Another fundamental idea in the conception of space is the role of religion in public life. Until secularism became prominent, mainly during colonialism, Muslim societies saw a fusion of religious, political, economic and social life, as Ernest Gellner comments that the association of Islam with temporal authority,

> has one important sociological consequence: the absence of accommodation with the temporal power. Being itself Caesar, it had no need to give unto Caesar.[14]

This said, there was always a recognition within Muslim societies of distinction between the public and private, and political and religious domains leading to a *de facto* division of powers. However, this was not as pronounced, particularly in the case of the latter, as in modern secular states.

During early Islamic history, Muslim scholars derived specific geo-political terms to define the way in which the law should apply to Muslims living within and outside the Muslim territories. The region that was under Muslim rule was defined as *dār al-Islām* (abode of Islam) and the 'other' regions were variously described as *dār al-ḥarb* (abode of war), *dār al-kufr* (abode of unbelief), *dār al-ʿahd* and *dār al-ṣulḥ* (abode of treaty), *dār al-amn* (abode of security), etc. Many more definitions were coined, but by far the most common were the first two, leading to what Tariq Ramadan calls 'a binary vision of the world':[15] the world of Islam and the world of 'others'. The implication this had on jurisprudence was great. Though there were differences among the various schools, most of them disliked that a Muslim should live outside *dār al-Islām*. Limited permission was granted for traders, students, preachers, etc., but these were generally seen as exceptions granted for a minimum time. This was inter-linked with related issues that arose among the scholars of the time: If a Muslim lives in a non-Muslim society, what are his duties towards that society? What are his duties towards the *Sharīʿah*, i.e. the law of the 'homeland'? What if a person (living in a non-Muslim society) converts to Islam, should he/she migrate to *dār al-Islām*? The opinions of scholars were quite diverse. While Abū Ḥanīfah (d. 767) disliked that Muslims should reside in non-Muslim territories and Mālik ibn Anas (d. 795) felt it was strictly prohibited, Abū'l-Ḥasan al-Māwardī (d. 1058), on the other hand, was of the opinion that if a Muslim could practicse his religion in a non-Muslim land, that land could be seen as part of *dār al-Islām*. Jaʿfar al-Ṣādiq (d. 765) suggested that at times it might be better for a Muslim to live in non-Muslim territory.[16] Upon close scrutiny one can deduce that the vital criteria of *dār al-Islām* were seen to be factors such as personal security, justice, freedom of worship and avoidance of corruption. Thus, in the context of North Africa – to where Muslims were fleeing from persecution encountered in Spain and Southern Europe – one finds very categorical Mālikī *fatwās* urging Muslims not to live in *dār al-ḥarb*.

One may, therefore, raise questions about the ironic situation today, where in some cases Muslims have been forced to flee from Muslim countries and seek refuge in countries in the West because of political problems. It is bearing these factors in mind that some contemporary scholars are questioning the whole approach of this binary vision.[17] Is it possible in this globalised world to have such a vision, especially when no such entity exists that the scholars can unanimously identify as *dār al-Islām* against which a *dār al-ḥarb* can be defined? Fathi Osman, Yusuf al-Qaradawi and Faisal Mawlawi are noteable scholars who have been writing and speaking on this issue over the last decade. Their views now seem to be filtering into US and European Muslim circles, especially as the latter two scholars are involved in a European *fiqh* council established in 1997.[18] Along with others,[19] these scholars have questioned the contemporary validity of the above terms pointing out that such definitions were a matter of juristic opinion, *ijtihād,* and are not found in the Qur'ān or the *Sunnah.* The Qur'ān reminds us that: "to God belongs the East and the West",[20] that regardless of political or moral expression in different countries the *whole* earth belongs to the Creator.

3. *Community*

Community here means all the people that one lives among, Muslims and non-Muslims alike. The Qur'ān relates the story of many messengers, saying that God sent the messengers 'to their brethren',[21] who were non-Muslims. The Prophets addressed their community as 'my people!'[22] (*qawmī*). Hence there is a fraternal relationship between the Muslim and his community, regardless of their belief. The Muslim is one of 'them', 'they' are part of the *qawm.* The Qur'ān further clarifies this:

> O mankind! Behold, We have created you from a male and female, and have made you nations and tribes, so that you might come to know one another. Verily the noblest of you in the sight of God is the one who is most conscious of Him...[23]

Thus, plurality of cultures and ethnic groups is acknowledged as a positive factor to enhance human life, rather than be a cause of prejudice.

At the same time there is the notion of belonging to a single 'community of faith', an *ummah.* This notion, often expressed in terms of brotherhood, is intended to be essentially faith-based rather than being ethnic, cultural or linguistic, though these notions have their place. This creates a very strong affinity and trans-national link. Sophie Gilliat-Ray comments that:

Nationalist ties appear to be a secondary means of identity for many young British Muslims. Given the racism so deeply embedded in parts of British society, feelings of 'belonging' to this country may be insecure, while at the same time they do not feel that an identity based upon being of Pakistani origin offers a viable identity in this country. Religion provides a way out of this identificational *impasse*, and presents a secure foundation for identity based upon time-honoured religious myths and rituals.[24]

However the notion of *ummah* does not negate one's duties to those who are neighbours, fellow countrymen or part of one's *qawm*. The idea of the concept of *ummah*, as theoretical as it may be, is to transcend the bonds of kinship, language, region and ethnicity. Such ties, identified as ʿ*aṣabiyyah* by the fourteenth-century Muslim historian and sociologist Ibn Khaldūn (d. 1395), are frowned upon when taken as the normative in group cohesiveness. In reality all Muslim societies struggle, and have struggled since the dawn of Islam, in trying to balance the idea of an *ummah* of Islam, with ties of faith alone, with the human desire to aggregate on the basis of lineage, language or class. We will consider this a little further in the next section when looking at national identity and Islam. Having looked at the notions of self, territory and community, let us look at the era of the Prophet Muḥammad and his Companions, to see how they dealt with the issue of identity:

1. Although the Prophet prescribed that the believers were to "be different from the disbelievers"[25] a close examination shows that this applied to those aspects of life that dealt specifically with religious symbolism, or acts that were distinctly opposed to Islamic teachings. However, when it came to issues of social interaction, such as trade, marriage or even consumption of food, then not only was allowance granted for Muslims to interact with people outside their

faith, but the Qur'ān goes out of its way to declare that, "The food of the People of the Book is lawful unto you and your food is lawful unto them".[26] This shows that the outlook of the early Muslim community was not one of isolation.

2. The Prophet Muḥammad (pbuh) respected diversity within the community. Bilāl was from Abyssinia, Salmān from Persia and Ṣuhaib from Rome, yet they became the Prophet's close comrades. When Salmān once faced a taunt from one of the Arab Companions, the Prophet intercepted saying that Salmān was from *ahl al-bait,* the Prophet's family. His statement that "no Arab is superior to a non-Arab",[27] his statement that "wisdom is the lost property of the believer, wherever he finds it, he should partake of it"[28] all show that Muḥammad (pbuh) was not a monocultural person, on the contrary he was keen to learn from, and interact with, people who were different, people who had other experiences than himself. Yet today Muslims urgently need to rediscover the appreciation of pluralism that is evidently present in their history.

3. Muḥammad (pbuh) laid down a simple guideline for being part of an 'ethnic' group: a man once visited the Prophet's mosque in Madinah where he saw Companions like Bilāl and Ṣuhaib and said, "If the tribes of Aws and Khazraj support Muḥammad (pbuh), they are his people, but what are these people doing here?" Muḥammad (pbuh) was disturbed when this was reported to him; he went to the mosque and summoned people and addressed them, "O people, the Lord and Sustainer is One. Your Ancestor is one, your Faith is one. The Arabism of anyone of you is not from your mother or father. It is no more than a tongue (language). Whoever speaks Arabic is an Arab."[29] With this sweeping statement Muḥammad (pbuh) took

away the privileged position that the ethnic Arabs occupied within Muslim society. Thus he empowered 'others' to become equals and encouraged the pursuit of a common language. He also showed that in his estimation birth and lineage counted for much less than what a person could choose to become. He emphasised that a cohesive community must be a united one and that, "He is not one of us, whoever asserts any race over another, or fights on racist grounds or dies in a racist cause."[30]

4. The spread of the early Muslims to neighbouring regions after the death of the Prophet and the expansion of the boundaries of the Islamic society show that they did not go on a 'Quraishising' or 'Arabising' mission. Rather the cultural diversity that we can see to this day, from Morocco to Malaysia, is a testimony to the respect they had for local traditions and cultures.

5. Islamic law recognises the revealed law of those before Islam (*sharā'i' man qablanā*) under certain conditions as legal precedence. In addition, custom (*'urf*) is recognised as a possible source of law where there is no contradiction with established laws. This shows that, contrary to the beliefs of some, Islam did not come to eradicate whatever was achieved before it. It is not a destructive force or even a revolutionary force; rather it tries to build on the positive aspects of previous civilisations. Muḥammad (pbuh) summarised his whole life by saying that he had been "sent to complete and perfect good conduct."[31] the emphasis here on 'completing' gives a sense of continuity and progression rather than replacement.

The emphasis on the Oneness of God has led Muslims to develop a *tawḥīdic weltanschauung*, there is one Book, one final Messenger, one *Dīn*, one *Ummah*. However, embedded within this unity lies a strong sense of plurality. The acceptance of different faiths, different opinions in *fiqh*, differences of ethnicity, the encouragement of juristic reasoning, all show this deep sense of pluralism that lies at the heart of Islam. Ultimately, the Qur'ān teaches, "...you will be brought back to God and He will show you the truth of the things about which you differed".[32] Meaning that the plurality of opinions held among people in this life will not be resolved and are not meant to be resolved, but we should live with each other in respect. "And if God had willed, He could have made you one people..."[33]

This pluralism extends into cultural expression also. Although many Muslims often speak of 'Islamic Culture', it is difficult to pinpoint one particular cultural expression in the Muslim world and label it 'Islamic' to the exclusion of others. The points mentioned above indicate that Islam is something of a moral backdrop, a framework, rather than a culture in itself. This explains the diverse Muslim cultural expressions that can be seen around the world. However, this does not mean that there are many 'Islams', but rather that there are many expressions of the Muslim way of life. Islam encapsulates values and ideas that lead to a cultural manifestation in the context of the particular area of the world where those values are implanted. This manifestation takes on the colour of the society it resides in and remains willing to change with time.

BEING A MUSLIM AND HAVING A NATIONAL IDENTITY

Islam does not give much importance to nationalistic identities; on the contrary, as mentioned before, it frowns upon those who divide themselves up on this basis, rather than unite around the common bond of faith. However, this does not mean that a Muslim cannot hold a piece of land dear to his or her heart and even identify with that territory, state or country. Surely, it is only natural for people to have a land they call home. For some Muslims living in Britain that homeland may be Pakistan, for others Bangladesh, and yet others that feeling of homeland, of home, finds its locus in the British Isles.

This can cause some tension for those who remember Britain as a colonial empire, or who feel aggrieved at some of Britain's policies at home or abroad. Some of these matters will be dealt with in the section on 'Objections to Accepting Britain as a Homeland'. Perhaps the point most often made is "how can you belong to a non-Muslim country?" Yet few would say that it is wrong to talk of 'Indian Muslims', although this is a clear example of a country where Muslims are in a minority, where there are political problems with Kashmir, and where the majority culture is not Islamic. We are used to hearing of 'Indian Muslims', because somehow that is more acceptable than the terms British, French or American Muslims.

What does all this mean for Muslims who live in Europe or the West? Can one be Muslim and be British or French? The answer to this rings out clearly if we ask the question with regard to those who convert, for what else could they be but British or French Muslims, etc? Let us look at the issue in a more controversial way, what does it mean to be Bangladeshi or Egyptian? What makes these nations Islamic? All the territories around which these nations were formed were at one time inhabited by people who were non-Muslims as were all other places including Saudi Arabia. It cannot be a matter of Islamic rule, as most would contest the 'Islamicity' of these governments. Is it then just a matter of presence or numbers, i.e. that Muslims in these countries are in a majority? Well how about Indian Muslims then? Or Malaysia where the population is about 50% Muslim?

It seems that the issue really is an emotional one. Perhaps it is the case that historically so much animosity has existed between the Muslim world and the West and that even today there is so much tension between some Muslim countries and some Western countries that people find it difficult to appreciate that Muslims now live in the West as Westerners themselves.

For some Muslims it is not a question of opposing the adoption of a Western nationality, but any nationality, *per se*, is wrong. Therefore one may hear, at times, the predictable, radically framed statement – "I am not British or Pakistani, just Muslim!" We must acknowledge that while Islam frowns upon nationalism as a primary tie of association, there are acceptable forms of adherence to national ties. The Prophet Muḥammad (pbuh) and most of the Companions around him were Arabs and they were not ashamed of their Arab heritage where it did not contradict Islam. The tribes were acknowledged as a reality and even in the latter part of his life, after the conquest of Makkah, Muḥammad (pbuh) gave the keys of the Kaʿbah and the privilege of providing water for the pilgrims to individuals knowing that their clans would hold on to these traditions. If one needed further proof, then the statement of the Prophet on his return to Madinah from a journey is clearer, "...this mountain loves us and we love it..."[34] referring to the mountain of Uḥud (which symbolised his approach to Madinah) and also the well-known anguish that Muḥammad (pbuh) and many of his Companions faced in fleeing from Makkah, their beloved home. It is related that while leaving Makkah, Muḥammad (pbuh) looked back and said:

> Of all God's earth, thou art the dearest place unto me and the dearest unto God, and had not my people driven me out from thee I would not have left thee.[35]

What Islam is against is the type of nationalism that degenerates into tribalism, of support for one's kinsfolk while putting aside ethical concerns. When one thinks "My countryman right or wrong". The deciding factor is, then, justice. That is where the ultimate loyalty of anyone should lie.

> O believers, stand up for justice, as witnesses unto God, even if it be against yourselves, your parents or closest of kin. And whether it is against rich or poor, for God's claim takes precedence over either of them. And follow not your desires lest you swerve from justice...[36]

This means that conflicts are handled and measured on the scale of justice. If one's own country, Muslim or non-Muslim, does something wrong then it is one's duty to make this clear and stand against the injustice. If another country, Muslim or non-Muslim, aggresses against one's country unjustly, then it is only right that one stands up to defend his/her country. This principle of justice is further enunciated in the Qur'ān.

> O believers, be steadfast in your devotion to God. And never let the hatred of a people lead you into the sin of deviating from justice. Be Just! This is the closest to being God conscious...[37]

Muḥammad (pbuh) further said, "Help your brother, whether he is an oppressor or is oppressed." The Companions asked, "We know how to help the oppressed, but how do we help the oppressor?" He replied, "Stop him from doing wrong. That will be your help to him."[38]

The question of physical manifestations of belonging is another point of debate. As a citizen, can a Muslim engage in acts of patriotism – perhaps the most visible of which are acts such as displaying the flag or reading or standing for the national anthem? According to Shaykh Faisal Mawlawi:

> Muslims living in non-Muslim countries are to respect the symbols of those countries such as the national anthem, national flag, etc. This is part of what citizenship dictates as

per modern customs. Thus, standing up for the national anthem is not a form of prohibited loyalty. If a Muslim is to change a wrong action in a majority non-Muslim country, let him do that through Da‘wah, wisdom and fair exhortation. At the same time, he should not obey any rules that involve disobedience to Allah.[39]

One other question that is often posed is "which are you first: Muslim or British?" In light of the above discussion on justice, such a question is actually a non-issue. In fact, there are two distinct identities involved here: one is a religious and philosophical identity and the other is a national or territorial identity. Just as one could be Christian and British, or Humanist and British, so one can be Muslim and British, without the need for contradiction, tension or comparison between the two.

At the centre of debates such as Muslims expressing an identity that is British, or indeed engaging in the political process of a Western country (that may be at odds with some section of the Muslim world) is the notion of loyalty (walā'). To whom is loyalty due? According to a fatwā of the European Council for Fatwa and Research walā' can be divided into two areas:

1. Loyalty in religious matters. It refers to creedal loyalty, which lies in believing in Allah and shunning other beliefs that run counter to the Oneness of Allah. This kind of walā' is due to Allah, His Messenger and the believers. Almighty Allah says: "Your friend can be only Allah; and His messenger and those who believe, who establish worship and pay the poor due, and bow down (in prayer)".[40]

2. Loyalty as regards worldly matters: This refers to transactions between people living in the same society or between different societies, regardless of the distance and the religion. It is permissible for Muslims to engage with non-Muslims in commercial transactions, peace treaties and covenants according to the rules and conditions prevalent

in those countries. Books of Jurisprudence do contain many references about such kind of dealings.[41]

Loyalty is hence multi-faceted and operates at different levels. Each one of us regularly balances loyalties to ourselves, our families, our work commitments and careers, our friends, the community, the nation, etc. Often these loyalties can clash, but this is not a case just for Muslims, but for all people. A person with a passion for the environment, for example, may have personal views about how to live and consume that do not agree with the views of the majority, or at least with some state policies. Living in any society involves a constant negotiation of our different values and ideas, allegiances and loyalties. The very framework of most modern constitutions, as well as international treaties on Human Rights are designed to facilitate this by giving room for freedom of individual thought and belief.

BRITISHNESS AS A CHANGING PHENOMENON

As has been mentioned a number of times previously, identities are not static but dynamic. Historically, the British Isles have been host to so many different groups of peoples including the Celts, Romans, Vikings, Normans, Saxons, and more recently, from the twentieth century onwards, migrants from almost all other parts of the world. Each group has in some way, even if small, added something to what is now known as Britishness. It is important to realise that when we talk of Britishness we are not talking of a monolithic or homogenous identity. Even today, if one travels the British Isles the range of different regional customs and habits, norms and subcultures and dialectual variations, is quite amazing.

When one stereotypically pictures this country – as John Major did talking of long shadows on the cricket grounds, warm beer, green suburbs and old maids cycling to communion in the morning mist – one often sees very romantic and quaint notions of Britishness or, more specifically in this case, Englishness. But it is interesting to note that some of the very popular symbols of Englishness such as the St. George's Cross, Christianity, afternoon tea, the Royal Family and fish and chips all have major foreign influences. The legend of St. George was brought to England by crusaders returning from the Middle East. Christianity, of course, also originated in the Middle East, tea comes from the Far East, the Royal Family is a result of trans-national marriages and fish and chips are thought to be a combination of Jewish and Irish culinary skills. Even the English language is classified as a Germanic language coming from the Indo-European family of languages.[42]

While Britishness has, in recent years, become acceptable and inclusive for non-whites, Englishness remains more elusive. In the words of Bernie Grant who is happy to call himself British, "It would stick in my throat to call myself English."[43] What is it about Englishness that is so exclusive? While we do not wish to go into this in detail here it is worth raising as an issue for future concern. It is possible that non-whites find it so difficult to call themselves English, and as a society we find it difficult to accept non-whites as English, because the implicit definitions of Englishness are related to ethnic origin, skin colour, or perhaps even religion. For some, to be truly English, (or even British), one must be of Anglo-Saxon descent and Christian. Yet who has defined these terms? Does anyone have a right to freeze a nation in time and use such a snapshot to define it?

For so long the rhetoric of the far right has been that Britain must be preserved for the British, meaning that it must be kept white. Yet this is not far removed from the comments of those who say that Englishness or Britishness are defined by ethnic origin. Why is Englishness so important? Because it is very likely that its pertinence will increase as regional consciousness increases within the UK. Already we can see that the cross of St. George has become much more common over the last few years. As a reaction to growing Welsh and Scottish consciousness, Englishness is bound to increase. Hence, if it is not today, it will become a serious debate tomorrow. It is important that Muslims are able to play a pro-active role in this debate before they are taken through the rigmarole of a whole new series of loyalty tests and put under the identity spotlight yet again.

Whatever the age-old concepts of national identity, in this globalised age of citizenship-based nation-states it seems valid to question the use of ethnic or racial criteria to define a national identity, be that Pakistani, Welsh, Scottish, or English. In the developed world, and indeed most parts of the whole world, it is very rare indeed to find a group of people that have remained completely racially isolated. The question then is where does one draw the line? Does one stop at the Roman influx into Britain, or the Viking, Norman, or twentieth century? The obvious answer is that one cannot draw such lines; nations are constantly changing and one cannot take a snapshot in time to define a nation for ever. For some, they would be comfortable in looking at colour, for others it is a matter of cultural practice, for others allegiance, but even these cannot be defining criteria – often these are only posed for those who are under suspicion of not belonging, of being 'other', of being disloyal. A white person, be they of Anglo- Saxon (which is in itself heterogeneous), Scandinavian, Jewish, or French Huguenot origin would rarely be questioned about their Englishness or Britishness – it would be assumed and taken for granted. Such an allowance cannot be granted to non-white people – especially in the case of Asians and Muslims, all the more so since 11th September 2001. Is it any surprise then that such thinking is described by some as racist?

The implication of this is serious because the success of the integration process of Muslim communities (or indeed any other community) is heavily dependent upon how included these communities are made to feel. Integration is a very problematic word to use as people have varying definitions. Here it is used as opposed to assimilation or segregation, as a middle way in which minority communities can become part of society while maintaining something of their values and religious and cultural norms. Attempts at assimilating migrant communities could ironically lead to the formation of stronger barriers between communities. For evidence of this one could compare the situation of Britain's 'minorities' with France where the policies have been much more assimilationist, or Germany, which has only recently officially accepted that is has something called immigration![44] Britain, with some justification, prides itself on its treatment of 'minority' communities – yet things are far from perfect and it is with great dismay that such communities continue to watch political parties treat the issue of race as a political football. In 2002 the Home Secretary, David Blunkett talked of asylum seekers 'swamping' British schools, harkening back to Thatcher's statement in 1978 "that this country might be rather swamped by people with a different culture".[45]

OBJECTIONS TO ACCEPTING BRITAIN AS A HOMELAND

These are not the only problems that face the Muslim community in the integration process. Those from within the Muslim community who are not convinced of the need for integration, for acceptance of a British Muslim identity, often raise a number of points as challenges (in addition to some of those presented beforehand). These can be summarised as:[46]

1. Religious-theological barriers:
   - Britain is considered as *dār al-kufr* or *dār al-ḥarb*.
   - One must migrate to the Islamic State once it is established, so our stay here is temporary.
   - The conflict between Islamic and British law.
   - Immoral practices.

2. Social-Political barriers:
   - The aggression by Britain against Muslim countries – historical and contemporary.
   - The taxes of Muslims used for the above.
   - The conflict of loyalties (for example in a military situation).
   - Muslims will never really be accepted as British anyway and are often treated negatively and in a prejudiced manner.

It should be pointed out firstly that these objections are often raised by people who have themselves made Britain their home. They chose to live in Britain, are protected by the state and in some cases claim financial support from the state. Naturally, this somewhat undermines such objections in the first place. As far as the question of the terminologies of *dār al-Islām* and *dār al-ḥarb* are concerned, we have mentioned that these were used at a particular time and place and are not part of the revealed body of knowledge. They are not relevant in today's globalised world, where Muslims sometimes flee from 'Muslim' countries and seek refuge for their very lives and well-being in 'non-Muslim' countries, or where one finds greater freedom to practise and debate about Islam in some 'non-Muslim' countries than in some 'Muslim' countries. Some have even stipulated that ideally Muslims should migrate to a Muslim country in order to 'preserve their faith' citing the example of the Prophet migrating from Makkah to Madinah. The condition of migration (*hijrah*) to an Islamic territory is one that is deeply misunderstood, as though it would be a practical feat to transport the millions of Muslims that live as minorities around the world to the Muslim world. The Companions of the Prophet affirmed that, "there is no further migration after the conquest of Makkah."[47] *Hijrah* as a physical,[48] religious obligation was a special condition for early Muslims because the situation in Makkah was very dangerous for those who believed in Islam and in Madinah they would be free from any molestation. Furthermore, the migrant community was a relatively small one.[49] Where possible, Muslims today are expected to live where they are and to build their own future and contribute to the lives of people around them. With respect to the conflict between Islamic and state law, this is the situation in all parts of the world, as there is no country that applies the *Sharī'ah* in full. However, some scholars argue that the objectives of the *Sharī'ah*[50] are better achieved in a country like Britain than under despotic rule, as in some of the Muslim world. Furthermore, the contractual status of Muslim communities living within non-Muslim states necessitates that they respect the norms and laws of the land.

The argument about morality in Britain or the West is a red herring; as if the Muslim world does not have vice and corruption. The people that the Prophets throughout the ages were sent to were not 'good practising believers', they were people who were criminals, worshipping false gods, or who were oppressing the weak. These were the very people the Prophets called their brethren, their people. Are we then in any way better than the Prophets? If we look closely at the story of Muḥammad's life, the Makkah he fled from was dominated by *mushrikīn* (idol worshippers), yet he felt it was his home. The whole Arab identity was one that revolved around the culture of idolatry, a culture in which baby girls were buried alive and in which drink and promiscuity were common. Yet the Prophet never asked the Muslims to deny their Arab identity, he simply redefined it, redirected it. He took the good things from it, like the honouring of guests, sticking to one's word, chivalry and courage, and discarded what was unacceptable. In fact, this is why the Qur'ān uses the phrase *amr bil-ma'rūf wa nahy 'anil-munkar*, promoting the good and discouraging the wrong. *Ma'rūf*, commonly translated as 'good', actually means in Arabic 'the things that are common and well known', established in society – the common good. Hence you simply take on those things that are good and reject those that are bad. There was never a revolution where the Prophet suddenly changed the lives of people, it was a gradual process of change.

It is true that there has been much historical animosity between Britain and parts of the Muslim world and that to this day there are many grievances about foreign policy matters. Yet were the Arabs not at odds with Muḥammad? Did that ever cause him to deny his Arabness? Even when the Quraish were oppressing the Muslims, this was no reason for the Muslims to denounce their Quraishī ancestry. Furthermore, many 'Muslim' countries are the chief perpetrators of crimes against other Muslim nations – would we expect Iraqis to denounce their Iraqi identity because their country attacked Kuwait, or the Pakistanis to denounce their Pakistani identity because they allowed the US to attack Afghanistan? This is also true in terms of how tax-payers' money is used. The conflict of loyalties can be resolved by considering our previous discussion on loyalty, justice and national identity. Within a military context, Muslims living in the West have recourse to conscientious objection. The Qur'ān goes even as far as stating that if Muslims are unfairly treated in a country that has a treaty with an external Muslim community, the latter need not intervene if this would breach the agreement for the treaty must be respected:

> yet if they ask you for help against persecution, it is your duty to help them – except against a people between whom

and yourselves there is a covenant: for God sees all that you do.[51]

It was on this basis that when asked about a few British Muslims who wanted to go to Afghanistan to fight alongside the Taliban (against British troops), Shaykh Abdullah al-Judai[52] answered as follows:

1. As far as the *Sharīʿah* is concerned, the situation of Muslims living in the UK is that they are under contractual obligations to the state in which they live. This is a natural consequence of the citizenship that we all bear. By accepting to live here, we have taken up a social contract to live within the framework of the English Legal System whilst practising and perfecting our Islamic faith. We have to realise that these agreements are ratified between two parties, i.e. the state and the individual. Therefore, even if the state breaches its contract with any other party with whom the individual has a connection of some sort, be it Muslim or otherwise, the individual remains bound by the contract between him and the state. It is totally and completely unlawful from the Islamic point of view for a Muslim individual to actively seek to breach or contravene this agreement.

2. There is nothing in the Islamic sources that compels a Muslim living in Britain to go to Afghanistan to fight. In addition to what was aforementioned in the first point, there is no obligation upon Muslims to respond to the call to fight with Muslims elsewhere because the source of such an obligation, such as an oath of allegiance or a Muslim ruler, to whom obedience is obligatory, is absent. It is important to note that even if such a source was available, such as a Muslim ruler, responding to his call to take up arms falls only unto those who have pledged their allegiance, and such an oath cannot run concurrently with a ratified agreement or contract with the opposite party.

3. The ruling of the *Sharīʿah* in such a case is clearly expressed in the Qur'ān in Sūrah al-Anfāl. The verse is categorical, that Muslims are not allowed to take up arms

against a party that they are in a treaty with, even when this is to go to the defence of other Muslims, as abiding by agreements and treaties is one of the most crucial aspects and features of Islam.

Following this, it is not allowed for British Muslims to go to another country to fight in such a way that British forces would be attacked by Muslims.

As regards people not accepting Muslims, this is a legitimate concern for it is difficult to 'belong' to a place if there is a perception of not being accepted. It is important that the reciprocal nature of the relationship between belonging and acceptance is highlighted in policy discussions that are gravitating towards citizenship tests and other measures to 'encourage' people to integrate. If people are constantly reminded that they do not belong, whether on the crude level of the rhetoric of far-right groups, or the more challenging day-to-day discrimination that they may face, or when the government fails to listen to their concerns and request for needs, it is only a matter of time before they will feel alienated and lose the desire to belong. Having said that, Muslims must also realise that in this arena there is much that Muslims must work at, while realising that in all societies some unsavoury people will exist. Just to give some hope, one can see the tremendous impact that Asians and Blacks have already had on Britain. Perhaps a rather flippant example is that curry is one of the most popular dishes in the UK! But on a more serious note, it is easy to see that most people are happy to accept and even celebrate the diversity of contemporary British society. And with time and concerted efforts real change can be brought about. For example, in the 1970s the Local Authority in Leicester placed advertisements in Ugandan newspapers asking the Asians being expelled by Idi Amin not to come to the city – yet Leicester is now held as a model of a multicultural, multifaith city, having won beacon status for its community cohesion in 2003.

IMPLICATIONS FOR MUSLIMS IN BRITAIN

In order to understand the importance of the debates around British Muslim identity, one should consider some demographic facts about the Muslim community in Britain. A large proportion of Muslims in the UK are young. Data from the 2001 census shows that 52% of Muslims are under the age of 25, compared to the national figure of 31%. As the youth are most actively engaged in thinking about identity issues the subject is directly relevant to a very large sector of the Muslim community. To compound this it was also found, in a 1997 survey carried out by the Policy Studies Institute (PSI),[53] that 90% of ethnic minority children under the age of 16 were born in the UK, whereas 90% of ethnic minority adults aged 35+ were born outside the UK. Meaning that in addition to the normal generation gap, there is likely to be a wide culture gap between the first two generations of Muslims in Britain. Another factor that bears on the situation is that there seems to be a heightened sense of religious consciousness among the Asian community as compared to the white community. According to further results from the PSI survey, 96% of people of Pakistani origin and 95% of those of Bangladeshi origin said they were Muslims, compared to 68% in the general white population who said they were Christians. The same survey showed that 66% of Pakistanis said that they think of themselves 'in many ways' as being British, 90% also said the same regarding being Pakistani. 23% said they were not British and 4% said they were not Pakistani. It therefore seems that a large number see themselves as both British and Pakistani forming hyphenated or hybrid identities.

Why is the question of identity so crucial to British Muslims? It is because of the consequence of the answers. By accepting that Muslims are British and this is their home, they move on to discuss as a consequence:

1. How to build a place for themselves in Britain and,
2. How to contribute to the lives of the people in Britain, I would say, "my people".

Integral to both of these challenges is that Muslim communities become more open to people around them (and vice-versa) so that there is increased mutual understanding and trust, as well as an appreciation of that which is in common – which is far more than that which is different.

The duty of Muslims is not just to ask about their rights and privileges, but to contribute, to help build this society. This is why it is necessary that Muslims understand that this is their society, that the people around them are their people.

The Prophet never isolated himself from the people, he always interacted with them, engaged with them, talked to them, lived with them. It was by seeing his behaviour, his personality that people were most impressed. That's how he began to tackle the Islamophobia that started to arise at his time. When some Muslims talk of 'Islamic activism', they often think of proselytising by giving talks, organising conferences, or even going to the neighbourhood knocking on people's doors or handing out leaflets. Yet faith in Islam requires something far more profound than that; that Muslims live in British society and involve themselves in it fully – that they simply live Islam rather than talk of Islam. Muslims should have ideas to contribute when it comes to health, education, crime, unemployment, homelessness, and all other areas of life. It would be a shame if they were to sell themselves short by being boxed into a niche, labelled as commentators on 'religious matters' or 'Islamic matters' alone.

If Muslims are to really make their contribution to British society there must be open and frank dialogue and interaction in both directions. Muḥammad was known as 'the Trustworthy', 'the Honest', 'the Truthful'. How many Muslims in Britain have the same reputation? Muslims need desperately to sort out their own house and also tackle prejudices that hamper people's views of them. But this too is not enough for they also have to know their people. How many Muslims have a deep understanding of the history, literature and traditions of Britain? How many actively interact and engage with their non-Muslim co-citizens? Yet how many lead lives that involve almost no interaction with non-Muslims in their day-to-day affairs in some meaningful way? Unless Muslims are able to feel the pulse of society they will not talk *to* people, but talk *at* them, and their words will have very little effect. This again shows exactly why Muslims need to be in tune with their Britishness.

There is also much to be said for removing the cultural obstacles that can get in the way of communication. Murad Hofmann asks Muslims to think of:

> ...separating religion and civilization. Only if we can peel away the many layers of civilizationary, local lacquer can Islam become universally relevant...[54]

The idea implied here is that if Muslims are able to apply the principles of Islam to a Western environment, a new Western Muslim cultural expression will develop that may be more akin to meeting the challenges of future generations of Muslims than say Asian or Arab culture. While there is some obvious credence in the idea, some care needs to be taken, especially given the reality of globalisation, for cultures are now in flux, more so than ever before. Is such a detachment from history and tradition an ideal way to deal with the contemporary? And is it possible that a sudden stripping of imported culture would leave a vacuum that would create an identity 'crisis' rather than address one? Perhaps Muslims can in some ways also enrich Western culture with parts of their 'cultural baggage'? Food is a prime example of this. In any case, it may be that the process of distinguishing between Islam *per se*, and Muslim cultural accretions, is a healthy exercise, for it may allow a whole generation of Muslims in the West to see Islam for its principles rather than its application. This can indeed be a revitalizing opportunity and one of the challenges for Muslims living in Britain. In the process of discovering their new British Muslim identity, they may well re-evaluate important issues such as the participation of women in society, the attitude towards people of other faiths, political participation and engagement in civil society.

CONCLUSION

For Muslim communities today the impact of nationalism, globalisation and the diasporic nature of large numbers of Muslims is something that cannot be ignored. This means that around the globe, one can see a tremendous interchange of cultures and ideas, and at times upheaval, taking place within the Muslim world. The debates around issues such as identity, how to deal with the West, how to cope with modernity have common threads that weave them together. Muslims living in the West are in a unique position; they are at the coal-face of the debates.

The cultural acclimatisation of any group of people is not an easy process and there are natural and organic sociological processes that will take time, perhaps generations. As the British Muslim community matures it becomes more and more evident that setting it 'cricket tests' and 'loyalty tests' are not the right way forward. In any case, Lord Tebbit's cricket test is reduced to a farce when you have a cricket team once captained by someone called 'Nasser Hussain' and a football team managed by someone called 'Sven-Goran Eriksson'; a football team composed of about one-third non-white players who are valiant fighters for England on the pitch, but cannot easily fit into the definition of English off the pitch. British Muslims need time to settle down – this can be made easier by giving them space to ease into British society, yet it can be made more difficult by perceptions of forced assimilation. One needs to also realise the impact of Islamophobia on Muslims in Britain. The fact that some cannot accept brown skinned Muslims as truly British is a standing argument for those who would say, "this country will never accept you so why bother?"

We have seen that we cannot afford to hold onto static notions of 'Britishness' or 'Englishness' and many prominent symbols of our nation, whether they are Christianity or the flag originated in far-off shores. This leads one to think that perhaps one day, Islam can also be 'normalised' and seen as an indigenous British faith. Britishness is of course a national debate and there seems to be no clear answer as to what it is precisely. But perhaps this is itself an opportunity for those wishing to catch the boat. For as long as there is openness in exploring the meaning of Britishness there is also the chance to contribute to it, add to it and subtly redefine it. This is exactly what 'minority' communities and migrants have done in Britain over the last 2000 years.

At the heart of the debate around British Muslim identity lies an acute sense of protecting oneself from 'the vices of the West', the erosion of religious and community values by modernity and individualism. Some would wish to preserve their values by isolating themselves; others would throw caution to the wind and give up their religious identity for a secular one. Somewhere in between there is a balance that could be struck. In an attempt to deal with Western cultural influence, some Muslims have decided to become more Eastern in their consumption of culture; satellite and cable stations can give a regular dose of Zee TV or Bangla TV.[55] But this begs the question – will such a defensive strategy be successful in the long term? Is it necessary? Is a film that flouts Islamic norms of decency any better because it is transmitted in Arabic, Hindi or Turkish?

By exploring the Islamic sources regarding notions of identity, and in addition looking at Britishness itself, we can see that there is no contradiction in a Muslim taking up full citizenship in British society and considering it his/her own country. In fact this is exactly what is needed if Muslims are to really build a place for themselves and for their future generations in Britain. Only as confident, assertive and engaged citizens can Muslims continue to shape British society and be of service to it. This necessitates that they complete the paradigm shift that has already begun, to realise that Britain belongs to them and they to Britain.

Chapter 4

Locating the Perpetuation of 'Otherness': Negating British Islam

Mohammad Siddique Seddon

INTRODUCTION

Definitions of what (and who) is 'British' and what is 'something other' have historically been the exclusive privilege of the dominant ruling Protestant English. But in a post-imperial, multi-cultural, multi-religious pluralistic United Kingdom is the preservation of Anglo-Saxon 'Britishness' established by negation of all other interpretations of 'Britishness' and by the perpetuation of a projected 'otherness'? When the former Labour Foreign Secretary, Robin Cook proudly proclaimed Britain's favourite dish as Chicken Tikka Masala, it was in response to claims that the nation's 'Anglo-Saxon culture' was being undermined. According to the former Conservative Minister for Employment, Norman Tebbit, in comments he made some years earlier, the acid test of 'Britishness' could be decided by a test cricket match – England versus Pakistan. For Tebbit, to support England is a manifestation of 'Britishness' whereas to support Pakistan is to be 'something other'.[1] In addition to these comments the present Home Secretary, David Blunkett, has fuelled the debate by insisting that immigrants, 'should try to feel British'. This comment comes in the light of the summer race riots of 2001 in the North of England and the 11th September 2001 US terrorist attacks. The attacks have led to increased specific racial and religious polarisation and suspicion towards Muslim minorities in the West. Beyond the party political jingoism and rhetoric lie important questions of identity and belonging for Britain's Muslims the most pertinent being, "are they British Muslims or simply Muslims in Britain?"

This chapter will seek to explore some of the root causes of this exclusion by examining the politics of racism and the development of 'national identity' as a consequence of the modern nation-state. Notions of 'Britishness', myths and realities, etymological and geographical definitions, the making of England and the development of so-called 'Anglo-Saxon Britishness' will be examined and measured against the idea of 'British' as an identity. An exploration of the creation of a nationality as a shared sense of 'belonging' partly born out of the tensions between the empirical sciences of the Enlightenment and Protestant Christianity will be undertaken. The Reformation and nationalism as a cause of Protestant 'choseness' and the demonisation (through religious polemics and theological negation) and the sensualisation (by misrepresentations of Muslim sexuality) of Islam[2] via Orientalism are other themes covered. The effects of imperialism, 'common-sense' racism and post-colonial migration will also be discussed. In the light of the on-going debate on 'Britishness' this chapter will explore the implications of ethnicity, race and national identity within the context of religious and cultural pluralism. Finally, British Muslims' perceptions of their ethnicity, race and national identity in the light of their responses to recent global events will be undertaken to evaluate their notions of 'Britishness'.

The formation of a sizeable Muslim community in Britain is a relatively new phenomenon that began in the late nineteenth century through the processes of imperialism and colonisation. As a result, British history and Islamic history have become interwoven and in the modern period neither can really be studied in isolation. The Britain into which Muslim communities were introduced was initially at the peak of its imperial power. In 1930, Dr Khalid Sheldrake, President of the Western Islamic Association, interestingly noted that the British Empire was, 'the largest Islamic power in the world' and that King George V had 'more Muslim subjects than Christian'.[3] As a consequence of Britain's global hegemony the introduction of various colonial communities into the 'Motherland' of the empire was not envisaged as a threat to the then very distinct and dominant British culture. However, the decline of Britain's Empire and the settlement of large post-colonial migrant Muslim communities occurred almost simultaneously. The tensions that surfaced as power shifted from ex-colonial masters to former colonial subjects during the period of independence has undoubtedly added to an increased polarisation between both. Compounding the colonial liberation experience was the sizeable existence of ex-colonials in Britain particularly when the common shared perception was that the migrant Muslim worker's presence here was a temporary one. But as patterns of migration changed, migrant workers began to form settled communities.[4] The social and political inclusion of this large Muslim population as full, equal and participating British citizens is primarily hindered by external perceptions and projections rather than internal conflicts that may occur as a result of shifting identities experienced through the migration process. These ideas in relation to the 'Britishness' of Britain's Muslims have been crystallised in the comments above made by politicians from both ends of the political spectrum. Scrutiny of ethnically 'other' communities has intensified through the new media obsessions with 'asylum seekers' and a revisit to the 'clash of civilisations' discourse as a post-11th September reaction.

THE REFORMATION, NATIONALISM AND 'ANGLO-SAXON BRITISHNESS'

An etymological and pedantic definition of the word 'British' might be, 'relating to, denoting, or characteristic of Britain or any of its natives, citizens or inhabitants of the United Kingdom'.[5] If one studies the historical development of the British nation we would find that this all-inclusive and ubiquitous definition of 'British' reflects the true composition of its people. Clearly being British is to be part of an eclectic multi-racial (if not multi-coloured) phenomenon. This development is a continuous almost evolutionary process certainly in terms of a multi-ethnic synthesis into a cultural monolith. It would appear however, that the greatest impediment to inclusion in this process is the colour of one's skin. Geographically, everything lying north of the European continent including the Orkneys, Shetlands, and Ireland belongs to what we call the British Isles.[6] The earliest inhabitants of these Isles were at some prehistoric timeline introduced to the Celtic language.[7] Opinions are divided and hypotheses are complex as to exactly which strand of Indo-European Celtic early Britons spoke. Ireland's Celtic is noteably different from mainland Britain.[8] Mainland Celtic had many similarities to Gaulish – no doubt the invading Romans would have noticed these similarities. Ironically, one of the first recorded inhabitants of Britain, the Celts, may have originated from Asia Minor.[9] Britain takes its name from the Roman conquerors that named the Isles Britannia. Before the Isles were renamed by the invading Romans Britain was known as Albion. This is the oldest name for Britain and can be traced back to around the fourth century BC. Albion or Britannia was always inviting invasion and many must have stood on the shores of France and wondered what lay beyond those elusive white cliffs. The year 43 CE brought Britain into the Roman Empire and with it came a new fusion of languages, religions and civilisations. The Romans were a multi-racial entity due to the inclusivity of their particular form of imperialism. This strange synthesis of indigenous Britons and invading Romans resulted in a distinct Romano-British culture. However, a *Novus Britannia* was short-lived and by 410 CE the Romans could no longer defend their small outpost on the far-flung reaches of their now diminishing empire so they retreated.[10] Romano-British culture although vibrant for some four hundred years, did not survive and the indigenous Britons reverted to what some historians call a 'sub-Roman Celtic Britain'.[11] At around the same time the abandoned Britons, left to defend themselves, were suffering from major Saxon incursions from the Southeast and invasions from the Picts and Scots from the North.[12] The advent of the Anglo-Saxons, three Germanic tribes – the Angles, Saxons and Jutes – has a semi-mythical chronology and whatever the facts concerning their eventually invited invasion,[13] their arrival changed and reshaped the political geography of Britain. The Anglo-Saxon arrival in the fifth century was not just another colonisation of the indigenous Celtic people of these Isles; it was the beginning of a new hybrid race – the English. These new invader settlers marginalised British language, religion and culture through their dominance. But the Anglo-Saxons did not bring Christianity to Britain, instead they were pagans.[14] It was later Roman Christian missions patronised by pagan Anglo-Saxon kings that eventually led to the Christianisation of Britain. The Britons or 'Welsh'[15] as they came to be called were either exiled into the western and northern highlands or integrated into the evolving Anglo-Saxon sovereignties. The achievement of the Anglo-Saxons was the making of England, not the United Kingdom or even Great Britain, but more or less what we mean by England today. Anglo-Saxon rule lasted for six centuries, two more than the Romans. However, the usurpers were eventually themselves usurped. Firstly by invading Viking Danes and then by the Viking Norsemen or Normans as they became. As a result of these invasions the English today are now predominantly 'English' by language only, racially they are a conglomeration of Celtic, Roman, German, Nordic, Norman and even Flemish peoples.[16] The myth of 'Anglo-Saxon Britishness' as a definite and cognitive national identity is akin to the legendary King Arthur – did he ever really exist except in the hearts and minds of romantic mythmakers and ancient sentimental tribesmen?

The Western European concept of identity through national and racial constructs has really been as a result of the creation of modern nation-states with their own particular defined laws, boundaries, languages and ultimately race. It would be wrong to absolve Protestant Christianity from the developed ideologies of racism that emanated via the Enlightenment – an intellectual movement developed from the ideas of historical and empirical critical analysis and a response to Christian theological reformation. Therefore, a brief examination of post-Reformation Protestant theology both before and at the advent of the Enlightenment must be undertaken. The origins of Pietist Protestant domination can be traced to 31st October 1517 when Martin Luther nailed up his catalogue of contentions with the medieval Church upon the Castle Church doors at Wittenberg.[17] Luther's monumental 'Ninety-Nine Theses' was a list of disputations he wished to discuss with theological professors.[18] The theme of the theses was the doctrine of indulgence, a minor point in Catholic theology but Luther's largely esoterical theses were seen and interpreted by most to be directed against the Church hierarchy and the papacy. This was because Luther had questioned the infallibility of both the general councils and the Pope.[19] One could argue that Luther's protests were more than a theological dispute; his complaints against Papal theocracy had social, political and economic ramifications. More importantly, his sentiments were echoed throughout Western Europe. The two major themes of Luther's reformation movement were individualism, in rights and responsibilities, and egalitarianism. These reforms saw institution and the authority of the Church disempowered and Christianity demystified. Absolution by priests was no longer needed in Reformation Christianity for salvation could be sought through 'works'. Reformist thinking undermined feudal society and in a sense laid the foundations for modern Western democracy.[20] The decentralisation of the institutionalised Church gave rise to the phenomenon of Christian 'sects'.[21] This apparent religious plurality not only questioned traditional Church dogmatics; it also instigated the birth of the secular nation-state. Al-Faruqi has correlated the advent of denominational Christianity and the emergence of nationalist movements formulated on racial and ethnic identities.[22]

In England, Henry VIII turned theological schism into political opportunism. The Protestants, as the Reformists came to be called, through an asserted religious piety and self-appointed chooseness began an intolerant and irreconcilable polarity not only with Papist Christians, but also with Muslims and Jews. Luther wrote in 1529, 'May our dear Lord Jesus Christ, help and come down from heaven with the last judgement, and smite both Turk and Pope to the earth'.[23] This newly developed Protestant chooseness theorised eschatology with distinct imperialist and racial assertions. Beyond dogmatic refutations there arose a greater hostility formulated around the ideas and differences of otherness and through racial stereotyping paving the way for Old Testament inspired religious conquering.[24] The later developed Protestant obsession with Jewish 'restorationism', a peculiar form of non-Jewish Zionism preached that if the Jews could be restored to Palestine they would rise-up and annihilate the Muslims. Thereafter, the Jews would convert to Christianity.

The removal of Islam *and* Judaism would give England control of Jerusalem in preparation for the Messiah. This reductionist and literalist religious ideology served both English secular imperialist dreams and Protestant millenarianist eschatology. Some view it as remarkable that three centuries later this *Pax Britannica* vision for the Holy Land was partially realised in the creation of the State of Israel in 1948 in what was then British controlled Palestine.

THE POLITICS OF RACISM

The processes and formulations of an institutionalised, structured racism are too complex to document in precise detail particularly within the limits of this chapter.[25] However, a concise examination needs to be undertaken to trace the evolution and development of racism as a tool for exclusion and xenophobia. Racist ideology is systematically evolved and infused within society through its institutions and organisations. Racism is of course not particular or unique to Britain; it is part of a global phenomenon structured within the framework of the capitalist world economy.[26] Recent global power shifts show that just as economies develop and transform either by 'meltdown' or 'bullish' trading,[27] so too does racism along the same political economic structures and social formations.[28] By way of example one could compare the plight of pre-eighteenth century European Jews who were brutally victimised by endless medieval pogroms and expulsions. This is in stark contrast with the fully Europeanised Jewish communities in existence today. This process was in part the result of Wilhelm Christian Dohm's efforts for Jewish emancipation. He declared in 1781 that Jews were capable of enlightenment and should therefore be fully assimilated into European society.[29] This begs the question, do Muslims, who are still largely treated as the outsiders in twenty-first century Europe, need to be afforded the same concession? Although Marxist studies on racism would pinpoint and focus largely on the economic roots of the current crisis, in reality the evolution of racism encompasses the combined effects of economic, political, ideological and cultural processes.[30] Racism as it exists in Britain today cannot be treated merely as a sociological phenomenon, it has to be located in the historical development of the political and religious structures of society. Whilst some scholars like Matar and al-Faruqi have meticulously traced the roots of British racism to nascent sixteenth-century colonialism and Renaissance England's imperial aspirations,[31] George Mosse and Edward Said, cite the Enlightenment as the major contributor in the construction of a systematic and institutionalised racism.[32] The tensions between the seventeenth-century Enlightenment movement and Western theocratic Christianity surfaced as empirical rationalism versus religious emotion – science versus faith. The Enlightenment's reliance on, and aspirations of, Greek classicism, imposed anthropological notions, value judgements and ideas of physical beauty and intelligence based on criteria derived from Ancient Greece.[33] Thus, according to Mosse, creating a 'scientific' pretext for racism through evolutionary theories.[34] Both phrenology (skull reading) and physiognomy (reading the face) have their origins in eighteenth-century anthropology.[35] These racist ideologies reinforcing notions of superiority helped to maintain, justify and perpetuate the European slave trade.

Colonialism, with its primary economic function, reinforced racist ideologies formulated via empirical sciences which were further condoned in the form of religious supremacy and Protestant revivalism. Religious zeal may have helped to provide a moral and spiritual validation for Britain's empire building which began in the reign of Elizabeth 1. Initial encounters and confrontations coupled with the changing representations of other races and civilisations from the Renaissance period onwards, serve only to example and chronicle the developing theories of racism by their misrepresentations and demonising of the 'other'. It is at this point that Islam began to be singled out. In many respects, for the Renaissance English the 'unevangelised pagan' fared better than his Muslim counterpart. For religious reasons the 'Noble Savage' was infinitely preferable to the 'Saracen Infidel', a common misnomer for Muslims. This was because the perceived racially and intellectually 'primitive heathen' was deemed to be innocent in his religious ignorance and therefore ripe for the Christian missionary and conversion experience. The Muslim on the other hand, had professed a 'false' religion that was portrayed as an aberration of Christianity and, therefore, worthy only of damnation. It was in this context that proselytising Christianity offered a noble pretext for British imperialism. A British official in colonial India declared it a divine plan to "spread the Christian faith in its purest form among the heathen[s]".[36] Beyond the racist ideologies formulated by evolutionary theories came a theological justification. A man's colour had become a defining characteristic and determining factor in his salvation. In the sixteenth century it was believed that the African's blackness was 'Biblical' in that it represented Ham's original disobedience to Noah.[37] Within Christian cosmology racism was transmogrifying 'others' into 'devils' whose external 'blackness' was an open manifestation of an even greater darkness within. Medieval religious polemics had already laid the foundations for demonising Muslims through racism. Hagarens, Saracens, Moors, Turks, etc., all helped to project Islam as primarily a racial rather than a religious other.[38] It was by this process in Renaissance Britain that English antagonists tried hard to rekindle ancient crusader spirits. By the beginning of the nineteenth century Britain and Europe's global politico-economic dominance was transformed into military might. Waines notes that, "The European challenge also raised the spectre of a modern crusading era as Muslim lands were occupied once again by Christian armies".[39] As a result of two world wars in the twentieth century, the Muslim world had been dismantled and neatly carved-up between its European beneficiaries. The sub-conscious fear of Ottoman military supremacy and Muslim economic dominance experienced in medieval times had now been allayed. British colonialism brought an influx of immigrant workers to the UK in two distinct waves. The first saw a small number of colonial subjects in the late nineteenth and early twentieth centuries.[40] This first wave tended to divide into two very distinct groups; wealthy merchants along with colonial 'white-collar' officials and then sailors or dockworkers. These seamen became known as Lascars.[41] The second wave came after World War Two when the British government, prompted by industrialists, encouraged large numbers of migrant workers, predominantly South Asian commonwealth subjects, during Britain's postwar economic boom.[42] Although, as we have seen, an institutionalised structured racism was set in place long before Britain received its first black and Asian immigrants, the general perception is that the presence of ethnic minority communities in Britain are 'invading' or 'threatening' the indigenous culture. The introduction of 'others' into Britain as a post-colonial phenomenon has been used to ignite racist fears of being 'dominated' or even 'overrun' by the beliefs and customs of newly introduced racial minorities. Given that the largest religious grouping amongst Britain's ethnic communities are Muslims, one might conclude that Islam would therefore, represent the biggest 'threat' to the 'British way of life'. A visible manifestation of this common distorted belief is sometimes expressed through 'Islamophobia'.[43]

This perceived threat led to race riots in the late 1950s after tensions mounted in the face of rising racial discrimination against the new migrant worker communities. The Lascars of Bristol, Cardiff, Liverpool and South Shields were the subjects of race violence back in 1919 and the 1930s.[44] Race riots have been an integral historical feature of British racism and their roots can be traced, via medieval religious polemics, to twelfth and thirteenth-century Jewish pogroms at York and Norwich. This was as a result of the heightened hostilities between Christians and Muslims resulting in the Crusades which in turn had a 'knock-on' effect upon the Jewish community in medieval England. The Jews were interwoven with Muslims into notions of the demonic other. In the twentieth century, whilst the Labour Party condemned the later 1958 race riots and opposed racial discrimination and immigration controls, a Conservative government in 1959 introduced a Bill to control commonwealth immigration to Britain.[45] This act of legislation seems to confirm the opinion that ethnic minorities were 'invading'. The political parties have ever since capitalised on the fears of racists and ethnic minorities alike, playing each against the other with both parties gaining much political capital in the process. Whilst the real problems, issues and root causes relating to racism are never addressed, endemic institutionalised racism is nurtured and perpetuated.[46] Politically, being British has no relation to being either 'white' or 'black' but historically the very notion of Britishness has been associated with race and ethnicity. Hence, the reality is that being British is synonymous with being English and Christian, therefore racially and religiously exclusive.[47]

ORIENTALISM AND THE PERPETUATION OF OTHERNESS

The Reformation in Europe gave rise to the hybridisation of English Christianity through Protestantism as a 'localised' theocracy where the secular sovereign doubled as spiritual leader. Thereafter English Protestantism provided a new cultural and religious framework in which all else was evaluated. As a consequence Catholicism, Judaism and Islam were demonised through eschatological theology and then mythologised through erroneous interpretations, projections and preoccupations with all things other. Perhaps by geographically locating Islam (and Judaism) in the East, through the discourse of Oriental Studies, 'Christendom'[48] became the *weltanschauung* by which all else was measured. Orientalism as a system of scholarship began in the early fourteenth century with the establishment by the Church Council in Vienna, which initiated a number of chairs to promote an understanding of the Orient.[49] The study of the Orient through the discourse of 'Orientalism' has helped Europeans define themselves in terms of what they are not as well as providing a monolithic construct by which the East is comprehended and evaluated. The transformation of Orientalism from an academic discipline into a multifaceted hydra of interchangeable meanings and perceptions is a subject that Edward Said's scholarly critique and deconstruction has detailed. What then is Orientalism? Said succinctly describes it thus: "a style of thought based upon an ontological and epistemological distinction made between 'the orient' and (most of the time) 'the occident'".[50] In terms of mythology, Orientalism has contributed in isolating and locating the Muslim in the typography of Sodom, a wicked and depraved city in ancient Palestine which was destroyed for its evil-doing (Genesis, 18-19). The notion of the 'other' was reinforced by the misrepresentation of Muslim sexuality by portraying Muslims as Sodomites. The Abrahamic people, i.e. 'The Arabs', were made to personify the inhabitants of Sodom. Eroticism and uninhibited sexuality was attributed to Orientals via imaginative travelogues, contemporary plays, popular novels and low-brow art – all contributed and still do in 'placing' Orientals as the descendants of the Biblical city of Sodom. The forbidden sexual deviations practised by the Sodomites have become a Western theological manifestation of the 'forbidden fruit' of Adam and Eve. This has become an extraordinary ideological interpretation of 'paradise lost' transposed on to Islam. The geographical location of Sodom – centrally placed in the Middle East – conveniently spatially and culturally distances its despicable immorality from the West and genealogically links it to Muslims, thereby creating a theologically demonised other. The fact that Christianity emanated from the same location and shares the same religious history and culture, must be unequivocally denied for the purposes of perpetuating otherness.[51] Using Orientalism as an ideological tool, Western colonialism and imperialism gave rise to the most arrogant and abhorrent form of racial superiority. To quote one of its unfortunate by-products and victims, Salman Rushdie:

> Four centuries of being told that you are superior to the Fuzzie-Wuzzies and the wogs leave their stain. This stain has seeped into every part of the culture, the language and daily life; nothing much has been done to wash it out.[52]

For British racism the 'quaint foreigner' remained the acceptable 'other' only when contained within his or her colonised geographical boundaries. English Renaissance writings are littered with a fascination and an obsession with the 'other', highlighted in the studies by Chew (1937)[53] Matar (1999),[54] Said (1991)[55] and Kabbani (1994).[56] Abdur Raheem Kidwai has also produced a very informative critique on the subject of perceptions of Muslims in English literature.[57] This obsession is often reflected in popular literature, E. M. Forster's, *A Passage to India* (1967), being a modern classic example. Once the 'other' wishes to domicile in the country that has been made the focus of his/her material ambitions and aspirations, quaintness becomes an abhorrent foreignness.[58] The politics of perpetuating 'otherness' globally and nationally as we have seen relies upon Britain's imperial past coupled with a developed racist theology. These institutionalised structures of racism are filtered down to the white working (and other) classes in the form of popular 'common-sense' racist ideologies. The ideologies exploit the themes of 'the British nation', 'the British culture' and 'the British people'.[59] The term 'common-sense' is used to describe and denote a 'down to earth' practicality, opinion or 'good sense' and is used as an appeal over the intellectual logic of argumentation and discussion to what all people know in their 'heart of hearts' to be 'true'. Lawrence attributes this phenomenon to the political ideology of Antonio Gramsci.[60] Tracing its origins to the development as concept, 'common-sense' logic was used by seventeenth and eighteenth century empiricists and philosophers battling against theology. Here 'common sense' was used as a confirmation of an accepted general opinion or commonly held belief. In reality, 'common-sense' values are largely situational and are fashioned and moulded by the evolving social, political and economic events of society. Translated to the specifics of racism, in Britain today we would witness 'common-sense' ideology as stereotyping and perpetuating fallacies that Black cultures are still 'primitive' and that Asian cultures, which also although to a lesser degree exhibit primitiveness, are still underdeveloped in comparison with the West. In 'common-sense' terms it would follow that most, if not all, Blacks or Asians would carry these disadvantages – regardless of their 'Britishness' in terms of their national and cultural identities. The effect is a 'common sense' justification of continued racist ideas rooted in imperialism and colonialism.

ETHNICITY, RACE AND NATIONAL IDENTITY

This chapter has examined the connection between the development of modern European nation-states and the Reformation, a connection which, Turner observes:

> Whatever the contradictory relationships between a capitalist economy and organised religion, Christianity came to provide a crucial basis of legitimacy for emerging nation-states.[61]

Within this process of nation building, constructed around state government and state religion, social entities outside this framework would naturally be seen as something 'other'. By way of example, Turner makes mention of the 'continuing isolation' within the emerging English nation-state of 'social minorities' which he says are 'characteristically religious minorities' referring to the large presence of Irish and Scottish Catholics or what he terms as the 'Celtic fringe'.[62] Into the descriptions of defining social minorities as 'others' came the usage of the term 'ethnic'. The word originates from the Old Testament Hebrew and was translated to *ethnos* a derivative of *ethnikos* a Greek word which originally meant heathen or pagan.[63] The word was used in this context in the English language from the fourteenth century until the mid-nineteenth century when it gradually became used within the developing terminology of race.[64] Thereafter its meaning lent itself almost exclusively to describe other races. The connotations of the word 'ethnic' are, in a sense, locked into the idea of 'other' created by the process of the English nation-state which is based on race and religious identity. Scholars such as George Mosse and Ismail Raji al-Faruqi hold the view that the Church provided an exclusive state religion and national identity mostly founded on race. Within the context of the British colonial experience, 'ethnicity' could be used as a political descriptive for non-white and mostly non-Christian colonised 'others'. As a consequence, throughout the geographical expanse of the British Empire, to paraphrase George Orwell, all were British but some were most definitely more British than others! The process of migration by post-colonial South Asians to Britain is now well documented and some commentators compare the settlement and formation of these communities with that of the earlier settlement of the Irish Catholics – the earliest community of 'social minorities'. Social scientists' observations and theories of settlement patterns and migration experiences are largely responsible for the perpetuation of religious, social and ethnic minorities being viewed as the 'other'.[65] Most studies focus on a particular geographical ethnic minority community, which is often then presented as the normative experience of Muslims throughout Britain. Beyond the intra-Muslim politics and theological differences that this genre of research produces, these works also explore the 'challenges' of 'multiple' identities among British Muslims whose heightened sense of 'Britishness' is often represented as a considerable contention with their 'traditional' Muslim or 'ethnic' identities. These studies also tend to over emphasise (and equate) ethnic culture and language with religion, again suggesting that Islam is incapable of rooting itself within British culture and civilisation, that it is somehow linguistically 'chained' to somewhere else. This assumption is a misconception, representative of outdated ideas of otherness normally critiqued in Postcolonial discourse. Leela Gandhi describes this form of representation as, 'procedures whereby the convenient Othering and exoticisation of ethnicity merely confirms and stabilises the hegemonic notion of 'Englishness'.[66] By presenting their ethnic, national and religious identities as 'multiple identities', the suggestion is that a synthesis with their British culture and identity is impossible.

Whilst an occasional passing reference is made to indigenous converts to Islam, these studies generally never examine the notions of the 'Britishness' of this new religious entity. Larry Poston[67] has produced a study which explores the concept of Islamic *da'wah* (invitation to Islam) in contemporary Western societies. His work seeks to understand the ideologies, movements and organisations that are proactive in introducing Islam to non-Muslims. Poston is also engaged with trying to offer a psychological profile of the typical Muslim convert in an attempt to explain the dynamics of conversion to Islam.[68] This expanding area of academic study seems to permeate a subconscious fear and impression of the imminent encroachment and invasion of Islam in the West. Whilst this fear is unqualified one cannot deny the increase in conversion to Islam in Britain and the West. This phenomenon began in the late nineteenth century during the height of the 'British Raj' in India resulting in a significant number of British dignitaries and notaries converting to Islam. Attention should be drawn to the growing epistemology of the 'conversion to Islam' experience by indigenous Muslims.[69] A recent study of Muslim converts has identified some of the problems faced by new adherents to Islam in Britain. Amongst some of the issues raised in the research are the difficulties faced by the transition from a culturally and traditionally dominant religion (Christianity) to a minority and ethnically perceived religion (Islam). This transition is documented through interviews with new Muslims who generally report their earliest conversion experience as an initial feeling of a spiritual 'no man's land'.[70] The problems normally associated with identity shifts, as a result of religious conversion, are somewhat compounded and exacerbated for new Muslims in Britain. This is in part because the community into which the converts are entering is itself experiencing a shift in identity from its ethnic, geo-cultural traditions into a new environment and social setting with a religiously heightened and culturally hybrid form of Islam. Whilst the search for identity as a modern/post-modern phenomenon is a growing preoccupation with all sections of British society, the situation of British Muslims is perhaps further complicated as a result of their migration history and experience. Jacobson's study[71] observes the effects of this process on second and third generation Muslims in Britain. She notes:

> The very nature of the historical background and current circumstances of the ethnic minority population in Britain

would seem to suggest that the evolution of hybrid and fluid identities may be an especially evident process within minority communities.[72]

This new emerging expression of Islam, essentially British in its cultural manifestations, is shared between new Muslims, or converts to Islam, and second and third generation British-born Muslims who are becoming increasingly disconnected from the inherited form of Islam that first generation migrants imported from their original homelands. It is fair to say that in some cases first and third generation British Muslims are gulfed by their cultural superficialities whilst both still adhere to fundamental Islamic beliefs and practices.

Resistance and reticence to engage with their new socio-political surroundings, its customs, culture and civilisation have been displayed by some sections of the British Muslim community who are at odds with contextualising and identifying themselves as minority status Muslims. This unwillingness by a small number of Muslims to integrate into a new environment has manifested itself in a number of ways and although these responses are in the minority they are sometimes an exaggerated or extreme reaction to the perceived predicament. The problem for this sub-group, here in the West, is how to separate and transpose their religion from their culture. This group believes that to 'Anglicise' Islam is to commit an innovation and aberration. Trapped into this way of thinking this visibly distinctly introspective minority are culturally and geographically bound elsewhere and are therefore, in the West but not of it.

Unwittingly, other Muslims have fallen into the trap of asserting their cultural, ethnic and linguistic identities in preference to their religious one. This has usually been done to procure local or central government financial assistance or 'special needs' in education, employment or housing. An unfortunate consequence of reliance and insistence on cultural and ethnic identities, in preference for an aculturalised religious one, has been the secularisation of some second and third generation British Muslims. In any society, however multicultural or religiously pluralistic, it is inevitable that the dominant culture will prevail and saturate others. Maintaining minority cultures and traditions, devoid of a religious dimension, becomes increasingly difficult when the geographical origins of an ethnic sub-group are so physically distant. Each new generation is more inclined towards the dominant culture and further removed from its ethnic roots. Added to this problem is the aspect of exclusion due to race and colour. Young people of Asian origin may believe that they are completely semiotically acculturated into British society, but despite their full participation in mainstream British society, the ultimate hurdle is acceptability on racial grounds. Many youths that have experienced this form of discrimination, often repeatedly, soon become disaffected and disenfranchised which leads to social isolation and in extreme cases an outright rejection of British culture. When this is experienced *en masse* the results are catastrophic. The race riots in the North of England throughout the summer of 2001 were the result of racism and social exclusion.

Some commentators prefer the all-inclusive 'majority ethnic' identity for political reasons.[73] The danger of undermining a religious identity in preference for a non-specific 'ethnic' or 'Asian' identity could result in reinforcing the notion of 'otherness' as being 'all the same' – a very retrogressive step. Insistence on such umbrella ethnic terms as 'Asian' generally inhibits the specifics of religious and cultural identities normally exhibited in developed multi-cultural pluralistic societies. The overall result being, that the cultural, ethnic and linguistic elements of their identity have largely given way to a hybrid British one, and whereby funding bodies and civic concessions made to accommodate the former are now being slowly withdrawn or refused. In some cases funding has been refused where applications have been made by the same group which has preferred its religious identity to its ethnic one. Confusion amongst financial assistance agencies is also often a consequence of minority communities shifting the emphasis from ethnic identities to religious ones. It may have been more appropriate for first generation migrants in Britain to identify themselves within a broader ethnic identity, for example describing themselves as 'Asian', thereby grouping together smaller minorities of multi-ethnic cultural and religious groups. Under such an umbrella the ethnic identities of first generation minority groups would have had many common shared experiences and would therefore have formulated a larger and more significant political voice. The question is then, has British society understood the processes and dynamics of these transforming or shifting identities and the changing emphasis from geo-cultural ethnicities to specific religious entities? Furthermore, as an increasingly secular national identity develops, how far is central and local government prepared to support minority religious groups both politically and economically? For Muslims experiencing migration and new environments, religious identity, its preservation and promulgation, has always taken precedence over cultural and ethnic ones. This is because whilst Islam is universal or global in its essence and fundamentals, it is not monolithic in its specific practice or cultural manifestations. Therefore, ethnic and cultural identities *can* be evolved, negotiated, redefined, transformed, reinvented, adopted, absorbed or integrated.

Where representation and provision for 'Asianness' via multiculturalism has been in abundance in all social spheres, the reassertion and re-identification of a distinct religious identity has been less accommodated. These new or shifted identities with the focus on religion rather than race raise some suspicions connected to duplicity in funding and beyond this a heightened sense of religiosity does not always fit well into a secular structured society. This reticence is not restricted to British society, Muslims in Europe are also met with resistance when manifesting and asserting their religious identity. In acknowledging that national and religious identities amongst 'new minorities' are as unlikely to dissolve as those of older minorities, Lewis adds, "in such a situation, the specificity of British civic culture with its strong Christian colouring needs to be acknowledged as a major asset".[74] Whilst there is a scriptural basis for Christian kindness and tolerance towards the 'stranger', Britain is now only traditionally Christian with secularity becoming the dominant experience. Many observers have alluded to Muslims being isolated and disadvantaged by what they express as anti-Muslim sentiment, xenophobia and Islamophobia.[75] Mason explains the influence of this developing and disturbing phenomenon in Britain as the controversy surrounding *The Satanic Verses*. Across Europe the Gulf War and a rise in what he calls 'Islamic revivalism' has, he claims, increased Muslim-Christian polemics and, "provided a focus for inter-ethnic hostilities in such countries as Britain".[76]

As if to add substance to the discussions surrounding British Muslims' national allegiances and loyalties, Muslim leaders moved quickly to distance themselves and Islam from the terrorist attacks on the US on the 11th September 2001, placing themselves 'shoulder to shoulder' with the Prime Minister. A genuine feeling of shock and outrage was experienced by most British Muslims and Muslims in the West generally. The horrific events further polarised Muslims into two quite distinct camps and loyalties were clearly divided between the fanatical minority which is deeply anti-Western to the point of acute Occidentalism[77] and the vast majority who are manifestly British, Western and Muslim. The public pronouncement of British Muslim identity was soon frustrated and compounded when the government committed troops to America's bombing of Afghanistan. British Muslims supported punishment for the perpetrators of the terrorist acts on New

York and Washington unconditionally, but the bombing of Afghanistan was seen as an indiscriminate act of aggression by America and Britain upon the Afghan nation. The Muslim Council of Britain (MCB), an umbrella organisation raising Muslim issues nationally, after an all-faiths meeting with the Prime Minister at Downing Street, publicly condemned the bombings and rightly questioned their validity. Here Muslims were forced once again to adhere to their global community, the *Ummah*, in preference to their national identity. The ground had been covered before during the *Satanic Verses* affair when protests about the publication of the *Satanic Verses* resulted in a number of Muslim deaths in Pakistan and elsewhere. After this came the Gulf War and whatever the rights and wrongs of Saddam Hussain's dictatorial regime in Iraq, British Muslims could not support the relentless bombing of innocent Iraqi civilians. This apparent shift in allegiance and identity once again forced the question – are they British Muslims or Muslims in Britain? Yet the same questions of allegiance and identity are not transposed on to non-Muslim anti-war campaigners or political dissenters. Indeed significant religious others are never scrutinised in respect of their loyalties and belonging.[78] British Catholics are not suspected of subversion of the monarchy because of their loyalty to Rome and the Pope. Nor are the majority of Irish Catholics suspected members of the IRA. British Jews who are afforded the luxury of dual nationality, British and Israeli, are not asked to prioritise their oaths of allegiance even after many have offered their military service in Israel. Perhaps other minority religious 'others' have proved their Britishness simply through the vicissitudes of time. Muslims are not exclusive to religious victimisation in Britain, there is no doubt that Catholics and Jews alike have historically experienced victimisation, intolerance and discrimination often resulting in pogroms and expulsions. If British Muslims must also inherit the role of the 'demonic other' as a systematic process in achieving religious credibility, cultural capital and general acceptability, then it is a damning indictment of the very nature of what it means to be British.

CONCLUSION

British Muslims, are equally British and Muslim with both components being a part of how they identify themselves. This sense of national and religious identity is not unique to British Muslims; Christians, Jews, Hindus, Buddhists, etc. would all manifest a distinct British/religious identity. Protestants have the privilege of being largely excluded from scrutiny when their religious convictions are in contention with their national identity. When there is a contention it is usually presented or contextualised as a matter of moral conscientious objection rather than a question of allegiance or loyalty. Although other religious minorities in Britain have been historically persecuted, Catholics and Jews are much less maligned than Muslims in respect of their loyalty and belonging. In today's political climate there is much mileage in exploiting ignorant fears and suspicions based on race and religion. Unfortunately it appears that Islam and Muslims are largely singled out for the purpose of political scapegoating. Laws dealing with anti-Semitism, introduced as a result of hideous European pogroms and the Holocaust, have helped to protect Britain's Jews from suffering a repeated fate. But should not all minorities and religions be protected from discrimination? A collective social responsibility needs to be exerted to eliminate all forms of discrimination and racism from Britain and Europe in order that the experiences of recent history, mass racial and religious genocide are not repeated. New definitions of nationality and citizenship that extend beyond the existing specifics of race and religion need to be formulated to realistically and practically reflect a modern multi-religious and multi-racial Britain. The evolution of the British nation is the historical result of an amalgamation of many races and ethnic groups. Although Anglo-Saxon centred, it is an identity that is continually evolving. The impact of the Reformation on European Christianity and ideas of nationality have resulted in clearly defined nation-states with their identities built around a distinct Protestant Christianity. As a result, any social entities present but existing outside the conceptions of this framework are treated as other – sometimes even demonised. The impact of the Enlightenment on Europe culminated in a dichotomy between faith and reason. Perhaps because during this period the mind had been engaged more than the heart, reason was crowned the new king and faith was forced to abdicate. Secularisation bifuracated the profane and the religious to the public and private spheres respectively. Perhaps a visible Muslim presence in a developed modern secular nation-state is seen as problematic because Islam defines itself as a *dīn* – 'a way of life', a holistic belief system rather than a religion in the traditional Western sense. As such it is all-encompassing and cannot be reduced or compartmentalised simply into the realm of the spiritual and the private. This comprehensive and dynamic universality might make Muslims an anomaly within the framework of a predominantly profane and secular environment. Here in Britain, as the role and importance of Christianity in the construction of national moral and social mores is somewhat reduced and undermined, Islam would seem by contrast to empower the individual. This is perhaps because Muslims insist on de-secularising spaces and their understanding of the Divine, instead offering a spiritual worldview which establishes religion in the public domain. The idea that British Muslims cannot synthesise into the predominant Christo-nationalist identity is largely projected as problematic of the outsider minority rather than as a result of theological negation or identity exclusion. To add to this, Muslims are continuously viewed in expressed terms of 'perpetuated otherness' and are measured by their responses to their religious convictions and national identities, particularly when there is a contention. Whilst the reality of a shifting identity that is increasingly British is experienced by Muslims, finding a voice to express and manifest it is difficult because of marginalisation. This is perhaps because the 'Britishness', which Muslims possess, is a new element – even hybrid – which belongs to the historical evolution of Britishness. Despite how British the large majority of Muslims may actually be or feel, social exclusion, racism and 'perpetuated otherness' inhibits their full and integrated participation in British society. No doubt, there is a minority element of Muslims who feel that they cannot and should not acculturalise. Due to their 'traditional' and cultural interpretations of Islam, this tiny element cannot conceive of themselves as 'minority status' British Muslims. For them there exists only the binary perception of the world based on medieval interpretations of the terms *dār al-Islām* and *dār al-ḥārb*. This group would identify with diplomats, foreign students, visitors, migrant workers and any other group who are temporarily in Britain, as 'Muslims in Britain'. Leaving them as mentioned earlier, in the West but not of it.

Chapter 5

'Friends, Romans, Countrymen?'

Nadeem Malik

During the 4th century AD, a Berber from North Africa crossed the Mediterranean to live in Milan. His mother later joined him there. Being a pious Christian woman and used to fasting on Saturdays in accordance with the practice of the church in her native city, she was disturbed to discover that this custom was not followed among Christians in Milan. On the other hand, fasting on Saturdays was, she knew, the norm in Rome. She therefore asked her son, who would later become known to the world as Saint Augustine, how the problem should be resolved. He in turn put the question to his guide and mentor, Saint Ambrose, the Bishop of Milan. Saint Ambrose counselled that in order to avoid giving or receiving offence, one should keep the custom of the church in the place in which one was living at the time. The gist of his advice has subsequently become proverbial, for he suggested that she should do what he himself did, namely not fast on Saturdays in Milan but 'when in Rome, do as the Romans do'.[1]

INTRODUCTION

'When in Rome, do as the Romans do', an excellent piece of general advice, but how many a racist has used that phrase to justify and condone their prejudicial views? The idea that a person who migrates from one place to another must, in some sense of 'paying for the privilege', give up their own culture, values and beliefs, may sound reasonable at first. After all, why should the host community have to change, even by way of accommodation, to allow for these 'newcomers' to feel more comfortable? They may feel justified in expressing a sense of right and ownership; 'we were here first after all'. The host community has its own set of values and culture, often developed over many centuries. There is a common language, a common set of norms, accepted ways and forms of social behaviour. Some things are acceptable whilst some are frowned upon or expressly forbidden. There are often sacred principles, deeply held sets of mores and a refined sense of morality. Why then, should all of this be questioned and changed just to allow a few people to live more comfortably?

Surely those who are migrating ought to have some responsibility to do as much as they can to respect the values and way of life of their new host community? If they expect to reap the benefits of this new place, to be welcomed and provided with shelter, security, company, warmth and food – all basic human requirements which to varying degrees are the motivating factors behind most migration. Then is it not for *them* to do the changing? A fair and rational argument, at least at first glance. But where do the limits lie? History bears witness that it is often not this way. It is often more to do with power and a sense of superiority. Or indeed, a case of simply wanting to remain the way you are, but in a different part of the world. Two simple examples serve to highlight these submissions. In modern history, several nations have colonised others. Be it the French, the Dutch, the Italians or indeed the British, each have taken control of lands and sought to change the whole environment to suit themselves. Language, values, culture, even names are changed to allow for the manifestation of the colonial master's own culture –

to ensure that it becomes the dominant culture as quickly as possible. Take the British in India. Every attempt was made to 'civilise' the barbarians and ensure British cultural dominance. Here a very small number of 'migrants' ensured, through political and military might, that they certainly did not do in Rome as the Romans do.

Alternatively, and much more peacefully, take another very recent example. When the Commonwealth immigration legislation was changed in the 1960s, there was an influx of economic migrants from the Indian sub-continent. It seemed that the coloniser was now in need of some of its subjects to come over and work the cotton mills. So, they came. They came initially as young men and then sought to bring over their wives. They came to work, and then to leave. But while they were here, they had to eat. Despite the historical connection, their palates had not quite adapted to Yorkshire Pudding and mushy peas, not every day at least! So they began to cook their own food. It needed certain ingredients that were not readily available, so they were imported. Slowly these communities began to be noticed. A few streets in Bradford, another few in Manchester and some more in Leeds. These streets began to display common traits. Shops selling 'exotic, foreign foods'. Children running around the streets wearing 'exotic, foreign clothes'. Women walking the streets speaking 'exotic, foreign languages'. Small houses being converted into Mosques for 'exotic, foreign worship'. These small communities of 'exotic, foreign people' were certainly not doing in Rome as the Romans did.

Despite the bouts of oppression and prejudice that these communities suffered, they tried to live their lives as peacefully as possible. In doing so, they did not seek to dominate the host community politically or militarily, they simply wanted to live in a different place according to their own customs, values and beliefs. Within a few decades, those 'exotic, foreign' foods have become some of Britain's best sellers.

Those smelly 'exotic, foreign' chicken dishes are now Britain's most commonly eaten cuisine. Would this country be as rich and diverse as it is if these communities had simply cloned themselves to be as much like their hosts as possible? Would we benefit from the multicultural society that we now enjoy? The contribution of these 'exotic, foreign' people to the economic, social, academic, political, diplomatic and military development of these Isles is well documented.

So where then, do these boundaries lie? Where are the walls of Rome? If I, a person having been born and bred in Birmingham, decide to move to Scotland, Wales or Ireland, should I change my accent, my values, my dress and my beliefs? What if I were to move to Liverpool or London? Both cities having indigenous peoples who would struggle to understand the accent of a person from the other side of town, let alone another city. Do we extend the phrase to "when in London, do as 'Cockneys' do," or "when in Birmingham, do as 'Brummies' do?" Obviously most rational people would argue against any such suggestion. It would be considered pedantic and ridiculous. But what *are* the criteria then? Arguably to ask someone to change their accent so that they can be understood by more people is more reasonable than asking them to give up their beliefs, dietary habits and culture. Unless and until these boundaries are more clearly defined, it will be almost impossible to legislate and advance policies that are fair in form, as well as fair in practice. Until the walls of Rome are agreed upon and visible, they will not be defended. If we want to create a society that exudes justice, honour, respect and community-minded engaged citizens, then we must ensure that the balance between assimilation and co-existence is well defined and legislated for. When is it fair to insist that a migrant community assimilate and 'do in Rome as the Roman's do' and when is it fair to respect their rights and identity and ensure that they are able to co-exist in a safe, secure environment without having to give up who and what they are?

This chapter will consider these issues from several perspectives. Having discussed the difficulties that the existing discrimination legislation presents with regard to an effective legal remedy for discrimination against Muslims on the basis of their faith, effects of the 11th September 2001 and some other pieces of legislation that directly impact on British Muslims in a previous chapter, this chapter will address the issue of citizenship. It will consider the basis of citizenship in general, specific issues affecting British Muslims as obstacles to citizenship, community cohesion – the British experience and various theories of citizenship and their compatibility with Islam. It will conclude that there is a link between the actions of the legislature, the judiciary and the executive and the direct impact that this has on the Muslim community's ability to not only *exist* in, but to *participate fully* in contemporary British society.

THE CITIZENSHIP LINK

Is there a link between legal recognition and the idea of citizenship? Why is it necessary to bring both of these, at first quite separate, discussions together? How does the Muslim community in Britain manifest its citizenry, if indeed it has one at all? Before these questions are answered, it is helpful to recall what it actually means to be a citizen in the first place.

MADE, NOT BORN – DO WE EVEN *WANT* TO BE CITIZENS?

The seventeenth-century philosopher, Spinoza,[2] is said to have concluded that "Citizens are made, not born". This profound statement was probably an established principle even at the time of Spinoza, yet he felt the need to make that statement so eloquently. Why? Because we often forget. An easy trap to fall into is to assume that one's simple existence makes one a citizen. That being a citizen is associated more with being alive than with upholding rights and responsibilities. Beyond this, even for those who are quick to assert their 'rights', and including the few who are able to accept their 'responsibilities', there is a greater concept of *engagement and participation*. This is a concept that seems to have been struck a fatal blow by post-industrial capitalism and globalisation. The idea that good citizens are those who busy themselves with 'getting ahead' in life by obtaining more material wealth and leaving 'politics to the politicians' has become an acceptable part of modern democracy. Simply considering the apathy shown to voting in recent elections is proof enough of this fact.[3]

Was it always this way and is this something specific to the Muslim community? Obviously it was not and it is not. There is no doubt that political participation and engagement in civil society activity is on the decrease throughout British society as a whole, the election results attest to this fact. The reasons for this are complex and are not simply because of a society that has genetically mutated into one that simply does not care or is lazy beyond imagination! A nation's apathy cannot be understood easily, and this is certainly not the place for that discussion. What needs to be assessed here are some reasons for the apathy that exists and then how the situation with regard to Muslims is aggravated. It is reasonable to begin with a basic assumption that people do want to be involved with shaping the society they are part of and helping to create the future. Arguably, this is a most fundamental quality that makes us all human. Indeed, even ancient civilisation honoured this human condition. In 395 BC, Thucydides[4] stated:

Here each individual is interested not only in his own affairs but in the affairs of the state as well: even those who are mostly occupied with their own business are extremely well informed on general politics – this is a peculiarity of ours: we do not say that a man who takes no interest in politics is a man who minds his own business; we say he has no business here at all.[5]

The opposite of this basic assumption then, is that people have no interest in politics. That they are not created as a species '*politicus*' but as a species '*frigidus*', so cold and uncaring about others that they are entirely unconcerned with political activity. Such a view would no doubt find opposition with most people who would agree that deep inside man is a *species politicus*, even if that political activity is to improve society for the good of themselves, for as Aristotle said:

Every art and every kind of inquiry, and likewise every act and purpose, seems to aim at some good: and so it has been well said that the good is that at which everything aims. But a difference is observable among these aims or ends. What is aimed at is sometimes the exercise of a faculty, sometimes a certain result beyond that exercise. And where there is an end beyond the act, there the result is better than the exercise of that faculty.[6]

Therefore whether or not a person seeks to engage in the politics of society around him simply because *he* will benefit ultimately from the result, or whether it is more altruistically to engage in the *process itself*, the person *will* want to engage in that process nonetheless. Where people *en masse* do not partake in such activity, one must begin to ask some deeply worrying fundamental questions.

The idea of what constitutes 'a good citizen' or indeed what it means to even be a citizen (beyond the very basic dictionary definition) is a subject of much discussion.[7] It may be best summarised for our purpose by David Miller[8] who states:

Citizenship – except in the formal passport-holding sense – is not a widely understood idea in Britain. People do not have a clear idea of what it means to be a citizen, as opposed to being one of Her Majesty's subjects. (Indeed, even passports have only referred to their holders as citizens rather than subjects since, appropriately, their jackets have turned from blue to red.) Citizenship is not a concept that has played a central role in our political tradition, in contrast, for example to France, where the revolutionary tradition of 1789 has made the idea of French citizenship a touchstone for debate ever since. We are still inclined to see citizenship as slightly foreign and slightly unsettling – the citizen is a busybody who goes around disturbing the easy-going, tolerant quality of life in Britain.[9]

It is fair to say that to provide a definition of citizenship in the post-modern democracy of Britain is not straight forward. That said, it is not so abstract a concept to render it obsolete. For the purpose of this chapter, let us consider citizenship as a sum of various components. These are defined by Gerard Delanty[10] as:

Citizenship as membership of a political community involves a set of relationships between rights, duties, participation and identity. These may be termed components of citizenship, the defining tenets of group membership.[11]

Each of these components has its own particular significance and discussion with regard to British Muslims, an emerging community that needs to engage in much internal debate to begin to address some of these issues.

To summarise, it can be said that the human need to participate in the politics of society has existed from the very creation of communities and social structures. To engage in the doing of good, whether for the pursuit itself or for some personal gain at the end, is something that all human beings desire. The reality in Britain today is that people seem to be becoming increasingly distant from this natural state and are moving towards a sense of cynicism and apathy. The reasons for this are complex but can be deconstructed by analysing various components of citizenship. Having established that context, there are specific factors that aggravate the shared sense of cynicism and disillusionment amongst British Muslims. Other than those already discussed, namely the lack of legal recognition and remedy, issues of racism, Islamophobia and community cohesion are instrumental in making it more difficult for Muslims to participate fully in social politics.

OBSTACLES TO CITIZENSHIP

Racism

It is worth mentioning briefly that because the vast majority of British Muslims belong to minority ethnic groups, they are potentially subject to racism. Racism in society is of course not something unique to Muslims, but it is something that cannot be excluded altogether when considering issues that lead to a decreased feeling of loyalty and belonging to the state one lives in. As Britain develops increasingly into a multicultural society, it is imperative that it considers the implications of the growth of different racial groups on the fabric of society. If communities begin to become isolated further on the grounds of race and culture, the ideal of a plural society respecting every individual for who they are becomes a distant dream. The need to address these issues and recognise that we live in a Britain that is a community of communities, each consisting of individual citizens who are not monolithic in nature but have individual rights and responsibilities, has been illustrated by a series of recent studies.[12]

Sadly, each concludes that there is absolutely no doubt that racism is rife in British society and that it manifests itself at all levels. The studies also confirm that Muslims, mainly Pakistani and Bengali males, suffer the worst, especially in employment.[13] The Singh Report found that in 1996, 39% of Bengali and 31% of Pakistani men were unemployed compared with 18% of white men. Similarly, 26% of Bengali women and 23% of Pakistani women were unemployed. For both men and women these rates of unemployment were the highest of any ethnic group.[14]

As a related point of note, this economic depravation also has a direct impact on an individual's ability to be a fully engaged citizen. Even in relatively progressive societies where issues of race have been debated for many decades and legislative changes introduced, such as America, economically deprived minority ethnic groups cannot participate fully as equal citizens. American society is especially indicative of this phenomenon:

> Until the 1960s, black Americans were virtually excluded from full and equal civil, social, and political citizenship rights accorded to the white native-born population and to naturalised immigrants. Thus, the boundaries excluding them were foremost racial, reinforced by social, economic, and political segregation. In the 1980s, blacks have gained formal citizenship equality. Yet, only middle class, and to a lesser extent working class blacks have been able to benefit from the new legal equality. The economically weakest members of the black population remain excluded. The boundaries that exclude them are primarily socio-economic and secondarily racial. The socio-economic dimension reflects the limited nature and institutionalisation of social citizenship in the United States.[15]

In Britain, there has been legislation to protect against racial discrimination for well over a quarter of a century, yet we find that there is very little semblance of true racial equality. This inequality manifests itself at all levels of society and even the most multicultural cities display alarming levels of inequality.

This racism continues to exist in both private and public sectors as well as the voluntary sector, albeit to a lesser degree. Amazingly, a local authority such as Birmingham City Council, with Birmingham having an estimated ethnic minority population of over 30%,[16] is alarmingly guilty of institutional racism. The Singh Report concludes:

> Our conclusions are clear. There can be no doubt about the strength of feeling in large sections of minority ethnic communities that institutions in the City are failing them and that their leaders and those who are accountable to them are not effectively tackling racism and racial inequality. Of particular concern is the City Council, who should play an important leadership role in driving forward race equality in the City, but whose efforts have been blunted by institutionalised racism. The institutions pointed to a wide range of race equality policies and initiatives. However, a combination of lack of effective implementation plans, leadership that is not always purposeful enough about achieving race equality and the tendency for race equality to be a 'bolt on' has meant that progress and therefore impact has been limited. Racial inequality and discrimination are still major blights on the lives of many minority ethnic people living in Birmingham today.[17]

If this is the conclusion that the investigation comes to with regard to a local authority (which one would assume to be better at enforcing racial equality than a private sector employer, especially since the Race Relations (Amendment) Act 2000 came into force on 3rd December 2001) such as Birmingham, one can only imagine how disturbing the situation is across the country.

ISLAMOPHOBIA[18]

Over the past decade, Muslims in Britain have been the focus of increasing public attention. One widespread form of such attention has been highly negative: Muslims have been portrayed in all kinds of media in very derogatory and vilifying ways. Among the effects of such depiction, which has contributed to what is now widely referred to as 'Islamophobia', Muslims in Britain have been subject to considerable discrimination and even violence.[19]

The media portrayal of Muslims that Steven Vertovec[20] is referring to is just one component of a pernicious form of xenophobia that has seen alarming levels of growth over the past decade. That xenophobia achieved national attention in 1997 when the Runnymede Trust[21] published a report called *Islamophobia – A Challenge for Us All.*[22] This report followed recommendations made by an earlier study carried out by the Trust which considered anti-Semitism in contemporary Britain: that study was published in 1994 and entitled *A Very Light Sleeper.*[23] The report recommended that a similar commission be set up to consider Islamophobia and that commission published its findings in 1997.

An immediate difficulty was how to define what Islamophobia actually means and the report offered the following definition:

> In recent years a new word has gained currency... 'Islamophobia'. It was coined in the late 1980s, its first known use in print being in February 1991, in a periodical in the United States. The word is not ideal, but is recognisably similar to 'xenophobia' and 'Europhobia', and is a useful shorthand way of referring to dread or hatred of Islam – and, therefore, to fear or dislike of all or most Muslims. Such dread and dislike have existed in western countries and cultures for several centuries. In the last twenty years, however, the dislike has become more explicit, more extreme and more dangerous.[24]

The report went on to articulate in detail the various manifestations and degrees of Islamophobia that exist in British society. It looked at the nature of anti-Muslim prejudice, at Muslim communities and their concerns, at media coverage of Muslims and rules of engagement, at the barriers to forming an inclusive society such as employment, housing and public bodies, at violence towards Muslims, at inclusive education, at inter-community projects and dialogue and at recourse to law. Each of these chapters contained within it detailed research and findings, each concluding that Muslims in particular, are subject to discrimination and therefore detriment, on the basis of their faith.

The report made sixty recommendations[25] under three broad headings; central and national government, regional and local authorities and private and voluntary bodies. Within each were recommendations under even more specific headings including: education, employment, health, law, monitoring and statistics, social exclusion, housing, police forces, employers' organisations, funding organisations, journalists, Muslim and non-Muslim organisations, political parties, press complaints commission, race equality organisations and monitoring groups. The sheer depth and comprehensive nature of these recommendations highlights the fact that Islamophobia was found to exist across all spheres and spectrums of life in Britain.

Following this report, various other studies have been conducted into the manifestation of Islamophobia, particularly with regard to legal remedies to religious discrimination. Two such studies were commissioned by the Home Office to specifically address the issue of religious discrimination. The first, *Religious Discrimination in England and Wales*,[26] was conducted through the University of Derby (here after 'the Derby Report'). The second, *Tackling Religious Discrimination: Practical Implications for Policy-makers and Legislators*,[27] was conducted from the Cambridge Centre for Public Law (here after 'the Cambridge Report').

The Derby Report was set the following objectives by the Home Office:[28]

1. To assess the evidence of religious discrimination in England and Wales, both actual and perceived.
2. To describe the patterns shown by this evidence, including:
   a. its overall scale
   b. the main victims
   c. the main perpetrators
   d. the main ways in which the discrimination manifests
3. To indicate the extent to which religious discrimination overlaps with racial discrimination.
4. To identify the broad range of policy options available for dealing with religious discrimination.

Using a variety of research methods, the Derby Report concluded that there was both actual and perceived discrimination on religious grounds in a number of public spheres. Specifically, the report studied issues in education,[29] employment,[30] criminal justice and immigration,[31] housing and planning,[32] health care and social services,[33] public transport, shops and leisure,[34] obtaining funding and benefits,[35] the media,[36] other religious traditions[37] and political and pressure groups.[38] Overwhelmingly the findings of the report were that minority faith groups, and especially Muslims, suffer from discrimination on religious grounds. Evidence of this is visible throughout the report, but it can best be illustrated by the results of a generic question asked in relation to how serious various problems were for people within each religious group. The exact question asked was: "How serious do you think the following problems/ experiences are for people within your religion?"[39] The results are as follows:[40]

How serious do you think the following problems/experiences are for people within your religion?

	Very serious	Quite serious	Not at all serious	Don't know	Total responses (100%)
Ignorance					
Buddhist	9%	36%	39%	15%	33
Christian	18%	55%	22%	5%	285
Hindu	21%	58%	9%	12%	33
Jewish	17%	49%	34%	0%	35
Muslim	42%	44%	5%	9%	66
Sikh	22%	63%	9%	6%	32
Indifference					
Buddhist	3%	13%	68%	16%	31
Christian	20%	46%	29%	4%	282
Hindu	15%	58%	24%	3%	33
Jewish	9%	35%	53%	3%	34
Muslim	30%	45%	13%	12%	60
Sikh	13%	53%	25%	9%	32
Hostility					
Buddhist	6%	13%	71%	10%	31
Christian	6%	25%	62%	7%	279
Hindu	35%	35%	13%	16%	31
Jewish	12%	32%	53%	3%	34
Muslim	37%	47%	8%	8%	60
Sikh	25%	47%	19%	9%	32
Verbal abuse					
Buddhist	6%	13%	71%	10%	31
Christian	6%	23%	63%	9%	279
Hindu	27%	36%	21%	15%	33
Jewish	12%	47%	38%	3%	34
Muslim	35%	40%	13%	13%	63
Sikh	36%	48%	12%	3%	33
Physical abuse					
Buddhist	3%	13%	71%	13%	31
Christian	4%	8%	75%	12%	277
Hindu	28%	17%	31%	24%	29
Jewish	11%	25%	58%	6%	36
Muslim	28%	38%	16%	18%	61
Sikh	23%	52%	23%	3%	31
Damage to property					
Buddhist	3%	6%	81%	10%	31
Christian	7%	25%	57%	11%	283
Hindu	47%	25%	9%	19%	32
Jewish	11%	40%	43%	6%	35
Muslim	30%	36%	19%	16%	64
Sikh	33%	48%	12%	6%	33
Policies of organisations					
Buddhist	7%	17%	70%	7%	30
Christian	3%	20%	59%	19%	273
Hindu	7%	38%	24%	31%	29
Jewish	12%	15%	68%	6%	34
Muslim	16%	43%	16%	25%	63
Sikh	10%	32%	32%	26%	31
Practices of organisations					
Buddhist	6%	16%	68%	10%	31
Christian	4%	20%	56%	20%	271
Hindu	10%	42%	26%	23%	31
Jewish	12%	15%	71%	3%	34
Muslim	21%	43%	16%	21%	63
Sikh	14%	34%	28%	24%	29
Coverage in the media					
Buddhist	6%	34%	47%	13%	32
Christian	19%	39%	35%	7%	275
Hindu	32%	29%	19%	19%	31
Jewish	11%	28%	58%	3%	36
Muslim	48%	38%	5%	9%	66
Sikh	21%	36%	27%	15%	33

Source: Weller, Feldman and Purdam, *Religious Discrimination in England and Wales*, Home Office Research Study 220, London, Home Office, 2001, pp. 1-2.

Out of nine issues, Muslims felt that the issue affected them 'very seriously' more than any other faith group in six issues. In another, 'physical abuse', they were jointly highest together with the Hindu respondents. In another, 'verbal abuse', only the Sikh community were higher by one per cent than the Muslim respondents. Therefore in almost eight out of nine categories, Muslims were worst affected.

The Cambridge Report was asked by the Home Office to identify and examine the main options open to policy makers and legislators for tackling religious discrimination in Great Britain.[41] The Report summarised the issues into thirty-three separate questions[42] and sought to provide answers to each.[43] The significance of this report for this purpose is to simply illustrate the degree of recognition that has already been given to the concept of discrimination against minority faith groups, in particular Muslims, and the various remedies that are available to help resolve it. The situation is clearly aggravated by Islamophobia which, as the table from the Derby Report above illustrates, is both perceived and actual (the question asked about *problems* and/or *experiences*).

Islamophobia, then, is clearly a well established phenomenon that has a deep-rooted history and wide-reaching impact. It manifests itself in almost all sections of British society to varying degrees. These range from subtle attacks on Muslims by the media, who are frequently guilty of portraying them as a fanatical monolithic group of people, to violence and physical attacks. Studies have been conducted to empirically ascertain the levels of Islamophobia, which most visibly manifests itself as religious discrimination. These studies go as far as to propose numerous methods of combating religious discrimination.

COMMUNITY COHESION –
THE BRITISH EXPERIENCE

> Community cohesion is a term that has recently become
> increasingly popular in public policy debates. It is closely
> linked to other concepts such as inclusion and exclusion,
> social capital and differentiation, community and
> neighbourhood. In this way it has indirectly been the focus
> of a number of policies and initiatives aimed principally at
> reducing social exclusion.[44]

This quote provides a useful definition of a term that is
becoming widely referred to. The idea that communities
currently exist *without* cohesion, living separate, parallel lives,
is gaining support from a wide range of social commentators.
For others, it is an obvious statement of fact. For the latter,
they walk amongst these communities on a daily basis, almost
oblivious to the neighbouring community that may exist only
across an invisible boundary. That invisible boundary is a
wall with many bricks, bricks such as language, faith, culture,
identity, tradition, economic standing, education, employment,
prejudice – the list goes on. It is apparent that situations such
as this are commonly found throughout Britain, both cause
and solution have been discussed at length from living rooms
in inner city Birmingham to meeting rooms at Number 10
Downing Street, via university research departments and
strategic planning units. For our purposes, community cohesion
can be understood as an ideal that is worth striving for, a
situation where communities consisting of a plethora of
different people are held together by a glue having a shared
sense of right and wrong and mutual respect as its ingredients.

Sadly, such glue is missing and therefore communities are
not held together very strongly, if at all. The events of summer
2001 in some of England's northern cities illustrate this fact
and a brief overview of those events serves to highlight some
of these issues – for it represents the British experience.

The disturbances were investigated by an independent review team, the Community Cohesion Review Team, which was chaired by Ted Cantle.[45] The team was asked by the Home Office to investigate the disturbances and present a report into them, which it did in December 2001.[46] The disturbances in question took place in Bradford at Easter and in July, and in Burnley and Oldham in summer 2001. It is estimated that over fifteen hundred people were involved in the events, that over four hundred police officers and sixty-five members of the general public were injured. The damage caused was estimated at £12 million. The brief given to the review team was:

> To obtain the views of local communities, including young people, local authorities, voluntary and faith organisations, in a number of representative multi-ethnic communities, on the issues that need to be addressed in developing confident, active communities and social cohesion.
>
> To identify good practice and to report this to the Ministerial Group, and also to identify weaknesses in the handling of these issues at local level.[47]

They did this in a number of ways and made sixty-seven proposals across various headings including: peoples and values, political and community leadership, political organisations, strategic partnerships, integration and segregation, younger people, education, disadvantaged and disaffected communities, policing, housing, employment and the press and media. Clearly the team felt that the tensions which were contributing to a lack of community cohesion could not be simply explained or attributed to a handful of issues. The proposals cover almost every spectrum of life and social construct.

Having made these proposals, the review team concluded by quoting from an earlier study which was carried out in 1997. They chose to use the following quotation:

> Equality and social cohesion cannot be built upon emphasizing 'difference' in a one-sided way...The emphasis needs to be on

common rights and responsibilities...It has to be a form of citizenship that is sensitive to ethnic difference and incorporates a respect for persons as individuals and for the collectivities to which people have a sense of belonging.[48]

Various theories of how these 'differences' can be equitably managed and leave people able to engage as active citizens have been considered by academics and policy makers alike. Some of these are now considered and their relevance to the British Muslim community discussed.

THEORIES OF CITIZENSHIP

Gerard Delanty[49] in his book *Citizenship in a global age – Society, culture, politics*,[50] outlines several models of citizenship including: the Liberal theory of citizenship,[51] Communitarian theories of citizenship[52] (including Liberal communitarianism, Conservative communitarianism and civic Republicanism), radical theories of politics: citizenship and democracy[53] (including direct democracy, discursive democracy and feminist citizenship), cosmopolitan citizenship[54] and human rights and citizenship.[55] Of these, the two most applicable to the British Muslim context appear to be the communitarian theory and the cosmopolitan theory. Each will be considered briefly in turn. Before doing so, it is worth remembering the classic definition of citizenship and its components. Again, Delanty puts it very well:

> Citizenship entails membership of a legally constituted political community, which may be called civil society; it consists of rights, duties, participation and identity.[56]

The concern for British Muslims is that not only is the space of civil society very limited *per se*, British Muslims are arguably not 'legally constituted' within it as they are not recognised as a legal entity. They therefore have fewer rights, inversely therefore, more duties, are much less able to participate fully[57] and have a confused shifting identity.[58] With each part of the definition posing problems, how can British Muslims feel a sense of citizenship?

COMMUNITARIAN THEORIES

This theory is based on the idea that citizenship is located in the public sphere. Over centuries the battle for where civic engagement should occur has been taking place. As considered earlier, in Greek and Roman times a public forum of civic participation existed. Modern theories of liberalism from Hobbes to Locke to Smith have created the market space as the forum for shared public culture and civil society. Thus a culture of wearing the same designer logos on jeans and shirts somehow creates a citizenship that replaces one of concern for the betterment of society, and the power to translate those concerns into a tangible process of change.

Social democracy then took this further and replaced the market by the state rendering any remnants of civil society dependent on social class – only those who can't afford not to, have to engage with others. Communitarian theories seek to redress this balance by shifting citizenship back into civil society and community rather than in the market (where liberalism places it) or in the state (where social democracy places it).

Referring to the four classic components, the focus is on participation and identity rather than on rights and duties. Historically, there have been proponents of the view that individuals do not, or should not, exist in selfish isolation, but should rather involve themselves in communities where they can come together to mutually agree morality, ethics and therefore laws that govern. This concept goes against notions of individualism and seeks to establish sets of values and norms based on common principles of shared ethics that can then be translated into governing principles. Thus, for Aristotle, it was the idea of *praxis* – the fusion of the ethical and the political; during the Renaissance it was termed 'virtue' and in modern discourse, Rousseau refers to it as a 'self governing political community'. The thread that binds them all is that 'community' is the foundation to civil society rather than the individual.

This basic theory has been extended, in various directions, with the degree of separation between community and individual often being the central point of debate. Delanty identifies three such variants, namely, Liberal communitarianism, Conservative communitarianism and civic Republicanism.[59] The detail of these is not necessary for this discussion; suffice to say that the central significance of these theories is that they propose that citizenship should be a much more politicised concept, giving people a public voice and greater power to influence than the state-led models of liberal social democracy provide.

Communitarian models of citizenship do not clearly deal with the relationship that would exist with democratic theory and neither do they adequately discuss matters of private domain. Thus, if the models are to be taken forward, these two critical areas need detailed discussion and development.

COSMOPOLITAN THEORIES

These theories are relatively new and therefore little has been written on them. The fundamental idea is that citizenship is a pure matter in that it does not recognise nation or state. The shift this time is from nation-state to local autonomy. There is a direct correlation between the emergence, growth and significance of these theories and an overwhelming recent phenomenon – globalisation. Globalisation enabled information, values, politics and almost everything else to be exchanged rapidly and with ease. With numerous obvious benefits as well as disadvantages, its impact on citizenship has been very significant. Referring once more to the four components, conceptions of rights, duties, participation and identity have all been influenced by globalisation. A young American man in New York will have the same sense of 'my rights and independence' as the same aged young Bengali man living in Dhaka. Socially and economically, the opportunities available to both, and indeed the social and economic responsibilities upon both (not considering the religious and moral values that might be different), will be quite different, yet the sense of what citizenship involves (often taught by Hollywood) will be similar. Most probably, that citizenship will focus more on rights and identity than duty and participation.

Obviously the impact of globalisation extends beyond the individual to the international arena, although its ability to impact on individuals attests to its power. Any recent readings of the proceedings of United Nations meetings, global environmental conferences, NATO meetings, World Bank policies (the list is endless) will testify to the fact that not only has globalisation actually had an impact in all of these arenas, but by globalisation often we mean Americanisation.

The consequence of this is that nations, states and indeed America, have acquired more power than most people would like to have given away. Very few people control their local environment, even fewer control the world. Cosmopolitan citizenship seeks to rectify this by giving power back to the individual and local communities.

Four such theories are identified by Delanty as: internationalism, globalisation, transnationalism and postnationalism. These correlate to four thematic concepts of citizenship, those being legal, political, cultural and civic respectively. Legal cosmopolitanism relates to the international politics of states and derives from the works of Immanuel Kant and Enlightenment universalism – the idea that government is supreme and that all are subject to the Rule of Law. Political cosmopolitanism considers the emergence of a global civil society and responds to the challenges of globalisation. It contests legal *government* and speaks of *governance* as a better suited form of managing civil society. Cultural cosmopolitanism addresses the idea that people are 'trans-national' in that they may move from one place to another either as migrants, forced or not, or by choice. They cannot therefore have their citizenship defined by locality or nationality. The theory builds on the ideal that as 'citizens of the world' people should have a sense of citizenship that can travel with them, and can also be accepted by whichever community they decide to base themselves in. Civic cosmopolitanism develops the idea that although people share sovereignty and locality, there is a sense of post-nationalism where the shared culture is based more in civil society than national society (which would consist of interest groups, non-governmental organisations, citizen initiatives and movements).

Within these theories, there are three concepts that will especially resonate with British Muslims. They are best expressed by the proponents themselves:

> The peoples of the earth have thus entered in varying degrees into a universal community, and it has developed to the point where a violation of rights in one part of the world is felt everywhere. The idea of a cosmopolitan right is therefore not fantastic and overstrained; it is a necessary complement to the unwritten code of political and international right, transforming it into a universal right of humanity. Only under this condition can we flatter ourselves that we are continually advancing towards a perpetual peace.[60]

This ideal of a global community is compatible with the Islamic notion of a global *ummah* (universal community). The right of an individual not to have their rights taken from them is a foundational principle of the Islamic *Sharīʿah* (law and code of governance) and the goal of attaining perpetual peace is a key objective of every Muslim.

> It is possible to combine the claims to citizenship status with a postmodernist critique, if postmodernism can be regarded as a form of pluralism. That is, we must avoid the equation of citizenship with sameness. In citizenship, it may be possible to reconcile the claims for pluralism, the need for solidarity and the contingent vagaries of historical change. If citizenship can develop in a context with difference, differentiation and pluralism are tolerated, then citizenship need not assume a repressive character as a political instrument of the state.[61]

For British Muslims in particular, a great fear is having to give up their belief and faith in order to be accepted as British citizens. Islam does not require such assimilation of people, having no compulsion in faith and providing citizenship rights and legal protection to people of other faiths living under Islamic rule. Thus, differentiation and pluralism are very acceptable concepts in Islam and Muslims would hope to benefit from the same concepts when living in lands where they are a minority.

When referring to global citizenship, Falk states:

> Its guiding image is that the world is becoming unified around a common business elite, an elite that shares interests and experiences, comes to have more in common with each other than it does with the more rooted, ethnically distinct members of its own particular civil society: the result seems to be a denationalised global elite that at the same time lacks any global civic sense of responsibility.[62]

This danger of global citizenship is again shared by British Muslims from a faith perspective. Leadership and political governance in Islam is regarded as a trust from the people. Thus, it is not sought after and when one is in a position of authority, one is obliged to seek out the needs and wishes of people, staying in touch with them and ensuring that whatever responsibility is given, is fulfilled in a responsible way – economically, socially, morally and environmentally. The concept of *khalīfah* (vicegerent) applies to both individuals in their duties to God, to one another and to the earth, as well as to those in positions of power and to those who appointed them.

By simply looking at some of these quotations it is clear that modern-day discourse on citizenship, especially in the realm of cosmopolitan citizenship, can be compatible with Islam. Thus, those holding the view that Islam and modern Western political and philosophical thought are fundamentally incompatible, are quite simply wrong. In fact, the opposite is true. Islam upholds every virtue of citizenship, it explicitly and in great detail not only emphasises the four components of rights, duties, participation and identity but provides detailed guidance on how each of these is to be manifested and secured.

CONCLUSIONS

This chapter has established that it is a well accepted part of the human condition to want to be socially engaged as a citizen. This is an ancient truth which remains more valid than ever today. For a number of reasons people are not able to fulfil this natural condition and this fact is evidenced by poor participation in local and national politics. More specifically, for minority groups there are other obstacles that act as impediments to their participation. For British Muslims, these are exemplified by racism and Islamophobia. The British experience is that communities are becoming more polarised and lack of community cohesion is becoming worse. A number of theories of citizenship have, and are still, being developed to try to help remedy this situation. For some of these at least, Muslims will encounter no difficulties in engaging with the discourse as it is wholly consistent with their belief system and way of life. If anything, British Muslims have a duty to share their thoughts and principles with society at large and take on the challenge fully. If Islam has the solutions, then it is time to process these and make them applicable to the British context, not in an attempt to convert everyone, but as a method of establishing a fair and just society where all people are respected, enabled and welcomed to become citizens in the true sense of the word. Not only must British Muslims be seen as 'friends and countrymen' but *they* too must see *all others* in society as their 'friends and countrymen' also.

The time to move the debate on is long overdue. The questions to be asked should no longer be: "Is Islam compatible with the West? Can Muslims be British citizens? Do Muslims want to engage with society?" Rather, the questions that need to be asked are: "What are the challenges of multiculturalism? Is the playing field level? Does British society cater for the legal and political recognition of minority groups?" Perhaps even more fundamentally, other questions need to be asked: "Why has civil society almost disappeared? Why are people so reluctant to vote and why do they show such resentment to those elected to represent them? Despite legislation to protect against it, why is discrimination on grounds of race and sex still so widespread in British society? Why are rates of crime, family breakdown and general dissatisfaction with life going up?"[63]

Britain will only begin to treat all of its citizens fairly and allow them the opportunity to become more fully engaged once it begins to deal with these and other specific issues relating to multicultural citizenship.[64] Only a society that has state-led respect for all communities, despite their differences, will begin to be able to successfully resolve some of these issues. Such an example can be seen in Canada about which Zohra states:

> Canada is a unique country in the world where preservation and advancement of multiculturalism is an official governmental policy. It is Canada's ingenuity and inner security that could allow freedom of cultures and their enhancement.[65]

The British Muslim position is clear – they would prefer to be part of a society that is more like the plural Canadian mosaic than the assimilationist American 'melting pot'.

Chapter 6

Councillors and Caliphs: Muslim Political Participation in Britain

Dilwar Hussain

INTRODUCTION

With the slow but steadily growing involvement of Muslims in the British political process, the Muslim community seems to be coming of age in its dealings with the 'establishment'. This has, however not been an easy process and still the degree of involvement with the state remains one that is easily influenced by a number of different factors. Among these factors are the climate of co-operation (which may depend in turn on local and international politics), the degree of acculturation or integration of the Muslim community and how responsive the Government appears to be to the sensitivities and needs of the British Muslim community.

There are numerous ways that Muslims have entered the political arena: as candidates for the political parties, as a lobby group entering into a dialogue with the parties, or by the setting up of an alternative political party. In addition to these 'engaging' approaches there are also cases of those who have sought to find a political niche outside the mainstream political system, and those who have vehemently opposed any attempt at dealing with the state, even voting. This chapter will look briefly at these various trends and approaches but it will also touch upon the arena of political action that is often forgotten, namely that of civil society (and also look at how the Prophet Muḥammad (pbuh) engaged with his society). Perhaps the largest component of Muslim effort is exerted in this arena – ordinary people changing their social space through collective efforts.

The chapter will also assay some of the Islamic legal opinions that lie behind socio-political participation in a political system that is not Islamic and also briefly look at the debates surrounding the involvement of Muslims in modern, democratically organised states. Such issues have been hotly debated within contemporary Islamic thought with some scholars even questioning the validity of Muslims living outside Muslim countries (see the chapter on British Muslim identity). Like so many of the issues discussed in this book, the themes are very much inter-related and inextricably linked. Despite the theoretical debates, there seems to be a growing consensus that Muslims are now permanent citizens of plural, Western, nation-states and they need to assert themselves to create a place for their future.

It is not only the internal factors relating to the Muslim community that determine how engaged British Muslims are with the politics of the nation. External influences such as the climate of political apathy in Britain and Europe naturally affect the British Muslim community. One may therefore see, as is the national trend, that younger people from the Muslim community are generally more apathetic to voting than their parents. Other significant external influences are international events that have brought the Muslim community under the spotlight, such as the Oil Embargo in 1973, the Iranian Revolution in 1979, the ethnic cleansing of Muslims in Bosnia and the Gulf Wars in the 1990s, the attacks of 11th September 2001 and the war in Afghanistan, and the war in Iraq in 2003. Likewise, there have also been a number of domestic issues such as *The Satanic Verses* affair, the campaign for state funding of Muslim schools or religious discrimination laws. In each case Muslims have been increasingly vocal as they have been forced to articulate responses or demands. This has meant engaging in lobbying, learning how to address the media, and meeting with government officials to articulate the views of the Muslim community. Such events have, step by step, brought the Muslim community into the public arena.

If one is to compare the response of the Muslim community during *The Satanic Verses* affair and that after the 11th September, there are marked differences in approach. With the events over a decade apart, there are signs of growing maturity in walking the corridors of power. It is likely that this has been aided by the fact that by 2001 the second generation of Muslims had reached either the leadership or prominent positions in many Muslim institutions, and were more articulate and well versed in the nuances of British society than their 'elders' were.

The discussion around political engagement partly impinges on the social, economic and political needs of the Muslim community, as well as on how established the Muslim community has become and is able to understand the opportunities available to articulate its needs, concerns and vision to the wider society. In order to look at this from a psycho-social perspective, one could refer to Maslow's hierarchy of needs which looks at human motivation. Important parallels can be drawn with how, not only individuals but also communities are motivated to act, thus giving us a basis for understanding the priorities and challenges that may face the Muslim community. This will be looked at in the section that discusses 'Why political participation?'

THE DEBATE AROUND
POLITICAL PARTICIPATION

The notion of Muslims participating in a non-Muslim political climate (including regimes in Muslim countries) has stirred strong opinions, for and against, within Muslim intellectual circles. As with the discussion on identity, this debate is also linked with how Islam relates to Modernity.

There are in fact two different issues, interlinked as they are:

1. Democracy and its acceptability to Muslims.
2. Sharing power as a minority with a non-Muslim authority.

Without going into the question of whether nations like Britain always behave democratically or not, or without actually discussing what democracy really is – both valid debates but ones that need their own time and place – this section will briefly look at some of the Muslim viewpoints in response to democracy.

The most vocal opponents of democracy are the Jihādī movements,[1] the Ḥizb al-Taḥrīr,[2] some of the Salafī movements as well as other traditional or conservative movements. Of course there are many others who defy categorisation. The reasons for opposition range from the thesis that democracy constitutes a form of polytheism (*shirk billah*), (by interfering with God's authority to rule), as God, not the consensus of people, is the ultimate source of legalisation and sovereignty (*ḥākimiyyah*), rests with God, to critiques that tap into the debate between traditionalism and modernity and highlight that Islam has its own paradigm based on consultation (*shūrā*), and does not need to borrow from a Western philosophical model, that to borrow the concept of democracy from the West would be to buy into the philosophy of modernism and secularism, if not consciously then by stealth.

The first significant encounter by Muslims of Western democratic systems probably occurred in the early nineteenth century as contact between Europe and the Muslim world began to grow. The most prominent advocates of democracy and a *rapprochement* with the West at the scholarly level, mainly figures such as Rifaʿah Taḥtawī (d. 1873), Jamāl al-Dīn al-Afghānī (d. 1897), Muḥammad ʿAbduh (d. 1905) and more recently Rachid Ghannouchi, Hasan Turabi and Abdulkarim Soroush, claim that democracy is not as alien to Islam as people often view it. Democracy as a mechanism of the political relationship of the individual to the state is distinct from the ideology of secularism and modernism. The principle of *shūrā* is in essence a democratic model that encourages participation. The other salient features of democracy – the ability to choose rulers and remove them if they deviate, and the freedom to criticise – are seen as Islamic values that have been taken up by the European Enlightenment and developed in a specific Western context at a time when the Muslim world had declined into a state of monarchy and dictatorship. This democratic alternative is seen as far more akin to the spirit of Islam than the *status quo* of the Muslim world. As regards the *ḥākimiyyah* of God – Muslim democracies would use the Qurʾān and *Sunnah* as a framework, or legislative source, within which to enact democratic policies.[3] This would ensure that overall sovereignty rests with God, but the process of decision-making is a democratic one. It is also pointed out there are different models of democracy and Islamic democracy would emerge and develop with its own nuances.

The first Muslim scholar to formally write about democracy was probably Taḥtawī, who in 1834, on his return from France, wrote of the virtues of French democracy in comparison with his experience of Egyptian/Arab society.[4] Taḥtawī, an *Imām*, felt that Muslim societies could borrow experiences from the West if they did not directly contradict Islam. Another early figure was Khairuddīn al-Tūnisī (d. 1899) who stressed that political reform was necessary to rejuvenate the Arab world. In order to appreciate the desire for reform, one should note that the Muslim world, having been superseded by Europe, was at the point of political fragmentation and the leading questions in the minds of Muslim intellectuals of this age were: 'how did the Muslim *ummah* come to such a state of decline?' and 'how should we deal with the West'? Al-Afghānī's answer to these questions were, similarly, that the Muslims had contributed to their own downfall by accepting despotism and that the way out was to learn from the West, as "wisdom is the lost property of the believer".[5] For al-Afghānī the absence of *ʿadl* (justice), *shūrā* and the lack of adherence of rulers to the constitution had brought the Muslim *ummah* to its declined state.[6] ʿAbduh, one of al-Afghānī's followers, took this notion further. ʿAbduh was known as a proponent of the Salafi trend, a return to tradition in the model of the first generations of Muslims (*salaf*). (However ʿAbduh's approach is not to be confused with the contemporary Salafiyyah movement, which although connected in some matters of methodology, has been much influenced by conservative Wahhābī[7] thought.) ʿAbduh's vision was one of combining traditional values and principles with a need for constant change in light of the modern. ʿAbduh declared that Islam is not a theocracy and that there is some distinction between the 'religious' and 'worldly'. He was very careful to use the term distinction (*tamyīz*) rather than separation (*faṣl*) for he believed that the two should co-exist, but not be separate.[8]

The ideas of al-Afghānī and ʿAbduh were taken on by Rashīd Riḍā (d. 1935) (albeit with a more conservative slant). Some of these views and approaches were adopted and contextualised by activist-scholars like Ḥasan al-Bannā[9] (d. 1949), who was able to popularise, within Muslim circles,[10] an approach towards the West that involved a strong critical stance towards colonialism but also a desire to learn from what was considered to be of benefit (*maṣlaḥah*) to the

Muslim world.[11] A document released by the Muslim Brotherhood elucidates the official viewpoint: that they believe in "...a representative council which is elected through free and fair elections...the term of presidency should be limited and should be renewed only for a fixed period, to ward off tyranny." Furthermore: "...the Muslim Brotherhood believe in the plurality of parties...[and that] The law would be applied through an independent judiciary away from the hands of the government..."[12] It is worth noting here that Sayyid Qutb (d. 1966), one of the prominent ideologues of the Muslim Brotherhood during the 1960s, seemed to have very different views. For Qutb, liberal democracies would lead to perpetual factionalism, and then there is the concern of sovereignty again. For others like Abdul Rashid Moten, democracy is a form of cultural imperialism that has fooled 'Westernised' Muslim thinkers into championing its cause. Democracy comes from the Enlightenment tradition[13] and cannot be separated from Westernisation.

Ghannouchi views such ideas as the misunderstanding of both democracy and Islam. He admits that liberal democracy may not suit Muslim society, but postulates that the mechanism of democracy can be used to develop a democratic tradition that is applicable to Muslims. Ghannouchi clarifies that the sovereignty of God cannot mean that God comes to earth to rule. On the contrary, the sovereignty of God implies the rule of God's law, i.e. 'the rule of law', a cornerstone of modern democratic states. For him, the idea of submitting oneself to the sovereignty of God is actually a liberating one; to remove the possibility of despotism, the totalitarian rule of another human being.[14] Another key argument posed against democracy is that the will of the people could be expressed in a way that runs counter to Islamic values, e.g. people could vote to legalise alcohol or usury. This is indeed the case in principle, but three considerations should be born in mind. Firstly, that as the framework or constitution of an Islamic democracy would be based on Islamic values, one would have to change the whole nature and ethos of the state in order to render it un-Islamic. This process is not as simple as just holding an election or referendum. Secondly, if the vast majority of people are adamant that they wish to depart from Islamic values then this raises more important questions about the Islamicity of that society and whether it is appropriate to observe Islamic laws in such an environment. The third, and most important, consideration is that any and every form of government could deviate from Islamic values. History is testimony to that. In a democracy it would take the majority to agree on this, but in a system where power is concentrated in the hands of a few, this is potentially even easier. History has shown how even scholars could be coerced or bought out to justify and legitimise tyranny. As the Prophet Muḥammad (pbuh) said, "My community will not agree upon an erronous matter,"[15] it seems better to leave power as widely dissipated as possible, in the hands of the people.

In terms of the second issue, sharing power, it is true that even among the milder critics of democracy, most still tend to participate (perhaps out of pragmatic reasons) in the system although they would not consider it ideal (or even legitimate in some cases) according to their own definitions. There are a few, such as the Ḥizb al-Taḥrīr and the Jihādīs who call for a complete abstention from even voting. Although it is interesting to note that the Ḥizb al-Taḥrīr did in fact enter the electoral process in 1954 and 1956.[16] Coming back to the objection, the argument again is similar to that given above for if one accepts that a system is non-Islamic, then one cannot share in the ruling of the system; that rule by other than God's revelations would be tantamount to wrongdoing (*fisq*), injustice (*ẓulm*), or even disbelief (*kufr*).[17] This argument is not restricted to the state level, but is also used in the context of, for example, a university student union where objections are raised about Muslims being party to a decision that may involve the sale of alcohol or other such actions that would run counter to Islamic values.

A counter argument is based on the maxim (*qā'idah*) of *fiqh* "if you cannot change a situation in its entirety then you should not leave it in its entirety". Secondly, another maxim, "choosing the lesser of two evils" is also cited, as well as the case of the Prophet Yūsuf ruling in Egypt within a non-Muslim system. The Qur'ān mentions the story of Yūsuf and how he was abandoned in the well by his brothers. Eventually Yūsuf finds himself in Egypt where he is first imprisoned wrongly and then gains favour with the ruler due to his ability to interpret dreams. He predicts the potential agricultural disaster of Egypt and offers his help in running the affairs of what could be considered the 'Ministry of Agriculture'.[18] Ghannouchi further mentions the Negus of Abyssinia ruling by Christian laws (while the Prophet indicated at the time of the Negus' death that he was a Muslim).[19] Ibn Taymiyah states regarding this:

> We know definitely that he could not implement the law of the Qur'ān in his community because his people would not have permitted him to. Despite that, the Negus and all those who are similar to him found their way to the pleasure of God in eternity although they could not abide by the laws of Islam, and could only rule using that which could be implemented in the given circumstances.[20]

A fifth argument is mentioned by Ghannouchi as being the *ḥilf al-fuḍūl* (the virtuous pact – see later), to which the Prophet Muḥammad (pbuh) was party; and finally the fact that ʿUmar ibn ʿAbdul Azīz found himself in a situation in which he was ruling over the Muslims as a monarch. A situation that befell him by right of inheritance and not one that he agreed with morally. However he tried his best to make gradual changes from within his post, rather than abdicate it altogether.

The argument is basically a pragmatic one, albeit rooted in jurisprudence (*fiqh*) that Muslims must engage with the system and influence it as far as they can. By standing outside they can only be conscientious objectors with no impact on the *status quo*. Close scrutiny of Islamic sources shows that neither the Qur'ān nor the *Sunnah* specified a particular form of government,[21] in fact Ibn ʿAqīl al-Ḥanbalī (d. 1130) defined *Siyāsah Sharʿiyyah* (Islamic Administrative Policy) as:

> that which brings people closer to good and distances them from evil, even if such actions were not advocated by the Prophet or revealed from the Heavens.[22]

As long as the practice of politics is described in such broad terms, it seems likely that Muslims will feel able to engage in any age and society, that they will be able to participate in political life in whatever society they are in and be able to take up their full roles in that society. Perhaps the clearest contemporary statement for political participation comes from a *fatwā* of Taha Jabir al-Alwani[23] in the US:

> ...it is the duty of American Muslims to participate constructively in the political process, if only to protect their rights, and give support to views and causes they favor. Their participation may also improve the quality of information disseminated about Islam. We call this participation a "duty" because we do not consider it merely a "right" that can be abandoned or a "permission" which can be ignored.[24]

EXAMPLE AND MODELS OF POLITICAL PARTICIPATION

Of the different models of participation, and indeed non-participation, the models mentioned below are presented as the main categories of the UK experience. It is very difficult to compartmentalise such entities into neat groups and there may be some overlap:

1. Working outside the system.
2. Working for an alternative system.
3. Joining existing parties.
4. Setting up a Muslim party.
5. Lobbying.
6. Local action and civil society.

Broadly speaking these groups could be divided into two: non-participative (1-2) and participative (3-6). It would be useful to look briefly at each model and mention some of the organisations or movements that are involved:

1. *Working outside the system*

The Ḥizb al-Taḥrīr typifies the anti-democratic, antiparticipation tradition. The solution is to work for the establishment of the Islamic State or *Khilāfah*,[25] but in a way that does not involve any participation with the '*kufr* system'. According to their recent and current literature, it is therefore wrong to vote, to join a political party, or to take up a post in government:

> As for the Islamic view on joining the political process and engaging in Western politics by becoming members of secular political parties, the view is clear – it is Haram – without a shred of doubt...The Muslims in Britain need to critically evaluate the call to participate in the political processes of the West. This call wishes to further the community away from Islam and accelerate the acceptance of Secularism as a basis for the Muslim political outlook. The Muslim community must resist this call.[26]

Working from outside the system, the party's strategy is to awaken Muslims to work for the *Khilāfah* by challenging and critiquing the prevalent beliefs of society. However, as

5 groups in approaches to muslim political engagement

mentioned before the party did put up candidates for election in Jordan in 1954 and 1956. The eventual goal is a revolution that will bring about the *Khilāfah*, which will then apply Islamic laws. In the late 1990s a split arose within the UK branch on the issue of where the attention for the *Khilāfah* should be centred, with one group saying that the focus should be a Muslim country and another group wanting to concentrate on the UK – this led to the split and formation of al-Muhajiroun, currently led by Omar Bakri Muhammad, who believes in the latter view.

As previously mentioned the Jihādī tendency would also come under this category of working outside the established system of politics. This tendency is typified, not as much by the desire to build an external *Khilāfah*, but by its aggressive stance and the articulation of *jihād* as a physical, military means of resolving the current dilemmas facing the Muslim world.

2. *Working for an alternative system*

The Muslim Parliament was launched in 1992 out of the Muslim Institute[27] under the leadership of Kalim Siddiqui (d. 1996). In 1990 Kalim Siddiqui launched a *Muslim Manifesto*, which laid out a vision for a 'minority political system'. The purpose was to create a political platform that would allow Muslims to debate issues of concern and formulate policies, while being accessible to the Muslim community. It was claimed that Muslims would never have real access to the corridors of power in Westminster and hence they needed their own version of 'parliament'. In fact, the organisation was originally called a council, but this was projected by the media as a parliament and then adopted by the organisation as such. The Muslim Parliament was composed of the leader of the house (Kalim Siddiqui), a speaker, four deputy speakers and around one hundred and fifty members (called MMPs – Muslim Members of Parliament) in the 'Lower House' as well as a planned 'Upper House'. This approach is quite different to the one adopted by the Ḥizb al-Taḥrīr, simply because it was in essence an approach towards building a future for Muslims in Britain through a gradual process but one that felt this future lay in parallel institutions, rather than within mainstream society. After the death of the founder in 1996 the Muslim Parliament has become less vocal and has lost many of its activists, some of whom have set up another organisation, the Institute of Contemporary Islamic Thought.

3. *Joining existing parties*

British Muslims began joining the mainstream political parties in the 1960s and the first councillor, Bashir Maan, was elected in 1970. Until quite recently the affiliation was almost exclusively with the Labour Party. Currently there are over 200 Councillors,[28] two Members of the House of Commons, four Members of the House of Lords and one Member of the European Parliament, that are of Muslim origin. It is difficult to estimate the number of Muslims that are members of the various parties.

Table: Number of Muslim Councillors according to Party in 2000.	
Party	**Number of Muslim Councillors**
Labour	166
Liberal Democrat	27
Conservative	20
Justice	6
Total	219

(Source: "Muslim Councillors in the UK: May 2000", compiled by *The Muslim News*, 2001)

However, it is still the case that few Muslims are placed in winnable seats and a recent tribunal found that there was race discrimination taking place within the selection procedure.[29]

According to the Institute of Public Policy Research (IPPR) there is still a strong case of under representation of ethnic minority candidates (including Muslims) in political positions.[30] The report, which calls for urgent positive action, found that there are only twelve black and Asian MPs, a figure which should be around forty-seven[31] in order to be more reflective of the demographic situation of the UK. 2.5% of the councillors are from ethnic minority backgrounds while there should be around 6% and there should be around six black and Asian members of the Greater London Assembly (GLA) whereas in reality there are only two.

Table: IPPR Estimate of Ethnic Minority Underrepresentation in Political Positions.

	Current Situation	MoreReflective Situation
No. of MPs	12	47
No. of Councillors	2.5% (530)	6% (1,272)
Members of GLA	2	6

(Source: Ali, Rushanara and O'Cinneide, Colme, *Our House? Race and Representation in British Politics*, London: IPPR, April 2002.)

On the whole, individuals rather than groups have participated in this manner, though at times some broadbased coalitions such as the pro-Kashmir lobby have encouraged Muslims to take up posts. Recent General Elections have seen a number of 'votesmart' campaigns (organised by *Q-News*, *Muslim News*, the Muslim Council of Britain and others)[32] highlighting areas with winnable seats and encouraging Muslims to vote strategically. The Muslim Council of Britain produced a document called *Electing to Listen* prior to the 2001 General Elections, which was formulated to encourage the different parties to take on board issues of concern to Muslims in a broad range of areas.

Muslims have traditionally been keen supporters of the Labour Party. However in recent years there has been a gradual increase in support for the other two mainstream parties as well. This has probably been because of dissatisfaction with some of the Government's foreign policy choices and also domestic stances on matters such as the repeal of Clause 28 and the lowering of the age of consent for gay relationships. The reasons for supporting the Labour Party find their roots in the immigration stance that Labour took in the 1970s, along with of course the fact that being factory workers, first generation Muslims would have had strong links with the unions. The local elections of 2003 saw Labour losing a large number of seats. Though there are no studies yet to prove why, it is thought that anti-war sentiment played a significant role in shifting votes from Labour to the Liberal Democrats. In Leicester for example, the previous four Muslim councillors (all Labour) lost their seats. At the same time there were four new councillors of Muslim background, but this time with affiliation to the Liberal Democrats. Patricia Hewitt, a Labour MP for Leicester, commented that Muslims were registering their protest against the Labour Party and acknowledged that she was not surprised by the lack of support for Labour in the Muslim community.[33] A number of groups including the Muslim Association of Britain (MAB) led vociferous campaigns asking Muslims not to vote for Labour out of protest for the Government's stance on the war in Iraq.[34]

4. Setting up a Muslim party

The Islamic Party of Britain, established in 1989, has been the only case of Muslims setting up a political party of their own to participate in mainstream elections in the UK.[35] However this experience has not been very encouraging. The party failed to secure a significant number of votes even in places like Bradford where some wards have high percentages of Muslim voters. In the Bradford North by-election in 1990 the Islamic Party attained 3% of the vote, and in the 1992 elections it lost its deposit. The reasons for this lack of support are quite complex but some of these may be: lack of trust in the group, lack of community involvement in setting up the party and the agenda of the party being perceived as too narrow. This may indicate that the Muslim community is more willing to vote for the mainstream parties than a party that makes Islam the issue of its manifesto. There is a possible correlation here with electoral behaviour in Pakistan and Bangladesh, for example, where large numbers of British Muslims originate from. Until recently overtly religious political parties in these countries have not enjoyed widespread success in elections, which is perhaps a sign of general cynicism towards religious figures entering the political arena. There is a caveat to this however, as in the last election in Pakistan, in which a broad spectrum of religious groups set up a coalition party (the United Action Forum), there were some significant gains.

5. *Lobbying*

The Union of Muslim Organisations (UMO) was set up in 1970 and pioneered the lobbying[36] of government for Muslim needs. In the wake of the *Satanic Verses* affair and the Gulf War in 1991 the UK Action Committee on Islamic Affairs (UKACIA) also made important strides in representing Muslim concerns to government. This eventually led to the creation of the National Interim Committee for Muslim Unity (NICMU), the precursor to the MCB which was established in 1997. The MCB has been active in lobbying government support for the inclusion of the Census question on religious affiliation, increase of Muslims in the House of Lords, funding for Muslim schools, changes to discrimination laws and a host of other matters. The MCB is the largest umbrella body, with over four hundred affiliate organisations from all over the UK. Its aims are:

1. To promote co-operation, consensus and unity on Muslim affairs in the UK.
2. To encourage and strengthen all existing efforts being made for the benefit of the Muslim community.
3. To work for a more enlightened appreciation of Islam and Muslims in the wider society.
4. To establish a position for the Muslim community within British society that is fair and based on due rights.
5. To work for the eradication of disadvantages and forms of discrimination faced by Muslims.
6. To foster better community relations and work for the good of society as a whole.

There are also other organisations (and indeed individuals) such as: Forum Against Islamophobia and Racism (FAIR), the Muslim College, al-Khoei Foundation and The Islamic Foundation, that have been able to establish good relationships with government institutions and have had some significant effects on policy matters.

A very recent development has been the rise of email based pressure groups like MPAC (Muslim Public Affairs Committee) styled upon some of the aggressive tactics of American lobbies. MPAC claim to have tens of thousands of email subscribers on their daily mailing list and alerts are sent out for action on a variety of issues ranging from writing complaints to biased programmes to attending marches and pickets. The group aims: "to politicise the Muslims and encourage them to get to know their Member of Parliament, and to feel confident in raising issues with them – it is after all their job to look after the interests of their constituents".[37]

6. *Local action and civil society*

Many local and national organisations have been involved outside the sphere of formal political authority within civil society as service providers and important catalysts in effecting change in society. Such organisations are too numerous to name but they range from small single-issue organisations that offer advice, counselling and support on specific issues to networks with thousands of people that encourage members to constantly write to MPs and the media and work on local capacity-building projects. Also of great importance here are the various mosques and mosque councils that are able to engage with the wider society. There is, no doubt, some degree of overlap between this category and the lobbyists above. Especially if ones look at movements such as the Stop the War Coalition which have organised a number of high-profile marches against the war in Iraq specifically and the War on Terrorism in general. This movement has attracted wide support from the left of the political spectrum, from the anti-globalisation movement, from Muslim groups as well as many non-aligned individuals and organisations creating a vibrant civil participation.[38] The sphere of civil society has become more prominent in recent years as people have begun to feel that states are too distant and aloof from their lives. Voter apathy seems to be on the increase, and while Fukuyama may have hailed 'The End of History',[39] Paul Hirst feels that "...liberal individualism and free-market capitalism have gained no decisive victory from this failure of socialism...".[40] Civil society is that sphere of public life that is between the state, the corporate sector and the family. It is the realm where people associate and come together for a plethora of different causes and pastimes that are non-governmental in nature, yet may be highly politicised, or indeed not. Often such organisations and associations can act as mediators between individuals, small groups and informal networks on the one hand and the state or statutory bodies on the other. The capacity-building work of civil society institutions or NGOs is well recognised as is their contribution to fighting social exclusion.[41]

The Role of NGOs

However a recent IPPR report highlights that there is much room for improvement in getting ethnic minority civil society organisations involved in the thinking and consultation process.[42]

An interesting model for civil society engagement is provided by the Citizen Organising Foundation (COF), formed in 1991 and inspired by the Broad Based Organising model very prominent in US Civil Society. The COF and its affiliated bodies, Young Citizens (in Birmingham) and The East London Communities Organisation (TELCO) have managed to bring thousands of volunteers from different backgrounds, including Muslims, together to work for issues of common local concern. The philosophy is to teach politics through action and to show that individuals can make a difference if they organise themselves together with others. The COF provides training for its affiliates and contacts to show how local community leaders can assess the power relations within communities, build connections with powerful people and press the right buttons to make things happen.[43]

WHY POLITICAL PARTICIPATION?

In order to bring some analysis to this scenario one must pose the question – why is it that Muslim organisations and individuals are participating in the political system? And furthermore, why is it important to be engaged in the political process? The obvious answer lies in the desire to affect power and to gain power. One of the definitions of power is 'the ability to do or act'.[44] Hence Muslims are trying to improve their lot by building their capacity to act. All too often this action has been to seek the needs of Muslim communities and so the focus has been to seek changes in service provision, public opinion or law. There has been little emphasis on contributing to the wider society. Abraham Maslow's (d. 1970) hierarchy of needs[45] for human motivation give us some useful insights into some of the complex needs and challenges that face human beings. It may help to describe the needs of British Muslims on a priority basis and thus allow the community to chart out an issue-based agenda for its future development. According to Maslow the following levels of needs motivate people:

1. Physiological: hunger, thirst, bodily needs, etc.
2. Safety/security: self-protection, shelter, order.
3. Belonging and Love: affiliation with others, be accepted.
4. Esteem: to achieve, be competent, gain approval and recognition.
5. Cognitive: to know, to understand, and explore.
6. Aesthetic: symmetry, order, and beauty.
7. Self-actualisation: to find self-fulfilment and realise one's potential.
8. Transcendence: to help others find self-fulfilment and realise their potential.

The first four are called deficiency needs and the second four are identified as growth needs. As this is a hierarchy, it is suggested that the growth needs are not felt to be important or applicable until the deficiency needs are met (at least partially). To transpose this on the Muslim community, it may be somewhat unrealistic to expect the community to engage in contributing to the wider society, for example, when it is still at the level of securing its own existence and at the stage of meeting physiological or security needs.

We have seen that some British Muslims choose not to engage in the political process out of principle. There however those who, due to their experiences, feel so frustrated with 'the system' that they end up losing confidence and faith in the political process altogether. This has been the case during every major event that has featured a perceived unjustified stance towards Muslims domestically or internationally by the government in power. It is surprising to see how many young (and not so young) people feel a sense of alienation. In some cases this may have led to radicalisation – a factor that deserves serious attention for it is a threat to both the Muslim community and society as a whole. Moderate and engaged Muslim organisations face a difficult job in convincing such people that isolation will be harmful. The day-to-day experiences of people in encountering racism, Islamophobia, feeling a sense of betrayal by their government, coupled with a sense of political impotence – not having a voice or the ability to affect the 'powers that be' – can result in serious harm as the riots in 2001 showed.

Much has been written and said about the disturbances in Oldham and other northern cities in 2001. Some have called into question the whole notion of a multicultural society, while others have tried to defend and justify the actions of one group or another. We need to separate the causes of the riots from the catalysts – some of the factors usually mentioned such as poverty and underachievement are, most likely, catalysts that may speed up the precipitation of a problem rather than the causes themselves. One could compare the attitude of the Asian first and second generations here and the way both have dealt with racism given their relative disadvantages. Among the list of causes would be issues such as provocation, Islamophobia and racism, thuggish behaviour, lack of sensible leadership, gang mentality, lack of access to power, and the inability of officials and authorities to relate to the needs of young people across cultures. This has led to a significant communication gap between the authorities and sectors of the communities in question.

A number of questions have arisen in the minds of onlookers: why are some communities in the same city leading such separate lives? Does having separate religious schools cause this? How did things get so bad – did we not solve the problem of racism a number of years ago? In order to understand why some communities live such separate lives, one needs to understand the nature and reality of community formation among migrants. When one arrives on the shores of a strange land where the culture, language, religion, norms are so different and sometimes hostile, one would find it natural to seek safety and security among one's 'own'. It is a reality that ghettoes, or enclaves, of migrants are formed throughout the world. Even the Europeans who migrated to Asia and Africa tended to live in their own quarters and cantons. But ghettoes are not just formed by people moving into certain areas, they are also formed by people moving out of areas – or 'white flight' as it has come to be known. This separation of people naturally brings with it certain challenges for society as identified in the Home Office report on community cohesion.[46]

Some have criticised religious schools (and more specifically Muslim schools)[47] for this 'self-imposed separation', yet the rioters, whether white or Asian, were not graduates of religious schools. It is a reality that in some British state schools, Asians form over 90% of the pupils, just as there are schools with over 90% intake of white pupils. Hence this separation is happening in state schools even when religious schooling is not an issue.

The fact of the matter is that these disturbances show racism and prejudice are still a problem on the streets of Britain, they never actually went away. Faced with prejudice and lack of opportunity second generation Asians, that have grown up in Britain, would not be as passive as their parents may have been. For they now felt that this is their own society, where they can be assertive. There is a striking parallel between these 'Asian riots', the 'Black riots' of the 1970s and early 1980s as well as the 'Battle of Cable Street' in London's Jewish neighbourhood in 1936. All had at their roots a conflict between discriminated minorities encountering bigotry and prejudice, all may have been signs of communities that were coming of age. Communities that were grappling with issues such as poverty, underachievement and discrimination, while at the same time being conscious that they were no longer 'guests' in society, that they were in a position to make demands. It could also be said that taking to the streets is not just a feature of underachieving migrant communities, but it has been the expression of choice by many groups of frustrated people in European history, particularly British history. The lack of understanding between people of different faiths and cultural traditions is, of course, deeply disturbing. Well intentioned attempts at the 'meeting of minds' through inter-faith and inter-cultural dialogue does not seem to penetrate to the grassroots level, or to young people – where it really matters in this context. Some observers claim that the solution lies in assimilating individual communities into the majority culture. But calls for assimilation are not the answer either for they produce a whole set of new problems and reactions. What is needed is greater and more positive interaction and engagement across all boundaries and at all levels, especially the political and social, so that the Muslim community can be empowered to feel more confident, a confidence that will bring with it a sense of calm and settlement.

The challenges that Muslims may face while living in a non-Muslim society like Britain are not an argument for social exclusion, if anything they are greater reasons to be involved and engaged. The Prophet Muḥammad (pbuh) lived for thirteen years in Makkah in a society that on the whole rejected his teachings, his views on morality, behaviour and conduct. Yet this did not deter him from trying to influence all the possible avenues of power in his society. He would meet whenever possible with the influential members and leaders of the Quraish. He would go to the Kaʿbah to speak to people around him. Perhaps one of the most vivid examples of social engagement is the case of the pact that came to be known as *ḥilf al-fuḍūl* (the virtuous pact). When the Prophet was about twenty years old a trader from Yemen came to Makkah and was wronged by one of the Quraish, Al-ʿĀṣ ibn Wāʾil, who bought goods from him and refused to give the agreed price. In those days people would be protected through their family/clan or an appointed protector and, knowing that the trader had no protection, Ibn Wāʾil felt that he would get away with this. The trader went to the Kaʿbah and pleaded for help. In response to this a group of people met in the house of ʿAbdullāh ibn Judʿān. Those present at the meeting formed a pact to protect the innocent and downtrodden. Some of the biographers of the Prophet narrate that those who were at the meeting went to the Kaʿbah and after washing their hands in a bowl, raised their right hands and made the pledge. The Prophet Muḥammad (pbuh) along with Abū Bakr, was party to this pledge. Later on in life, during the time of Prophethood, he is reported to have said: "I attended in ʿAbdullāh ibn Judʿān's home the formation of a covenant which I would not exchange for any material gain. If now after Islam I am called upon to honour it, I would certainly do so."[48] This incident shows clearly how Muḥammad (pbuh) was keen to stand up for issues in his society that needed attention. But beyond this it shows that he was willing to make a moral stance with other people, despite their different faith or values, for a common cause. A cause that not only affected one of his 'own' but another human being whom he did not even know. Some have argued that this all happened before Prophethood was declared and does not form a part of the exemplary life or teachings of the Prophet, however his clear statement praising the pact later in life shows that this is an erroneous view. We can also find other examples of how Muḥammad (pbuh) benefited from the help of other people, or was prepared to work with them, regardless of their own particular religious or moral backgrounds. When the small band of followers in Makkah faced severe treatment at the hands of the Quraish, it was to the Christian Negus of Abyssinia that the Prophet sent those who were able to leave, as we have already seen. When the Prophet was secretly leaving Makkah for Madinah at the time of the migration (*hijrah*), it was a polytheist guide that he employed and confided in to show them the way. During the time of famine in Makkah, when the Muslims were boycotted and placed under strict sanctions, it was non-Muslims like Al-Muṭʿim bin ʿAdiy who would secretly smuggle food to the Muslims and who were instrumental in bringing the boycott to an end.

The Qur'ān exhorts believers to stand up for justice, even if it be against their own kin. Furthermore it asks people, especially people of faith, to find common ground and work together for good causes. The example of the Prophet Yūsuf, that we have also seen before, shows how he took up a place in a non-Muslim government because in that was scope for him to promote good and prevent harm, not just for himself but for the whole of that society. This notion of promoting good and preventing harm is a central idea in the Qur'ān. Many Muslim scholars would say that it is *the* earthly purpose of the Muslim community. The basic Objectives (*Maqāṣid*) of the *Sharīʿah* (Islamic law) further elucidate this, for the law is designed to protect: (i) life, (ii) faith, (iii) intellect, (iv) progeny, and (v) property.[49] All of this is tied to the notion of justice, for the pursuit of justice can only be meaningful when people are granted dignity and their fundamental rights are guaranteed. Islam expects that Muslims will cooperate with others in the pursuit of justice; the Qur'ān states: "...and join together in pursuit of good and pious things...".[50] It further clarifies that our differences are there to be explored rather than to be obstacles to interaction:

O mankind! We created you from a single (pair) of male and female, and made you into nations and tribes, that you may know each other, (not that you may despise each other)...[51] [for] if God had willed he could have made you all one people...[52]

Before we complete this discussion it should be mentioned that with the ethnic, racial and 'religious' diversity among Muslims, despite the common bonds that tie them together, it is difficult to see them as a homogenous community. There are marked differences in the way different Muslim communities relate to the state and civil society, for example, those who migrated from regions where they became accustomed to living under authoritarian regimes may not be well versed in the art of organising within civil society. A difference in engagement can be perceived between Muslims that initially migrated from South and East Asia, where power is quite devolved and civil society is active and pronounced, and the Arab world or Turkey where there is a problem of centralised authority and rule, or even totalitarian rule, in which many Muslim organisations and movements have been banned. For those Muslims who had no chance of organising themselves outside the state in their inherited traditions, the state has always played an exaggerated role in their lives. Migrant communities would have brought their own culture of participation with them and passed these on, albeit in diluted form, to the new generations that have grown up in Britain.

Conclusion

In this chapter a brief overview of the different approaches that Muslim individuals and institutions have used to engage, or not, with mainstream political life in the UK has been presented. We have looked at some of the arguments presented for and against participating in the political reality that confronts us today. Politics is about power, and the pursuit of power for the Muslim community or individual groups within the community has been the driving force. Initially, one would expect that power to be used for certain parochial needs such as safeguarding the position of the Muslim community, i.e. lobbying for necessary changes to law, service provision and creating an acceptable public profile given the prejudices that exist in relation to Muslims. However that power must eventually be used to benefit people at large. Muslims need to devise strategies that will allow them to look ahead and plan their presence in this country, rather than stumble along, as has arguably been the case so far. Naturally, a number of different approaches need to be actively adopted to affect power, including lobbying, encouraging individuals to join political parties, and also working at the level of civil society. It would seem that setting up a Muslim political party would not be a useful step given the lack of support for this in the near past and the dichotomy this may create between 'Muslim' issues and 'non-Muslim' issues. It is probably much more realistic, and strategic, to encourage Muslim individuals to join the established political parties, based on their personal inclinations, and to work in those parties as individuals who aim to represent the whole of the local electorate, not just the Muslims.

Another question that needs to be posed is, where does power lie? Does the ability to act lie primarily with political parties and government? In modern societies globalisation has led to a radical re-shuffling of power and it may well be that financial and corporate power, the power of the media and entertainment industry far outstrip the power of politicians. If this is true, then it may be that the experience of the Muslim communities in influencing power will be an incomplete one, for there seems to be minimal effort in affecting the world of ideas through academic institutions, think tanks and policy forums; there seems to be little significant impact on the financial sector and perhaps less so on the media. The arenas of art, culture and entertainment do not even seem to feature in any serious form on the agenda of Muslim organisations. One should not forget that by engaging in these spheres of life Muslims can probably have as much, if not more, of a role in contributing to society and shaping the ability of people to act.

Notes

Chapter 1

Muslim Communities in Britain:
A Historiography

1. Weller, Paul, (ed.), *Religions in the U.K. 2001-3*, The Multi-Faith
    Centre at the University of Derby, 2001. This voluminous work is a
    directory of national and local religious organisations and places of
    worship that make up the landscape of multi-faiths present the UK. The
    book contains a useful introduction and outline to the history, beliefs,
    practices, and diverse theological groups and organisations of the
    Muslim community in Britain. The directory also contains a very
    resourceful extended bibliography and index of local and national
    Muslim organisations.

2. Geaves, Ron, *Sectarian Influences Within Islam in Britain: with
    reference to the concept of 'ummah' and 'community'*, Leeds,
    Department of Theology and Religious Studies, University of Leeds,
    1996.

3. According to *The Encyclopaedia of Islam*, "Umma(h) usually refers to
    communities sharing a common religion, whereas in later history it
    almost always means the Muslim community as a whole while
    admitting of regional, essentially non-political expressions." Bearman,
    P.J., Bianquis, T.H., Bosworth, C.E., van Donzel, E., and Heinrichs,

W.P. (eds.), *The Encyclopaedia of Islam*, Leiden, New Edition, Brill, Volume X, 2000, p.862.

4. For a detailed analysis of the historical symbolism of the *Hijra* see, Bashier, Zakaria, *Hijra: Story and Significance*, Leicester, The Islamic Foundation, 1983.

5. Anwar, Muhammad, and Bakhsh, Qadir, *British Muslims and State Policies*, Warwick, University of Warwick, Centre for Research in Ethnic Relations, 2003, p.7.

6. Arnold, T.W., *The Preaching of Islam: A History of the Propagation of the Muslim Faith*, 1896, (reprinted) Lahore, Sh. Muhammad Ashraf, 1979.

7. Pool, John J., *Studies in Mohammedanism: Historical and Doctrinal*, London, Archibald Constable & Co., 1892.

8. Arnold, op. cit., 1979, p.456.

9. Ibid, p.457.

10. For a detailed study on this subject see, Buaben, Jabal M., *Image of the Prophet Muhammad in the West: A Study of Muir, Margoliouth and Watt*, Leicester, The Islamic Foundation, 1996, and also, Reeves, Minou, *Muhammad in Europe: A Thousand Years of Western Myth-Making*, Reading, Garnet Publishing, 2000.

11. Pool, John J., op. cit, 1892, p.402.

12. Halliday, Fred, 'The Millet of Manchester: Arab Merchants and Cotton Trade', *British Journal of Middle Eastern Studies*, BRISMES, vol. 19, no. 2, 1993.

13. Ally, M.M., *History of Muslims in Britain 1850-1980*, Unpublished MA Thesis, University of Birmingham, 1981.

14. Khan, M.A., *Islam and the Muslims of Liverpool*, Unpublished MA Thesis, University of Liverpool, 1979.

15. Lawless, Richard I., *From Ta'izz to Tyneside: An Arab Community in the North-East of England During the Early Twentieth Century*, Exeter, University of Exeter Press, 1995.

16. A subject briefly covered by Ataullah Siddiqui in his paper, 'Issues of Co-Existence and Dialogue: Muslims and Christians in Britain', in, Waardenburg, J. (ed.), *Muslim-Christian Perception of Dialogue Today: Experiences and Expectations*, Leuven, Peeters, 2000, pp. 183-200.

17. For a detailed study see, Salter, J., *The Asiatics and England*, London, Selly Jackson, 1872. Also, see his other book, *The East in the West*, London, Partridge, 1895.

18. Collins, Sydney, *Coloured Minorities in Britain: studies in race relations based on African, West Indian and Asiatic Immigrants*, London, The Lutterworth Press, 1957.

19. Carr, Barry, 'Black Gordies', in, *Geordies: Roots of Regionalism*, Edited by Robert Colls and Bill Lancaster, Edinburgh, Edinburgh University Press, 1992.

20. The author's phrase, not mine.

21. Ibid, p.132.

22. In addition, the Western Islamic Association based in London and the Islamic Society affiliated to the Woking Muslim Mission, had both made representations on behalf of the Arabs to South Shields City Council and the Port Authorities as early as 1919 when there were race disturbances and employment discrimination. Perhaps because the community in its nascent period was continuously transient the development of a permanent religious centre, such as a mosque, was either difficult to establish and maintain or not a necessary facility. Dr Khalid Sheldrake, an English convert to Islam, of the Western Islamic *Association* had made efforts in August 1929 to establish a purpose built mosque for the South Shields Muslim community. He collected some donations from the Aga Khan and the Nizam of Hyderabad and bought a plot of land but the scheme never saw fruition. However, in the 1930s Shaykh ʿAbdullāh ʿAlī al-Ḥakīmī, a Yemeni scholar from the North African ʿAlawī *ṭarīqah,* established Sufi *zāwiyahs* (religious centres) throughout the Yemeni communities in Britain. In South Shields the Muslim community, mostly Arab, numbered around four and a half thousand catered for by some 60 boarding houses. Shaykh ʿAbdullāh had noticed that many Arabs had taken English wives and some had converted to Islam. Provision for these new converts (and their children) to learn about Islam was absent so al-Ḥakīmī set-up classes in South Shields in 1936. In 1938 the community purchased the Hilda Arms, a former Public House, on Cuthbert Street, and converted it into the 'Zaoia Allaoia Islamia Mosque'. The establishment of this Islamic centre transformed the religious identity of the community that had previously been cultural and perhaps somewhat peripheral. Public processions where held on the occasions of ʿId prayers and the birthdays of the Prophet Muhammad and that of the founder of the Sufi ʿAlawī order, Aḥmad ibn Muṣṭafā al-ʿAlawī.

23. Umar, Zubayda, 'Yemen to South Shields', *Afkar Inquiry*, May 1985, p.62.

24. Assimilation is a complex sociological process by which, usually, one culture is absorbed into a 'host society'. For a detailed study see, Gordon, Milton, M., *Assimilation in American Life*, New York, Oxford University Press, 1964.

25. Integration, the means by which a society's various elements hold together or bond with each other. Essentially in the context of ethnic minorities integration refers to the process by which different races fuse together through social, economic and political interaction. See, Abercrombie, Nicholas, Hill, Stephen, and Turner, Bryan S., *The Penguin Dictionary of Sociology*, London, Penguin Books, 1985, p.112.

26. Acculturation is, according to John Lewis, "the process by which culture is transmitted through contact of groups with different cultures, usually one having a more highly developed civilisation". For a more detailed explanation see, Lewis, John, *Anthropology Made Simple*, London, William Heinmann Ltd., 1982.

27. Zubayda, op. cit., 1985, p.63.

28. Halliday, Fred, *Arabs in Exile: Yemeni Migrants in Urban Britain*, London, I B Tauris & Co. Ltd., 1992.

29. Darlymple, William, 'The Arabs of Tyneside', *The Independent Magazine*, 7th October 1989.

30. Ibid.

31. Halliday, op. cit., 1992, p.iv.

32. Lawless, op. cit., 1995.

33. Halliday, op. cit., 1992, p.77.

34. Chain migration is described by Muhammad Anwar as "the movement in which prospective migrants learn of opportunities, are provided with transportation and have initial accommodation and employment arranged by means of primary social relations with previous migrants". Anwar, Muhammad, *The Myth of Return*, London, Heinemann Educational Books Ltd., 1979, p.14.

35. Other reasons for migration were sometimes political, as was the case of Shaykh ʿAbdullāh ʿAlī al-Ḥakīmī. Al-Ḥakīmī's story and journey to Britain in the 1930s has been detailed by Lawless and Halliday examples al-Ḥakīmī as a great innovator and networker amongst the Yemenis in Britain. The establishment of Sufi *zāwiyahs* in most of the major Yemeni communities and the production of a quarterly Arabic language newsletter, *al-Salām* were some of his achievements. He also founded religious educational classes for Yemeni Children and Muslim convert wives. He was also the voice of opposition to the Imam of Yemen via the 'Free Yemen Movement'.

36. Halliday, op. cit., 1992, p.97.

37. He also reports that by 1990 the Yemeni population in Liverpool was around 3,500. When North and South Yemen were unified in 1990, some Yemenis actually returned home.

38.   Ibid. p.140.

39.   Ibid. p. 129.

40.   For a further study into young British Muslims' views on arranged marriages see, Jacobson, Jessica, *Islam in Transition: Religion and identity among British Pakistani youth*, London, Routledge, 1998, pp.90-93.

41.   Halliday, op. cit., 1992, p.130.

42.   Anwar, Muhammad, *The Myth of Return*, London, Heinemann Educational Books Ltd., 1979.

43.   Jeffery, Patricia, *Migrants and Refugees: Muslim and Christian Pakistani Families in Bristol*, Cambridge, Cambridge University Press, 1976.

44.   It is the published form of her PhD Thesis, which was undertaken at Bristol University in Anthropological Studies.

45.   See Lewis' study on the Muslim community of Bradford, Lewis, Philip, *Islamic Britain: Religion Politics and Identity among British Muslims*, London, I.B.Tauris and Sons Ltd., 1994.

46.   Urdu is the *lingua franca* of South Asian Muslims and is traditionally associated with the Moghul Muslim dynasty and South Asian Islam.

47.   This skill was put to some use by the inclusion of a rather superfluous glossary in which most of the terms included do not actually feature in the text.

48.   Anwar, Muhammad, *The Myth of Return*, London, Heinemann Educational Books Ltd., 1979.

49.   The author describes it as having an 'Indian flavour'. This serves as an example of the typology used to describe the cultures and customs of ethnic minorities in the late nineteen sixties and early seventies. It displays a distinct lack of sensitivity and appreciation of the newly forming migrant communities and has the effect of reducing different cultures and ethnicities to a single homogenous entity.

50.   The issue of refugees and asylum seekers to Britain has not been dealt with in this chapter. Refugees and asylum seekers have their own unique circumstances and position in British society which is very different from the migration process experienced by most post-war first generation migrants in Britain. The growing influx of religious and political migrants to Britain is complex and multi-faceted. The reasons for migration along with the settlement patterns require detailed analysis far beyond the subject and limits of this chapter.

51.   Shaw, Alison, *A Pakistani Community in Britain*, Oxford, Basil Blackwell, 1988. Her work is again the result of a PhD in Social Anthropology.

52. Ibid. p.64.

53. Ibid. p.74.

54. It is another published work originally undertaken as a doctoral thesis. See, Lewis, op. cit., 1992.

55. According to the 2001 Census.

56. See, Ramadan, Tariq, *To be a European Muslim*, Leicester, The Islamic Foundation, 1999.

57. The research was originally undertaken in 1981 as the authors MPhil Thesis. See, Barton, Stephen William, *The Bengali Muslims of Bradford*, Monograph Series, Community Religions Project, Department of Theology and Religious Studies, University of Leeds, 1986.

58. Ibid. p.77.

59. Ibid. p.107.

60. *Purdah*, according to the Concise Oxford Dictionary is, "(1) a system in certain Muslim and Hindu societies of screening women from men or strangers by means of a veil or curtain, (2) a curtain in a house used for this purpose". Thompson, Della, (ed.), *The Concise Oxford Dictionary*, Oxford, Clarendon Press, 1995, P.1112.

61. Ibid. p.108.

62. Ibid. p.174.

63. Ibid. p.174.

64. Ibid. p.120.

65. *Jamāʿat-e-Islāmī*, a revivalist Islamic movement established by the prominent South Asian Muslim scholar, Abu'l Aʿlā Mawdūdī in the late nineteen thirties.

66. Barton, op. cit.,1986, p.149.

67. See, Dahya, B., 'The Nature of Pakistani Ethnicity in Industrial Cities in Britain', in, *Urban Ethnicity*, Edited by Abner Cohen, London, A.S.A. Monographs 12, 1974. And, another work by the same author, 'Pakistanis in England', *New Community*, Winter, Vol. 2, London, 1972-73. Pp. 25-33.

68. Joly, Daniéle, *Britannia's Crescent: Making a Place for Muslims in British Society*, Aldershot, Ashgate Publishing Ltd., 1995.

69. Ibid., p.2

70. Anwar, Muhammad, *British Pakistanis: Demographic, Social and Economic Position*, University of Warwick, Centre for Research in Ethnic Relations, 1996.

71. Modood, Tariq, *Ethnic Minorities in Britain: Diversity and Disadvantage*, London, Policy Studies Institute, 1997.

72. Joly, op. cit., p.6.

73. Ibid. p.7.

74. Ibid. p.75.

75. Ibid. pp.87-88.

76. Ibid. p.93.

77. Ibid. p.94.

78. Ibid. p.95.

79. Ibid. pp.108-110.

80. Ibid. p.183.

81. Geaves, Ron, *Muslims in Leeds*, Community Religions Project Research Papers, no. 10, (New Series), The University of Leeds, Department of Theology and Religious Studies, 1995.

82. Ibid. p.5.

83. Ibid. p.5.

84. Ballard, Roger, and Ballard, Catharine, 'The Sikhs: The Development of South Asian Settlements In Britain', in, *Between Two Cultures*, Watson, Oxford, James, (ed.), Basil Blackwell, 1977.

85. Geaves, op. cit., 1995, p.6.

86. Barton, op. cit., 1986.

87. Geaves, op. cit., p.11.

88. Ibid. p.13.

89. Ibid. pp.13-14.

90. Ibid. p.15.

91. Ibid. p.15.

92. Ibid. p.14.

93. Ibid. p.17.

94. Joly, op. cit., 1995.

95. Lewis, op. cit., 1992.

96. Jacobson, Jessica, *Islam in Transition: Religion and identity among British Pakistani youth*, London, Routledge, 1998.

97. Scantlebury, Elizabeth, 'Muslims in Manchester: the depiction of a religious community', *New Community*, Vol. 27, No.3, 1995, pp.452-35.

98. Ibid. p.452.

99. Ibid. p.426.

100. Ibid. p.426.

101. Nielsen, Jørgen, 'Muslims in Britain: Searching for an identity?' *New community*, vol. 13, no.3, 1987, p. 392.

102. Robinson, Francis, *Varieties of South Asian Islam*, Research Paper no.7, Coventry, Centre for Ethnic Relations, University of Warwick, 1988.

103. Werbner, Pnina, 'Manchester Pakistanis: Division and Unity', in, C. Clarke, C. Peach and S. Vertovec (eds.), *South Asians Overseas: Migration and Ethnicity*, Cambridge, Cambridge University Press, 1990, pp.331-47, and see her other studies, Werbner, P., 'Factionalism and Violence in British Pakistani Politics', in H. Donnan and, P. Werbner (eds.), *Economy and Culture in Pakistan: Migrants and Cities in a Muslim Society*, Basingstoke, Macmillan, 1991, pp.188-215.

104. Lewis, op. cit., 1992.

105. Scantlebury, op. cit., 1995, p.428

106. Ibid. p.428.

107. Werbner, Pnina, *Ritual and social networks: a study of Pakistani immigrants in Manchester*, PhD thesis, Manchester University, 1979.

108. 'West Pakistan' as opposed to 'East Pakistan', now known as Bangladesh.

109. Werbner, Pnina, 'Avoiding the Ghetto: Pakistani migrants and settlement shifts in Manchester', in Michael Drake (ed.), *Time, Family and Community: perspectives on family and community history*, Oxford, Blackwell Publishers, The Open University, 1994, pp.240-260.

110. Scantlebury, op. cit., 1995, p.429.

111. Ibid. p.430.

112. Ibid. p.430.

113. *The Islamic Banner*, July 1986, quoted in, Ibid. p.433.

114. Ibid. p.432.

Chapter 2
Equality? The treatment of Muslims under the English Legal System

1. As Ahmad Thomson (a Barrister and Author, he is also Deputy Chairman of the Association of Muslim Lawyers) put the position in a letter written to the University of Derby in December 1999.

2. The Convention was signed and ratified by the United Kingdom in 1951 and came into force in 1953.

3. The Human Rights Act 1998 came into force on 2 October 2000.

4. The Disability Discrimination Act 1995 mainly came into force on 2 December 1996. Prior to this the Disabled Persons (Employment) Act 1944 was in force which was alarmingly ineffective. There were only ten prosecutions under this Act, the last being in 1975.

5. In the case of *Jones v Tower Boot Ltd* (1995) IRLR 464 CA.

6. In the case of *Savjani v IRC* (1981) 1 QB 458.

7. s1(1)(a) Race Relations Act 1976.

8. See, *Zarcynska v Levy* (1978) IRLR 532 in which a barmaid was dismissed because she refused to follow her employer's instruction not to serve black customers. This was followed by the famous case of *Showboat Entertainment Centre Ltd v Owens* (1984) IRLR 7 in which a white manager of an amusement centre was dismissed because he refused to exclude black people from the centre.

9. s1(1)(b) Race Relations Act 1976.

10. See, *Tower Hamlets LBC v Qayyum* (1987) ICR 729.

11. See, *Raval v Department of Health and Social Security and Civil Service Commission* (1985) IRLR 370. The questions to be asked were:

    Does the applicant belong to the racial group or groups that s/he claims to belong?

    Has the respondent applied to the applicant any, and if so, what requirement or condition in the arrangements made by him for the purposes of determining who should be offered the relevant employment?

    If so, when was such requirement or condition applied to the applicant (the answer to such question being hereinafter referred to as 'the material time')?

    Did such requirement or condition apply to other persons not of the same racial group as the applicant?

If so, what are the relevant circumstances necessary to ensure that the proportionate comparison be made under s1(1)(b)(i) complies with the 'like with like' requirement in s3(4)?

Within what section of the community does the proportionate comparison fall to be made?

Does the application of the proportionate comparison within such community section result in a finding that the proportion of persons in the same racial group as the applicant who could comply with the condition or requirement at the material time is considerably smaller than the proportion of persons not of that racial group who could comply with it?

Can the requirement or condition be shown by the respondent to be justifiable, irrespective of any racial factor? If not,

Could the applicant at the material time comply with the requirement or condition? If not,

Was it to his/her detriment that he/she could not do so?

12. s3(1) Race Relations Act 1976.

13. *Mandla v Dowell Lee* (1983) 2 AC 548 HL.

14. See, *Seide v Gillette Industries* (1980) IRLR 427 EAT and *Westein v Misprestige Management Services Ltd* EAT/523/9, 19 March 1993.

15. See, *CRE v Dutton* (1989) IRLR 8 CA.

16. See, *Bogdeniec v Sauer-Sunderstrand Ltd* (1988) 383 IDS Brief 15 EAT.

17. See, *Cameron v Argon Borough Council* (1987) COIT 1713/71.

18. In the case of *Power v Northern Joint Police Board* (1997) S/101410/96 DCLD 32, it was concluded that the Scottish and English ethnic origins are distinct. However, in *Boyce v British Airways plc* (1997) S/400597/96 DCLD 32, a different judgement was given.

19. See, *Tariq v Young and Others* (1998) 24773/88.

20. See, *Bhatti v Sandwell Muslim Organisation and Others* (1993) Case no: 48589/92 DCLD 20.

21. See, *Kabir v Bangladesh Women's Association* (1993) Case no: 10026/92 DCLD 18.

22. Consultation Paper of Runnymede Trust, February 1997.

23. *The proof of adverse impact* – A paper presented by Robin Allen QC at a Discrimination Law Association seminar on Indirect Discrimination on 15 November 1996. Page 1 para 1.

24. See, *Griggs v Duke Power* (1971) 408 U.S. 404. Ibid., p.1, para. 2.

25. See, *Safouane & Bouterfas v Joseph Ltd & Hannah* (1996) Case no: 12506/95/LS & 12568/95, where the employer may have attempted to

prevent the Applicant's prayer mats being urinated upon, but then dismissed them for praying during lunch and tea breaks.

26. See, *J H Walker v Hussain and others* (1996) IRLR 11.

27. See, *Safouane & Bouterfas v Joseph Ltd & Hannah*, op. cit., 1996.

28. See, *Islamophobia – a Challenge for us all*, London, Runnymede Trust Report, 1997.

29. See, *Sardar v McDonald's* (1998).

30. See, *The Muslim News* No. 115, 27 November, 1998.

31. See, his paper – *Religious Discrimination & The Law* presented at the Commission on British Muslims Seminar on Religious Discrimination, 9/12/99.

32. *The European Convention for the Protection of Human Rights and Fundamental Freedoms* came into force on 3 September 1953.

33. Compare with the case of *Ansari v Ray's Plumbing Contractors* (2000) reported by the Florida Times on 3 April 2000. In this case, a Muslim man was awarded $105,216 because he was denied the right to leave work early on Fridays to attend prayers. In America, the *Civil Rights Act 1964* prohibits discrimination on religious grounds.

34. See, *Soering v United Kingdom* (1989) 11 EHRR 439 at para.89.

35. See, Ibid.

36. See, *Handyside v United Kingdom* (1976) 1 EHRR 737.

37. See, *Marckx v Belgium* (1979) 2 EHRR 330 at para.31.

38. See, Wadham, J., & Mountfield, H., *Human Rights Act 1998*, London, Blackstones, 1999, p.11.

39. Islamophobia has been explained as "Dread or hatred of Islam – and therefore fear and dislike of all or most Muslims". The Runnymede Trust, op. cit., 1997, p.1. The key aspects of Islamophobia are Exclusion, Discrimination, Violence and Prejudice. See, Ibid. p.12.

40. See, Ibid.

41. For a more detailed study of these principles see, Starmer, K., *European Human Rights Law*, London, Legal Action Group, 1999; Grosz, S., Beatson QC, J., and Duffy QC, P., *Human Rights: The 1998 Act and European Convention*, London, Sweet and Maxwell, 2000; Wadham, J. and Mountfield, H., op. cit., 1998; Lester QC, A. and Pannick QC, D., *Human Rights Law and Practice*. London, Butterworths, 1999.

42. Article 9 of the Convention.

43. In *X and Church of Scientology v Sweden* (1979) No. 7805/77, 16 DR 68, the Commission said "When a Church body lodges an application

under the Convention it does so, in reality, on behalf of its members. It should therefore, be accepted that a Church body is capable of possessing and exercising the rights contained in Article 9(1) in its own capacity as a representative of its members".

44. In *Kokkinakis v Greece* (1993) 17 EHRR 397 the European Court argued that "Article 9(1) is, in its religious dimension, one of the most vital elements that go to make up the identity of believers and their conception of life, but it is also a precious asset for atheists, agnostics, sceptics and the unconcerned. The pluralism indissociable from a democratic society, which has been dearly won over the centuries, depends upon it".

45. See, Wadham, J., & Mountfield, H., op. cit., 1999, p. 98.

46. See, *X v United Kingdom* (1981) 22 DR 27 (which arose from *Ahmed v Inner London Education Authority* (1978) QB 36).

47. See, *Stedman v United Kingdom* (1997) EHRLR 545.

48. See, *Kokkinakis v Greece* (1993) 17 EHRR 397.

49. See, Halliday, Fred, *Two Hours that Shook the World – September 11, 2001: Causes & Consequences*, London, Saqi Books, 2002, p.24.

50. See, Blair (2002), *The Power of World Community* p 124, chapter in Leonard (2002), *Re-Ordering the World: The long-term implications of 11 September*, London, The Foreign Policy Centre.

51. Home Office, *Race Incidents Rise*, 2001, 165 JPN 65, Issue 4.

52. Ibid., p. 65.

53. The Anti-terrorism, Crime and Security Act 2001, Part 5 - Race and Religion.

54. Section 29 of the Crime and Disorder Act 1998.

55. Ibid. Section 30.

56. Ibid. Section 30.

57. Ibid. Section 32.

58. Blunkett, H.C.Debates, 13th December 2001. Cols. 1112-1113.

59. Blunkett, H.C.Debates, 19th November 2001. Cols. 34-35.

60. R v Director of Public Prosecutions ex parte The Council of the London Borough of Merton (1998) E.W.H.C.Admin 1009.

61. See, Malik, Racist Crime: Racially Aggravated Offences in the Crime and Disorder Act 1998, Part II (1999) M.L.R. 62:3, p. 417.

62. Blunkett, H.C. Debates, 26th November 2001. Col. 701.

63. H.L. Debates, 10th December 2001. Cols. 1163-1165.

64. Hughes, H.C. Debates, 26th November 2001. Col. 675.

65. Chope, H.C. Debates, 19th November 2001. Cols. 69-70.

66. Key, H.C. Debates, 19th November 2001. Col. 78.

67. Wiltshire, H.C. Debates, 26th November 2001. Cols. 677-678.

68. Gummer, H.C. Debates, 19th November 2001. Col. 83.

69. Hughes, H.C. Debates, 26th November 2001. Col. 713-714.

70. See, Hare, *Legislating Against Hate – The Legal Response to Bias Crime,* 17 O.J.L.S., 415, 1997, and, Bowley, *A Cancer at the Heart of Societ,* N.L.J. 150, 2000.

71. Section 29 of the 1998 Act.

72. Ibid. Section 30.

73. Ibid. Section 31.

74. Ibid. Section 32.

75. Goldsmith, H.L. Debates, 10th December 2000. Cols., 1166-1167.

76. Lord Lester of Herne Hill was instrumental in framing the Sex Discrimination Act 1975, the Race Relations Act 1976, the Immigration Appeals system and indeed the Human Rights Act 1998.

77. See, his speech at the debate on Religious Discrimination in the House of Lords on 28 October 1999.

78. The Runnymede Trust, op. cit., Chapter 4.

79. Passed by 106th Congress Resolution 133 on 1 July 1999 in the Senate of the United States and by the 106th Congress Resolution 174 in the House of Representatives on 5 August 1999.

Chapter 3
British Muslim Identity

1. Jenkins, Richard, *Social Identity*, London, Routledge, 1996, p. 4.

2. See Modood, Tariq et al., *Ethnic Minorities in Britain*, London, PSI, 1997.

3. MORI Poll commissioned by *Eastern Eye*, November 2001.

4. Kahani-Hopkins, Vered and Hopkins, Nick, "'Representing' British Muslims: the Strategic Dimension to Identity Construction", *Ethnic and Racial Studies*, Vol. 25. No. 2, March 2002, pp. 288-309.

5. Without entering into a detailed discussion of what modernity means, the term is primarily used here to mean the product of (i) on the religious and cultural level – enlightenment rationalism and (ii) on the scientific and technological level – industrialisation.

6. Giddens, Anthony, *Modernity and Self-Identity*, Stanford, Stanford University Press, 1991, p. 70.

7. Gauntlett, David, *Media, Gender and Identity: An Introduction*, London and New York, Routledge, 2002.

8. Kahani-Hopkins, Vered and Hopkins, Nick, op. cit.

9. This refers to the 'push' from the original society of the migrants due to relatively poor economic, educational and health standards and the 'pull' from within the UK due to the labour shortage, especially in the industrial sector.

10. See *Hansard*, 23rd April 1968.

11. Quoted in Alibhai Brown, Yasmin, *Who Do We Think We Are? Imagining the New Britain*, London, Penguin, 2001.

12. Quoted in Malik, Kenan, *The Trouble with Multiculturalism*, in http://www.spiked-online.com/Articles/00000002D35E.htm. 18 December 2001.

13. Jenkins, Roy, *Essays and Speeches*, 1967. Quoted in Lewis, Philip, *Islamic Britain: Religion, Politics and Identity among British Muslims*, London, I.B. Tauris, 1994, p. 3.

14. Gellner, Ernest, 'A Pendulum Swing Theory of Islam', in Robertson, Roland (ed.) *Sociology of Religion*, London, Penguin, 1976, pp. 127-138.

15. Ramadan, Tariq, *To Be a European Muslim*. Leicester, Islamic Foundation, 1999.

16. Fadl, Khaled Abou El, 'Islamic Law and Muslim Minorities: The Juristic Discourse on Muslim Minorities From the Second/Eighth to the Eleventh/Seventeenth Centuries', *Islamic Law and Society*, Vol. 1, No. 2, Leiden, 1994, pp. 148-150.

17. See Ramadan, Tariq, op. cit.

18. The European Council for Fatwa and Research (*al-Majlis al-Urubbī li'l-Iftā' wa'l-Buḥūth*) which brings together scholars from different schools to consider the challenges facing Muslims living in the West, especially Europe.

19. Another member of this *Fiqh* Council, Abdullah bin Bayyah, regards the condition of Muslims in minority situations as *dār al-ʿahd* (abode of contract).

20. Qur'ān, 2: 115.

21. See Qur'ān, 7: 65, 7: 73, 7: 85, 11: 50, 11: 61, 11: 84.

22. Ibid.

23. Qur'ān, 49: 13.

24. Gilliat-Ray, Sophie, 'Back to Basics: The Place of Islam in the Self-Identity of Young British Muslims', in Clarke, Peter B., *New Trends and Developments in the World of Islam*, London, Luzac Oriental, 1998, pp. 93-103.

25. *Ḥadīth*, Bukhurī and Muslim.

26. Qur'ān, 5: 5.

27. Guillaume, Alfred (ed.), *Ibn Hisham, Life of Muhammad*, Oxford, Oxford University Press, 1955. Also narrated by Bayhaqī.

28. *Ḥadīth*, Tirmidhī. Though this *ḥadīth* is categorised as a weak narration, its meaning is said to hold true to the spirit of Islam.

29. Ḥafiẓ Ibn Asākir from Imām Mālik.

30. *Ḥadīth*, Muslim.

31. *Ḥadīth*, Aḥmad.

32. Qur'ān, 5: 48.

33. Ibid.

34. *Ḥadīth*, Bukhurī.

35. Lings, Martin, *Muhammad: His Life Based on the Earliest Sources*. London, Unwin Hyman Ltd., 1984, p. 118.

36. Qur'ān, 4: 135.

37. Qur'ān, 5: 8.

38. *Ḥadīth*, Bukhurī.

39. http://www.islamonline.net/fatwa/english/FatwaDisplay.asp?hFatwaID=79294 (Date of Fatwa: October 2002).

40. Qur'ān, 5: 55.

41. http://www.islamonline.net/fatwa/english/FatwaDisplay.asp?hFatwaID=78491 (Date of Fatwa: August 2002).

42. See *The Encyclopaedia Britannica*.

43. Paxman, Jeremy, *The English: A Portrait of a People*. London, Penguin Books, 1999, p. 74.

44. Though it is now declining, the term *Gastarbeiter* (guest worker) was used to describe the offspring of Turkish migrants in Germany, despite the fact that German Turks are now into the fourth generation.

45. *World in Action*, Granada Television, 30th January 1978. Quoted in: Alibhai Brown, Yasmin, op. cit, 2001, p. 78.

46. For a discussion of the challenges facing British Muslims in terms of expression of loyalty and belonging, see Seddon, Mohammad et al. (eds.), *British Muslims: Loyalty and Belonging*, Leicester, The Islamic Foundation and Citizen Organising Foundation, 2003.

47. Ḥadīth, Bukhurī.

48. A number of commentators of the Qur'ān have viewed the Qur'ānic injunctions on migration as a spiritual and moral advice for later generations, see Mawdūdī, Abu'l Aʿlā, *Tafhīm al-Qur'ān*.

49. Islamic Law, the norms of International Law, and above all common sense, would dictate that if contemporary communities were to face persecution, they should migrate to a place of security.

50. Protection of faith, life, intellect, family/lineage and property.

51. Qur'ān, 8: 72.

52. Shaykh Abdullah al-Judai is based in Leeds, UK, and is a member of the European Council for Fatwa and Research. This *fatwā* was issued in November 2001 and was titled, 'Fatwa on British Muslims Fighting in Afghanistan'.

53. Modood, Tariq et al., op. cit.

54. Hofmann, Murad, *Islam 2000*, Beltsville, USA, Amana Publications, 1996, p. 67.

55. Asian satellite channels.

Chapter 4

Locating the Perpetuation of 'Otherness': Negating British Islam

1. See, 'The Cricket Test: a note to Mr Tebbit', in Modood, Tariq, *Not Easy Being British: Colour, Culture and Citizenship*, Stoke-on-Trent, Runnymede Trust and Trentham Books, 1992.

2. A point noted by Watt, 'Sexual licence and promiscuity were held to be authorized by the Islamic religion', in, Watt, W. Montgomery, *Islamic Surveys 9: The Influence of Islam on Medieval Europe*, Edinburgh, Edinburgh University Press, 1972, p.73.

3. Richard I Lawless, *From Ta'izz to Tyneside*, Exeter, University of Exeter Press, 1995, p.117.

4. This development has been observed by Muhammad Anwar, in, Anwar, Muhammad, *The Myth of Return*, London, Heinemann, 1979.

5. *Collins English Dictionary: 21st Century Edition*, Glasgow, Harper Collins Ltd, 2000, p.200.

6. Thomas, C., *Celtic Britain*, London, Thames Hudson Ltd., 1986, p.16.

7. ibid. p.17.

8. ibid. p.17.

9. According to Thomas, "The adjective Celt means, in the strict and most pedantic form, 'of or pertaining to the Celtic group of Indo-European languages'". Thomas, op. Cit., p.16.

10. Hauerfield, F., *The Roman Occupation of Britain*, London, Oxford University Press, 1924, p.267.

11. Thomas, op. cit., 1986, p.38

12. Fisher, D.J.V., *The Anglo-Saxon Age C. 400-1042*, London, Longman Group Ltd., 1973, p.10.

13. It is suggested they came as invited mercenaries by the Celts and the Britons to fight the northern invaders, the Picts and Scots.

14. The weekdays, Tuesday, Wednesday, Thursday and Friday are a constant reminder of their hegemonic legacy and their pagan gods. See, Seddon, M. S., *An Inquiry into the Religious Beliefs of King Offa of Mercia (757-796)*, unpublished dissertation, Lancaster University, 1999, p.9.

15. The word 'Welsh' is from the Saxon word *Weahlish* meaning 'foreigner'.

16. Thomas comments, "the English, heaven knows, should find enough problems in defining their own identity without seeking to extend it to other peoples". Thomas, op. cit., p.13.

17. Bruce, Steve, *Religion in Modern Britain*, Oxford, Oxford University Press, 1995, p.4.

18. See, Long, Roy, *The Lutherian Church*, Exeter, Religious and Moral Educational Press, 1984.

19. See, Hillerbrand, Hans J. (ed.), *The Protestant Reformation: Selected Documents*, London, Macmillan, 1968.

20. Bruce, op. cit.,1995, p4.

21. ibid. p.5.

22. "The break-up of the church authority achieved by the reformation let loose particularistic forces, which grew, under Romanticism, into nationalist movements founded ultimately on race". Al-Faruqi, Ismail R., 'Common Bases between the two Religions', in, Siddiqui, A. (ed.), *Islam and Other Faiths*, Leicester, The Islamic Foundation & International Institute of Islamic Thought, 1998, p.231.

23. Noted by Matar thus, "It was (during) this post-reformation period in English history that the Christian hostility towards the Muslims was transformed from dogma to race: if the medieval mind, according to Spitzer, 'Knew hatred only on a dogmatic, not racial ground', then the early modern period witnessed the transformation of that hatred into racial stereotypes". Matar, Nabil, *Islam in Britain 1558-1885*, Cambridge, Cambridge University Press, 1998, p.154.

24. ibid. p.154.

25. As Lawrence notes, "It would be a mammoth task to attempt to trace these ideas back to their historical roots and then to reconstruct the subsequent histories of their gradual elaboration-paying attention to their complex articulations within specific historical social formulations-into the anti-black racist ideologies we are familiar with today". Lawrence, E., 'Just plain Common Sense: the 'roots' of racism', *The Empire Strikes Back: Race and racism in 70s Britain*, London, Routledge, 1982, p.60.

26. Ibid. p.10.

27. i.e. the collapse of the Soviet Union as a global political power and the emergence of the so-called 'tiger economy' of the Far East.

28. I can recall that geography lessons during my school days bore testament to the 'third world's' reliance on the West (the implied 'first world') in its efforts to 'catch-up' with the developed world's technologies and lifestyles. This was of course the justification for colonialism and imperialism.

29. Mosse, G., 'Eighteenth-Century Foundations', in, Bulmer, M. and Solomos, John (eds.), *Racism*, Oxford, Oxford University Press, 1999, p.43.

30. Lawrence, op. cit., 1982, p.11.

31. See, Matar, Nabil, *Islam in Britain 1558-1685*, Cambridge, Cambridge University Press, 1998.

32. As Mosse states, 'Eighteenth century Europe was the cradle of modern racism'. op. cit.,1999, p.41.

33. Ibid., p.41

34. "The world of ideal-types, of myth and symbol, was given its dynamic through concepts basically opposed to the Enlightenment: pietism, evangelism and pre-romanticism. The link between the Enlightenment and such a world view was forged by anthropologists who in their racial classifications would pass from science to art". Ibid. p.44.

35. Pseudo-sciences which promoted the ideas that 'white' races were both physically and intellectually superior over others and prompted evolutionary theories such as 'Darwinism'.

36. Waines, David, *An Introduction to Islam*, Cambridge, Cambridge University Press, 1995, p.214.

37. Lawrence, op. cit., 1982, p.60.

38. For a detailed study see, Masud, Muhammad Khalid, 'Naming the 'Other': Names for Muslims and Europeans in European and Muslim Languages', in, Ansari, Z., and Esposito, J.L., (eds.), *Muslims and the West Encounter and Dialogue*, Islamabad, Islamic Research Institute, & Washington, D.C., Center for Muslim-Christian Understanding, 2001.

39. Waines, op. cit., 1995, p.214.

40. Haliday, Fred, *Arabs in Exile: Yemeni Migrants in Urban Britain*, London, I.B. Tauris & Co., 1992, pp.17-58.

41. An Anglicised version of the Arabic, al-Askar, literally meaning 'the soldier' and the Persian *Lashkari*, denoting someone in military service.

42. Anwar, Muhammad, *Between Cultures: Continuity and Change in the Lives of Young Asians*, London, Routledge, 1998, pp.2-3.

43. Lawrence has noted that, "the 'alien' cultures of the blacks are seen as either the cause or else the most visible symptom of the destruction of the 'British way of life'". Lawrence, op. cit., 1982, p.47.

44. Halliday, op. cit., 1992, p.24.

45. Anwar, op. cit., 1998, p.10.

46. To quote Lawrence, "there is a link between the development of this racist ideology and the post-war forgetfulness which obscured the historical connections between England and her colonial Empire". Lawrence, op. cit., 1982, p.80.

47. Dodd, Phillip, *The Battle Over Britain*, London, Demos, 1995, p.44.

48. With regard to the usage of this term, Samuel Chew says, "The word 'Christendom' is generally used to embrace the Catholic and Protestant states of Western Europe but it is occasionally used in a wider sense". Chew, Samuel C., *The Crescent and The Rose: Islam and England during the Renaissance*, New York, Oxford University Press, 1937, p.viii.

49. Turner, Bryan S., *Orientalism, Postmodernism & Globalism*, London, Routledge, 1994, p.37.

50. Said, Edward, *Orientalism: Western Concepts of the Orient*, London, Penguin Books, 1991, p.2.

51. See, Nabil Matar's chapter, 'Sodom and the Conquest' in *Turks, Moors & Englishmen In the Age of Discovery*, Matar, Nabil, New York, Columbia University Press, 1999.

52. Rushdie, Salman, *Imaginary Homelands*, London, Granta Books, 1991, p.130.

53. See, C. Chew, Samuel, op.cit., 1937.

54. Matar, Nabil, op. cit., 1999.

55. Said, Edward, op. cit., 1991.

56. Kabbani, Rana, *Imperial Fictions: Europe's Myths of Orient*, London, Pandora, 1994.

57. Kidwai, Abdur Raheem, 'Perceptions of Islam and Muslims in English Literature: A Historical Survey', in, Ansari, Zafar Ishaq, & Esposito, John L., *Muslims And The West: Encounter and Dialogue*, (eds.), Islamabad, Islamic Research Institute, & Washington D.C., Center For Muslim-Christain Understanding, 2001.

58. Akbar Ahmed notes that, 'The Asian is an alien and threatening presence. No longer romantic and mysterious, he is contemptible and smelly. There is an inane triumphalism and, lurking not too far underneath it, bigotry and racism.' Ahmed, Akbar, *Postmodernism & Islam: Predicament and Promise*, London, Routledge, 1992, p.112.

59. Lawrence, op. cit.,1982, p.48.

60. Antonio Gramsci (1891-1937) an Italian communist and intellectual who became popular, posthumously, for his series of *Notebooks* and *Letters* which he wrote whilst in prison for political activism. The works were not published until after World War II when his ideas became popular. Some of the terms he used became household words, such as 'hegemony' which he applied to the twin task of understanding the successes and failures of socialism as a global movement and to the prevailing capitalist conditions in the world. Other important terms which, if not coined by Gramsci, acquired radical and new interpretations such as 'organic intellectual', 'national popular' and 'historical bloc', constitute effectively new formulations in the terminology of political philosophy.

61. Lawerence, op. cit., 1982, p.78.

62. Turner, Bryan S., *Max Weber: From History to Modernity*, London, Routledge, 1992, p.105.

63. Ibid. p.112.

64. Eriksen, T. H., *Ethnicity & Nationalism: Anthropological Perspectives*, London, Pluto Press, 1992, p.4.

65. Eriksen says, 'it gradually began to refer to racial characteristics'. Ibid. p.4.

66. Gandhi, Leela, *Postcolonial Theory: A Critical Introduction*, Edinburgh, Edinburgh University Press, 1998, p.126.

67. Chairman of the Department of Missiology at Nyack College, New York.

68. See, Poston, Larry, *Islamic Da'wah in the West: Muslim Missionary Activity and the Dynamics of Conversion to Islam*, New York, Oxford University Press, 1992.

69. Some notable indigenous authors in this field are, Muhammad Marmaduke Pickthall, Martin Lings, Charles Le Gai Eaton, Ian Dallas, T.J.Winter, Ahmad Thompson, Yusuf Islam, Harfiyah Ball-Haleem, Ruqaiyyah Waris Maqsood and Aisha Bewley to name but a few.

70. Adlin, Adnan, *New Muslims in Britain*, London, The Muslim College & Ta Ha Publishers, 1999, p.41.

71. See, Jacobson, Jessica, *Islam in Transition: Religion and identity among British Pakistani youth*, London, Routledge, 1998.

72. Ibid. pp.22-23.

73. Lewis, says, "From the perspective of ethnic majority, the term 'Asian' will continue to be serviceable to identify shared relations with, Hindu, Sikh and Muslim communities with regards to racial, educational or religious exclusion". Lewis, Philip, in, Modood, Tariq, & Werbner, Pnina, *The Politics of Multiculturalism in the New Europe: Racism, Identity & Community*, (eds.) London, Zed Books, 1997, p.142.

74. Ibid. p.143.

75. "A growing stigmatization of Muslims as unique and self-chosen outsiders", Mason, David, *Race and Ethnicity in Modern Britain*, Oxford, Oxford University Press, 1999, p.141.

76. Ibid, p.141.

77. Usually manifesting itself as an almost mythological demonisation of all things western and an extreme retrogressive interpretation of the traditional binary spaces of *dār al-Islām* (the abode of Peace) and *dār al-ḥarb* (the abode of War).

78. For an extended discussion on the issues of loyalty and belonging, see, Sayyid, S., 'Muslims in Britain: Towards a Political Agenda', in Seddon, Mohammad et al. (eds.), *British Muslims: Loyalty and Belonging*, Leicester, The Islamic Foundation and Citizen Organising Foundation, 2003, p.87-94.

Chapter 5

'Friends, Romans, Countrymen?'

1. Extract taken from Poulter, Sebastian, *English Law and Ethnic Minority Customs*, London, Butterworths, 1980, p. v.

2. Benedict De Spinoza was born in Amsterdam in 1632, into a family of Jewish emigrants fleeing persecution in Portugal. He was trained in Talmudic scholarship, but his views soon took unconventional directions which the Jewish community - fearing renewed persecution on charges of atheism - tried to discourage. Spinoza was offered 1,000 florins to keep quiet about his views, but refused. At the age of 24, he was summoned before a rabbinical court, and solemnly excommunicated.

3. The Electoral Reform Society's analysis of the 2001 General Election shows that from 1955 to 1992, turnout averaged 75.8%. Turnout in the 1997 election was the lowest since 1945, but in 2001 dropped by a further 12.1% to 59.4%.

4. An ancient Greek historian of the Peloponnesian War between Athens and Sparta. Thucydides began writing his *History of the Peloponnesian War* in 431 BC; during the time Thucydides composed his *History*, he was exiled from Athens because, as an Athenian general, he failed to save the town of Amphipolis from the Spartan general Brasidas; his *History* was published in 395 BC.

5. Thucydides, *History of the Peloponnesian War*, Book 2 Chapter 4, London, Penguin Books, 1954, pp. 118-119.

6. Aristotle, *The Nicomachean Ethics of Aristotle*, Book I Chapter 1, Cambridge, Cambridge University Press, 2000, p. 1.

7. See for example, Delanty, Gerard, *Citizenship in a global age*, Buckingham, Open University Press, 2000; Kymlicka, Will, *Multicultural Citizenship*, Oxford, Oxford University Press, 1995; Roche, Maurice, *Rethinking Citizenship – Welfare, Ideology and Change in Modern Society*, Cambridge, Polity Press, 1992 and Pearce, Nick, & Hallgarten, Joe, *Tomorrow's Citizens*, London, Institute for Public Policy and Research, 2000.

8. Official Fellow in Social and Political Theory at Nuffield College, Oxford. His publications include *On Nationality*, Oxford, Clarendon Press, 1995, *Principles of Social Justice*, Massachusetts USA, Harvard University Press, 1999 and *Citizenship and National Identity*, Cambridge, Polity Press, 1999.

9. Miller, David, 'Citizenship: what does it mean and why is it important?' in, *Tomorrow's Citizens*, Institute for Public Policy and Research, 2000, p. 26.

10. Gerard Delanty is Professor of Sociology at the University of Liverpool. His recent works include *Social theory in a Changing World*, Cambridge, Polity Press, 1999 and *Modernity and Postmodernity: Knowledge, Power, the Self*, London, Sage, 2000.

11. Delanty, Gerard, *Citizenship in a global age*, Buckingham Open University Press, 2000, p. 9.

12. See Parekh, Bhikhu, *The Future of Multi-Ethnic Britain*, London, Profile Books, 2000; Ouseley, Herman *Community Pride not Prejudice – Making Diversity Work in Bradford*, Bradford Race Review, 2001; Ritchie, David, *Oldham Independent Review Panel Report – One Oldham One Future*, 2001; Denham, John, *Building Cohesive Communities: A Report of the Ministerial Group on Public Order and Community Cohesion*, Home Office, 2001; Cantle, Ted, *Community Cohesion: A Report of the Independent Review Team*, Home Office, 2001 and Singh, Ray, *Challenges for the Future – Race Equality in Birmingham*, Birmingham City Council, 2001.

13. For example, see Singh, Ray, op. cit.

14. Ibid. p. 22.

15. Schmitter-Heisler, Barbara, 'A comparative perspective on the underclass', *Theory and Society* 20 (4), 1991, p. 468.

16. Singh, Ray, 2001, op. cit.

17. Ibid. p. 5.

18. The present discussion will focus on Islamophobia in Great Britain in the past decade. The issue is much more complex and has historical roots which can be traced to before the Crusades. It is also a global phenomenon which has varying degrees of intensity in different parts of the world.

19. Vertovec, Steven, "Islamophobia and Muslim Recognition in Britain", in Haddad, Yvonne, *Muslims in the West – From Sojourners to Citizens*, Oxford, Oxford University Press, 2002, p. 19.

20. Steven Vertovec is research reader in Social Anthropology at the University of Oxford and Director of the British Economic and Social Research Council's Research Programme on Transnational Communities.

21. The Runnymede Trust was established in 1968 and is an independent research and policy agency offering practical and strategic thinking on race relations and cultural diversity in Britain and Europe. See www.runnymedetrust.org.

22. *Islamophobia – A Challenge for Us All*, London, The Runnymede Trust, 1997.

23. *A Very Light Sleeper – The Persistence And Dangers Of Anti-Semitism*, London, The Runnymede Trust, 1994.

24. *Islamophobia – A Challenge for Us All*, p. 1, op. cit.

25. Ibid. pp. 62 – 64.

26. Weller, Paul, et al., *Religious Discrimination in England and Wales*, Home Office Research Study 220, Home Office, 2001.

27. Hepple, Bob, and Choudhury, Tufyal, *Tackling Religious Discrimination: Practical Implications for Policy-makers and Legislators,* Home Office Research Study 221, Home Office, 2001.

28. Weller, Paul, et al., 2001, op. cit.

29. Ibid. Chapter 3, pp. 23-36.

30. Ibid. Chapter 4, pp. 37-49.

31. Ibid. Chapter 5, pp. 51-61.

32. Ibid. Chapter 6, pp. 63-70.

33. Ibid. Chapter 7, pp. 71-77.

34. Ibid. Chapter 8, pp. 79-80.

35. Ibid. Chapter 9, pp. 81-85.

36. Ibid. Chapter 10, pp. 87-92.

37. Ibid. Chapter 11, pp. 93-99.

38. Ibid. Chapter 12, pp. 101-102.

39. Ibid. p. 106.

40. Ibid. pp. 106-107.

41. Hepple, Bob, and Choudhury, Tufyal, op. cit.

42. Ibid. pp. iii-v.

43. Ibid. pp. 17-65.

44. Cantle, Ted, 2001, op. cit.

45. Ted Cantle is an Associate Director of the Improvement and Development Agency for Local Government.

46. Cantle, Ted, 2001, op. cit.

47. Ibid. p. 5, para 1.1.

48. Modood, Tariq, *Ethnic Minorities in Britain: Diversity and Disadvantage,* London, PSI Publishing, 1997, p. 359.

49. See note 11 above.

50. Delanty, Gerard, op. cit.

51. Ibid. pp. 9-22.

52. Ibid. pp. 23-35.

53. Ibid. pp. 36-47.

54. Ibid. pp. 51-67.

55. Ibid. pp. 68-80.

56. Ibid. p. 4.

57. See Chapter 6, p. 173, of this publication.

58. See Chapter 3, p. 83, of this publication.

59. For a more detailed discussion see Delanty, Gerard, op. cit. pp. 24-35.

60. Kant, Emmanuel, "Perpetual Peace", in Reiss, H. (ed.), *Kant: Political Writings*, Cambridge, Cambridge University Press, 1970, pp. 107-108.

61. Turner, Bryan S., *Citizenship and Social Theory*, London, Sage, 1993, p. 15.

62. Falk, Richard, *The Making of Global Citizenship*, in Bart van, Steenbergen (ed.), *The Condition of Citizenship*, London, Sage, 1994, pp. 134-135.

63. Placing Muslims in the wider context of British and European societies is an on-going process of negotiation. For recent examples of the developing debate, see, Goodhart, David, 'Too Diverse?', in *Prospect*, February 2004 and Ramadan, Tariq, *Western Muslims and the Future of Islam*, Oxford, Oxford University Press, 2004.

64. For a detailed discussion about this issue see Kymlicka, Will, op. cit. and Kymlicka, Will, *The Rights of Minority Cultures*, Oxford, Oxford University Press, 1995 and Kymlicka, Will, and Opalski, Magda, *Can Liberal pluralism be Exported?* Oxford, Oxford University Press, 2001.

65. Husaini, Zohra, *Muslims in the Canadian Mosaic: Socio-Cultural and Economic Links with their Countries of Origin*, Alberta, Canada, Muslim Research Foundation, 1990, p. 98.

Chapter 6

Councillors and Caliphs:
Muslim Political Participation in Britain

1. A broad collection of networks that may not even have contact with each other, but are recognisable from their ideological standpoints. These groups come from a conservative Salafī background but are also highly politicised and radical in nature. They believe that the main vehicle for effecting change in the status quo of the Muslim world is military struggle, hence their name.

2. The Liberation Party, established in 1953 in Jerusalem.

3. i.e. the Constitution would be drawn up in reference to the Qur'ān and *Sunnah*.

4. Tamimi, Azzam, *Rachid Ghannouchi: A Democrat Within Islamism*, New York, Oxford University Press, 2001, p. 47.

5. *Ḥadīth*, Tirmidhī. Though this *ḥadīth* is categorised as a weak narration, its meaning is said to hold true to the spirit of Islam.

6. Tamimi, 2001, op. cit.

7. Pertaining to Muḥammad ibn ʿAbdul Wahhāb (d. 1792), a reformer of the Arabian Peninsula, known for his puritan approach.

8. Muslih, Muhammad, 'Democracy', in Esposito et al. (eds.), *Oxford Encyclopedia of the Modern Islamic World*, Oxford, Oxford University Press, 2001, p. 354.

9. Founder of the Muslim Brotherhood.

10. It is no surprise then to find that many of the current advocates of democracy in the Arab world, including Muhammad Imarah, Salim El-Awa, and Fahmy Huweidi have had at least an informal relationship with the Muslim Brotherhood.

11. Bannā, Ḥasan al-, *Risālat al-Taʿlīm* (*Message of the Teachings*).

12. 'The Muslim Brotherhood's Statement on Shūrā in Islam and the Multi-Party System in an Islamic Society', in *Encounters: Journal of Inter-Cultural Perspectives*, Leicester, The Islamic Foundation, Vol. 1, No. 2, September 1995, pp. 100-103.

13. *Encounters*, 3: 1, 1997, p. 4.

14. Tamimi, 2001, op. cit. p. 185.

15. *Ḥadīth*, Abū Dāwūd.

16. Tamimi, 2001, op. cit.

17. Qur'ān, 5: 44-47.

18. Qur'ān, 12: 1-56.

19. Ghannouchi, Rashid, 'The Participation of Islamists in a non-Islamic Government', in Tamimi, Azzam (ed.), *Power Sharing Islam?*, London, Liberty, 1993, p. 57.

20. Ibn Taymiyah, *al-Fatāwā*, 19: 218-219, quoted in Ghanouchi, Rashid, ibid.

21. Awa, Muhammad Salim al-, 'Political Pluralism from an Islamic Perspective', in Tamimi, Azzam, *Power Sharing Islam?*, p. 70.

22. Ghannouchi, Rashid, op. cit. p. 59.

23. Shaykh al-Alwani is Chairman of the North American Fiqh Council.

24. The actual *fatwā* is quite long and can be found on: http://www.amconline.org/fatwa/

25. For a more detailed understanding of the ideas behind this Islamic State, see: http://www.hizb-ut-tahrir.org

26. http://www.1924.org/comment/index.php?id=430_0_13_10_M

27. The Muslim Institute was set up in 1974.

28. Based on figures for 2000.

29. Ishaq v McDonagh and the Labour Party, Hull employment tribunal decision, 2 May 2000.

30. Ali, Rushanara and O'Cinneide, Colme, *Our House? Race and Representation in British Politics*, London, IPPR, April 2002.

31. According to Muhammad Anwar this figure should include about 20 MPs of Muslim origin, see Anwar, Muhammad, 'British Muslims: Socio Economic Position', in Seddon, Mohammad et al. (eds.), *British Muslims: Loyalty and Belonging*, Leicester, The Islamic Foundation and Citizen Organising Foundation, 2003, p. 65.

32. See, www.votesmart.co.uk

33. Hetherington, Peter, 'Lib Dem surge changes the landscape', *The Guardian*, Friday May 2, 2003.

34. The recently established Respect Party (February 2004) has also entered the political arena mainly on an anti-war agenda. Though it did not do that well in the June 2004 Local and European Elections, the Labour Party seems to have lost many local seats to the anti-war protest vote.

35. The Party has recently suspended campaigns to take up political posts and is considering other options such as restructuring as a think tank or pressure group.

36. As with other categories mentioned, this is a broad area and would include activities that represent the wider issues of the Muslim community including employment, health, education and media.

37. See, www.mpacuk.org

38. It is from this network that the Respect Party was launched.

39. See, Fukuyama, Francis, *The End of History and the Last Man*, London, Penguin, 1993.

40. Hirst, Paul, *Associative Democracy: New Forms of Economic and Social Governance*, Cambridge, Polity Press, 1994, p. 3.

41. *Strengthening the Black and Minority Ethnic Voluntary Sector Infrastructure*, The Home Office, 2000.

42. Ali, Rushanara, *Involving Black and Ethnic Minority Communities in Decision Making*, London, IPPR, May 2000.

43. See, Jameson, Neil, "British Muslims: Influencing UK Public Life – A Case Study", in Seddon, Mohammad et al., 2003, op cit.

44. *The Oxford English Reference Dictionary*, 1995.

45. See, Tosi, Henry et al., *Managing Organisational Behaviour*, Blackwell, 2000. Maslow initially listed five needs then later sub-divided some of the needs to form the final list.

46. See, *Community Cohesion: A Report of the Independent Review Team Chaired by Ted Cantle*, London, Home Office, 2001.

47. For a discussion on Muslim schools see Sarwar, Ghulam (ed.), *Issues in Islamic Education*, London, MET, 1996.

48. Salahi, Adil, *Muhammad Man and Prophet: A Complete Study of the Life of the Prophet of Islam*, Leicester, The Islamic Foundation, 2002, pp. 40-41.

49. According to Hashim Kamali, some scholars have added to this 'freedom' and 'economic development' among other items, Hashim Kamali, seminar on *Usūl al-Fiqh*, at Oxford Centre for Islamic Studies, June 2001.

50. Qur'ān, 5: 2.

51. Qur'ān, 49: 13.

52. Qur'ān, 5: 48.

Bibliography

—- A Very Light Sleeper – The Persistence And Dangers Of Anti-Semitism, London, The Runnymede Trust, 1994.

—- Islamophobia – A Challenge for Us All, London, The Runnymede Trust, 1997.

—- Strengthening the Black and Minority Ethnic Voluntary Sector Infrastructure, London, The Home Office, 2000.

—- The Empire Strikes Back: Race and racism in 70s Britain, London, Routledge, 1982.

Abercrombie, Nicholas, et al., The Penguin Dictionary of Sociology, London, Penguin Books, 1985.

Adlin, Adnan, New Muslims in Britain, London, The Muslim College & Ta Ha Publishers, 1999.

Ahmed, A., Postmodernism & Islam: Predicament and Promise, London, Routledge, 1992.

Ali, Rushanara and O'Cinneide, Colme, Our House? Race and Representation in British Politics, London, IPPR, 2002.

Ali, Rushanara, Involving Black and Ethnic Minority Communities in Decision Making, London, IPPR, 2000.

Alibhai Brown, Yasmin, *Who Do We Think We Are? Imagining the New Britain*, London, Penguin, 2001.

Ansari, Zafar Ishaq, & Esposito, John L., (eds.), *Muslims and the West Encounter and Dialogue*, Islamic Research Institute, Islamabad & Center for Muslim-Christian Understanding, Washington, D.C., 2001.

Anwar, Muhammad and Bakhsh, Qadir, *British Muslims and State Policies*, Warwick, University of Warwick, Centre for Research in Ethnic Relations, 2003.

Anwar, Muhammad, *Between Cultures: Continuity and Change in the Lives of Young Asians*, London, Routledge, 1998.

Anwar, Muhammad, *The Myth of Return*, London, Heinemann Educational Books Ltd., , 1979.

Anwar, Muhammad., *British Pakistanis: Demographic, Social and Economic Position*, University of Warwick, Centre for Research in Ethnic Relations, 1996.

Aristotle, *The Nicomachean Ethics of Aristotle*, Cambridge, Cambridge University Press, 2000.

Arnold, T.W., *The Preaching of Islam: A History of the Propagation of the Muslim Faith*, 1896, (reprinted) Lahore, Sh. Muhammad Ashraf, 1979.

Bart van, Steenbergen (ed.), *The Condition of Citizenship*, London, Sage, 1994.

Barton, Stephen William, *The Bengali Muslims of Bradford*, Monograph Series, Community Religions Project, Department of Theology and Religious Studies, University of Leeds, 1986.

Bashir, Zakaria, *Hijra: Story and Significance*, Leicester, The Islamic Foundation, 1983.

Bearman, P.J., et al. (eds.), W.P., *The Encyclopaedia of Islam*, New Edition, Leiden, Brill,Volume X, 2000.

Bruce, Steve, *Religion in Modern Britain*, Oxford, Oxford University Press, 1995.

Buaben, Jabal M., *Image of the Prophet Muhammad in the West: A Study of Muir, Margoliouth and Watt*, Leicester, The Islamic Foundation, 1996.

Bulmer M., & Solomos, John, (eds.) *Racism,* Oxford, Oxford University Press, 1999.

Cantle, Ted, *Community Cohesion: A Report of the Independent Review Team*, Home Office, 2001.

Chew, Samuel C., *The Crescent and The Rose: Islam and England during the Renaissance*, New York, Oxford University Press, 1937.

Clarke, C. et al. (eds.), *South Asians Overseas: Migration and Ethnicity*, Cambridge, Cambridge University Press, 1990.

Clarke, Peter B., *New Trends and Developments in the World of Islam*, London, Luzac Oriental, 1998.

Collins, Sydney, *Coloured Minorities in Britain: studies in race relations based on African, West Indian and Asiatic Immigrants*, London, The Lutterworth Press, 1957.

Colls, Robert, and Lancaster, Bill, (eds.) *Geordies: Roots of Regionalism*, Edinburgh, Edinburgh University Press, 1992.

Delanty, Gerard, *Citizenship in a Global Age*, Buckingham, Open University Press, 2000.

Delanty, Gerard, *Modernity and Postmodernity: Knowledge, Power, the Self*, London, Sage, 2000.

Delanty, Gerard, *Social Theory in a Changing World*, Cambridge, Polity Press, 1999.

Denham, John, *Building Cohesive Communities: A Report of the Ministerial Group on Public Order and Community Cohesion*, Home Office, 2001.

Dodd, Phillip, *The Battle Over Britain*, London, Demos, 1995.

Donnan, H., and Werbner, P. (eds.), *Economy and Culture in Pakistan: Migrants and Cities in a Muslim Society*, Basingstoke, Macmillan, 1991.

Drake, Michael, (ed.), *Time, Family and Community: perspectives on family and community history*, Oxford, Blackwell Publishers, 1994.

Eriksen, T. H., *Ethnicity & Nationalism: Anthropological Perspectives*, London, Pluto Press, 1992.

Esposito et al. (eds.), *Oxford Encyclopedia of the Modern Islamic World*, Oxford, Oxford University Press, 2001.

Fisher, D.J.V., *The Anglo-Saxon Age C. 400-1042*, London, Longman Group Ltd., 1973.

Fukuyama, Francis, *The End of History and the Last Man*, London, Penguin, 1993.

Gandhi, Leela, *Postcolonial Theory: A Critical Introduction*, Edinburgh, Edinburgh University Press, 1998.

Gauntlett, David, *Media, Gender and Identity: An Introduction*, London and New York, Routledge, 2002.

Geaves, Ron, *Sectarian Influences Within Islam in Britain: with reference to the concept of 'ummah' and 'community'*, Leeds, Department of Theology and Religious Studies, University of Leeds, 1996.

Giddens, Anthony, *Modernity and Self-Identity*, Stanford, Stanford University Press, 1991.

Gordon, Milton, M., *Assimilation in American Life*, New York, Oxford University Press, 1964.

Grosz, S., Beatson QC, J., and Duffy QC, P, *Human Rights: The 1998 Act and European Convention*, London, Sweet and Maxwell, 2000.

Guillaume, Alfred (ed.), *Ibn Hisham, Life of Muhammad*, Oxford, Oxford University, 1955.

Haddad, Yvonne (ed.), *Muslims in the West – From Sojourners to Citizens*, New York, Oxford University Press, 2002.

Halliday, Fred, *Arabs in Exile: Yemeni Migrants in Urban Britain*, London, I B Tauris & Co. Ltd., 1992.

Halliday, Fred, *Two Hours that Shook the World – September 11, 2001: Causes & Consequences*, London, Saqi Books, 2002.

Hauerfield, F., *The Roman Occupation of Britain*, London, Oxford University Press, 1924.

Hepple, Bob, and Choudhury, Tufyal, *Tackling Religious Discrimination: Practical Implications for Policy-makers and Legislators*, Home Office Research Study 221, Home Office, 2001.

Hillerbrand, Hans J., (ed.), *The Protestant Reformation: Selected Documents*, London, Macmillan, 1968.

Hirst, Paul, *Associative Democracy: New Forms of Economic and Social Governance*, Cambridge, Polity Press, 1994.

Hofmann, Murad, *Islam 2000*, Beltsville, USA, Amana Publications, 1996.

Husaini, Zohra, *Muslims in the Canadian Mosaic: Socio-Cultural and Economic Links with their Countries of Origin*, Ottowa, Muslim Research Foundation, 1990.

Jacobson, Jessica, *Islam in Transition: Religion and identity among British Pakistani youth*, London, Routledge, 1998.

Jeffery, Patricia, *Migrants and Refugees: Muslim and Christian Pakistani Families in Bristol*, Cambridge, Cambridge University Press, 1976.

Jenkins, Richard, *Social Identity*, London, Routledge, 1996.

Joly, Daniéle, *Britannia's Crescent: Making a Place for Muslims in British Society*, Aldershot, Ashgate Publishing Ltd., 1995.

Kabbani, Rana, *Imperial Fictions: Europe's Myths of Orient*, London, Pandora, 1994.

Kymlicka, Will, and Opalski, Magda, *Can Liberal pluralism be Exported?* Oxford, Oxford University Press, 2001.

Kymlicka, Will, *Multicultural Citizenship*, Oxford, Oxford University Press, 1995.

Kymlicka, Will, *The Rights of Minority Cultures*, Oxford, Oxford University Press, 1995.

Lawless, Richard I., *From Ta'izz to Tyneside: An Arab Community in the North-East of England During the Early Twentieth Century*, Exeter, University of Exeter Press, 1995.

Leonard, Mark, *Re-Ordering the World: The long-term implications of 11 September*, London, The Foreign Policy Centre, 2002.

Lester QC, A., & Pannick QC, D., *Human Rights Law and Practice*. London, Butterworth, 1999.

Lewis, John, *Anthropology Made Simple*, London, William Heinemann Ltd., 1982.

Lewis, Philip, *Islamic Britain: Religion, Politics and Identity among British Muslims*, London, I.B. Tauris, 1994.

Lings, Martin, *Muhammad: His Life Based on the Earliest Sources,* London, Unwin Hyman Ltd., 1987.

Long, Roy, *The Lutherian Church*, Exeter, Religious and Moral Educational Press, 1984.

Mason, David, *Race and Ethnicity in Modern Britain*, Oxford, Oxford University Press, 1999.

Matar, Nabil, *Islam in Britain 1558-1885*, Cambridge, Cambridge University Press, 1998.

Matar, Nabil, *Turks, Moors & Englishmen In the Age of Discovery*, New York, Columbia University Press, 1999.

Miller, David, *Citizenship and National Identity,* Cambridge, Polity Press, 1999.

Miller, David, *On Nationality,* Oxford, Clarendon Press, 1995.

Miller, David, *Principles of Social Justice,* Cambridge, MA., London, Harvard University Press, 1999.

Modood Tariq, and Werbner, Pnina, London, (eds.), *The Politics of Multiculturalism in the New Europe: Racism, Identity & Community,* London, Zed Books, 1997.

Modood, Tariq, *Ethnic Minorities in Britain: Diversity and Disadvantage,* London, Policy Studies Institute, 1997.

Modood, Tariq, *Not Easy Being British: Colour, Culture and Citizenship,* Stoke-on-Trent, Runnymede Trust and Trentham Books, 1992.

Ouseley, Herman *Community Pride not Prejudice – Making Diversity Work in Bradford,* Bradford Race Review, 2001.

Parekh, Bhikhu, *The Future of Multi-Ethnic Britain,* London, Profile Books, 2000.

Paxman, Jeremy, *The English: A Portrait of a People.* London, Penguin Books, 1999.

Pearce, Nick, & Hallgarten, Joe, *Tomorrow's Citizens,* London, Institute for Public Policy and Research, 2000.

Pool, John J., *Studies in Mohammedanism: Historical and Doctrinal,* London, Archibald Constable & Co., 1892.

Poston, Larry, *Islamic Daʿwah in the West: Muslim Missionary Activity and the Dynamics of Conversion to Islam,* New York, Oxford University Press, 1992.

Poulter, Sebastian, *English Law and Ethnic Minority Customs,* London, Butterworth, 1980.

Ramadan, Tariq, *To Be a European Muslim,* Leicester, Islamic Foundation, 1999.

Ramadan, Tariq, *Western Muslims and the Future of Islam,* Oxford, Oxford University Press, 2004.

Reeves, Minou, *Muhammad in Europe: A Thousand Years of Western Myth-Making,* Reading, Garnet Publishing, 2000.

Reiss, H. (ed.), *Kant: Political Writings,* Cambridge, Cambridge University Press, 1970.

Ritchie, David, *Oldham Independent Review Panel Report – One Oldham One Future,* 2001

Robertson, Roland (ed.) *Sociology of Religion,* London, Penguin, 1976.

Roche, Maurice, *Rethinking Citizenship – Welfare, Ideology and Change in Modern Society*, Cambridge, Polity Press, 1992.

Rushdie, Salman, *Imaginary Homelands*, London, Granta Books, 1991.

Said, Edward, *Orientalism: Western Concepts of the Orient*, London, Penguin Books, 1991.

Salahi, Adil, *Muhammad Man and Prophet: A Complete Study of the Life of the Prophet of Islam*, Leicester, The Islamic Foundation, 2002.

Salter, J., *The Asiatics and England*, London, Selly Jackson, 1872.

Salter, J., *The East in the West*, London, Partridge, 1895.

Seddon, Mohammad et al. (eds.), *British Muslims: Loyalty and Belonging*, Leicester, The Islamic Foundation and Citizen Organising Foundation, 2003.

Shaw, Alison, *A Pakistani Community in Britain*, Oxford, Basil Blackwell, 1988.

Siddiqui, Ataullah, (ed.), *Ismail R. Al-Faruqi - Islam and Other Faiths*, Leicester, The Islamic Foundation & International Institute of Islamic Thought, 1998.

Singh, Ray, *Challenges for the Future – Race Equality in Birmingham*, Birmingham City Council, 2001.

Starmer, K, *European Human Rights Law*, London, Legal Action Group, 1999.

Tamimi, Azzam (ed.), *Power Sharing Islam?* London, Liberty, 1993.

Tamimi, Azzam, *Rachid Ghannouchi: A Democrat Within Islamism*, New York, Oxford University Press, 2001.

Thomas, C., *Celtic Britain*, London, Thames Hudson Ltd., 1986.

Thompson, Della, (ed.), *The Concise Oxford Dictionary*, Oxford, Clarendon Press, 1995.

Thucydides, *History of the Peloponnesian War*, London, Penguin Books, 1954.

Tosi, Henry et al., *Managing Organisational Behaviour*, Oxford, Blackwell, 2000.

Turner, Bryan S., *Citizenship and Social Theory*, London, Sage. 1993.

Turner, Bryan S., *Max Weber: From History to Modernity*, London, Routledge, 1992.

Turner, Bryan, S., *Orientalism, Postmodernism & Globalism*, London, Routledge, 1994.

Wadham, J., & Mountfield, H., *Human Rights Act 1998*, London, Blackstones, 1999.

Waines, David, *An Introduction to Islam*, Cambridge, Cambridge University Press, 1995.

Watson, James, (ed.), *Between Two Cultures*, Oxford, Basil Blackwell, 1977.

Watt, W. Montgomery, *Islamic Surveys 9: The Influence of Islam on Medieval Europe*, Edinburgh, Edinburgh University Press, 1972.

Weller, Paul, (ed.), *Religions in the U.K. 2001-3*, The Multi-Faith Centre at the University of Derby, 2001.

Weller, Paul, et al., *Religious Discrimination in England and Wales*, Home Office Research Study 220, Home Office, 2001.

Index